TAILOR-MADE

Praise for Yolanda Wallace

The War Within

"*The War Within* has a masterpiece quality to it. It's a story of the heart told with heart—a story to be savored—and proof that you're never too old to find (or rediscover) true love."
— *Lambda Literary*

Rum Spring

"The writing was possibly the best I've seen for the modern lesfic genre, and the premise and setting was intriguing. I would recommend this one."—*The Lesbrary*

Murphy's Law

"Prepare to be thrilled by a love story filled with high adventure as they move toward an ending as turbulent as the weather on a Himalayan peak."—*Lambda Literary*

Lucky Loser

"Yolanda Wallace is a great writer. Her character work is strong, the story is compelling, and the pacing is so good that I found myself tearing through the book within a day and a half."—*The Lesbian Review*

TAILOR-MADE

by

Yolanda Wallace

2017

TAILOR-MADE

© 2017 By Yolanda Wallace. All Rights Reserved.

ISBN 13: 978-1-63555-081-8

This Trade Paperback Original Is Published By
Bold Strokes Books, Inc.
P.O. Box 249
Valley Falls, NY 12185

First Edition: December 2017

CREDITS
Editor: Cindy Cresap
Production Design: Stacia Seaman
Cover Design by Tammy Seidick

Acknowledgments

Few things make my heart beat faster than the sight of a woman in a suit. Except, perhaps, the sight of that same suit casually tossed on a bedroom floor. But I digress.

I received the inspiration for *Tailor-Made* from two sources: a trip to Seattle and a documentary about a company that makes bespoke suits.

While in Seattle for a literary conference, I had several conversations with readers who identified as gender fluid who were frustrated by the lack of representation in contemporary fiction. Thanks to those lengthy discussions, the character of androgynous bicycle messenger Dakota Lane came to me almost fully formed. Grace Henderson, the tailor Dakota meets at the beginning of the book, soon followed. I had a great time getting to know both characters and exploring their favorite New York haunts. Hopefully, I will be able to visit the locales in person one day instead of virtually. I also hope to make a return trip to Seattle someday soon to share this story with the people who helped inspire it.

As always, I would like to thank Radclyffe, Sandy, Cindy, and the rest of the Bold Strokes Books team for providing the fantastic support system that allows me to continue indulging my favorite hobby.

I would also like to thank the readers for their feedback. Your critiques help me become a better writer. That's the goal, anyway.

Last, but by no means least, I would like to thank Dita for her seemingly endless supply of patience. She's the best first reader (and wife) a girl ever had.

To Dita,

We're tailor-made.

CHAPTER ONE

Grace Henderson drummed her fingers on the fabric-strewn cutting table while she waited impatiently for her tardy prospective client to deign to make an appearance. Blowing out a breath, she checked her watch for the fourth time in the past fifteen minutes. The prospect, a model who had recently sent an email to the company's website to request an appointment for a fitting, was almost an hour late. Maybe she had decided not to show. Or even worse, perhaps she had received a freebie from one of the many design houses she modeled for and no longer needed Grace to craft a bespoke suit for her. Grace didn't like the idea of losing out on a sale, but she liked being disrespected even less.

"I've had it up to here with entitled athletes and self-absorbed celebrities who are more concerned with hanging out with their entourages and 'expanding their brands' than they are about the things that really matter," she said, venting her frustration. She pushed a container of straight pins away from her so she wouldn't be tempted to throw it across the room. Being forced to clean up the mess would make her even angrier than she already was. "My commission might pale in comparison to their exorbitant salaries, but my time is just as valuable as theirs. I have better things to do than sit around waiting for some cut-rate Chrissy Teigen to—"

"Careful." Lillie Washington, a seamstress who had been working for Henderson Custom Suits since Grace's father founded the business forty years ago, looked up from the blazer she was mending and stared at Grace over the top of her half-moon glasses. "If you get too steamed up, you're bound to sweat out that perm you paid good money for. You don't want that, do you?"

Grace unconsciously reached up to pat her chemically straightened hair with the heel of her hand as she stared at her reflection in the full-length mirror across the room. Her long locks, somehow free of gray despite the copious amount of stress her job heaped on her, fell past her shoulders. "I should just cut it all off and go natural. It's much cheaper and the upkeep requires far less maintenance."

"You've been threatening to cut your hair since you were knee-high to a grasshopper, and you still haven't done it yet." Lillie made the final stitch in the mended seam and briefly paused to admire her handiwork. The blazer belonged to the starting center for the hometown Brooklyn Nets. He was out for the rest of the season with a knee injury sustained in practice, but the garish prints he had selected for this suit and the nine others he had ordered guaranteed he would draw attention while he warmed the bench. Lillie placed the blazer on a wooden hanger and set it aside until the client's assistant could claim it. "I've got a pair of scissors right here if you're feeling brave."

Grace grabbed her hair with both hands and held it away from her face. The difference was striking, but the new look wasn't something she thought she could get used to seeing every day. Wearing her hair up was one thing. Getting rid of it altogether was another. She liked long hair. Both on her and the women she dated. She liked running her fingers through it, and she absolutely loved feeling it slide across her skin when her lover—

"Well, are you?" Lillie asked. "Feeling brave, that is."

Grace released her grip on her hair and turned away from the mirror. "Perhaps some other time."

"Mmm-hmm. I've heard that before." Lillie smiled knowingly, the pair of gold teeth in the upper plate of her dentures flashing under the fluorescent lights. "Who are we waiting for again?"

"Dakota Lane."

Lillie put her hands on her ample hips. "That skinny white girl who looks like she could use a double cheeseburger and an extra-large order of fries?"

Grace nearly choked on her bottled water. Dakota Lane was a woman who worked primarily as a male model. Images of her wearing men's suits, flirting with scantily clad women, and showing off her washboard abs while she modeled designer briefs had been appearing in print ads, on billboards, and in the tabloids for the past several years. Grace had seen several adjectives used to describe her—*mysterious, androgynous, butch, gender fluid,* and *smoking hot* were the most frequent terms bandied about—but Lillie's description was certainly the most colorful.

"No wonder you're walking around as nervous as a long-tailed cat in a roomful of rocking chairs," Lillie said. "We don't get many women in here. And when we do, it's usually church ladies from the neighborhood ordering something special for Easter Sunday, not someone who makes women, even straight ones, want to drop their drawers. Is Dakota your type?"

"I don't have a type."

"Child, please. Everyone has a type, whether they want to admit it or not. Sometimes, though, those preferences are subject to change. Take me, for example. I like my men tall, dark, and handsome, but I'll take short, light, and ugly as sin as long as he treats me right. Dakota might not be your type, but she definitely has you off your game. That's not like you." Lillie laid a hand on Grace's shoulder. "Your father picked you to help him run this place because you don't get starry-eyed when celebrities walk through the door. Actors, musicians, athletes, and other high rollers pay us a visit all the time, but you don't let their fame turn your head. Your sisters, on the other hand, would treat the business like a dating service until each of them managed to land a rich husband."

"I'm not looking for a husband."

Lillie pursed her lips. "You don't have to tell me that. I've known what you're about since you were ten years old and I caught you kissing one of your little playmates in the fabric room. You being a lesbian don't make no nevermind to me, Grace. I love you like family. I always will. All I'm saying is, you're treating this

Dakota person different from the rest of your female clients and you haven't even met her yet."

"What am I doing differently?"

"Isn't it obvious? Every other time a woman has come into the shop, you've treated their appointments just like everyone else's. You don't stress over them. You just go about your business. Not today."

"Because she's an hour late and I've got someplace to be."

"Where?" Lillie asked skeptically. "The only places you ever go are home, church, and work. I shake my tail feather more often than you do, and we both know I haven't done much of that since Cotton came to Harlem."

Grace tried not to laugh but failed miserably. Lillie had that effect on people. She was nearing seventy and had reached the age where she said what was on her mind instead of holding her tongue. Like now, the results were usually humorous rather than off-putting. "If you must know, I'm meeting someone for drinks tonight."

Lillie cocked her head so hard her wig nearly flew off. Thanks to her vast collection, she sported a different look every day. Unlike Grace, who had been rocking the same style since she finished college. Seven years was a long time, but Grace was in no rush to change a winning formula. She was, however, anxious to end her losing streak. She hadn't been in a serious relationship since she started apprenticing with her father ten years ago. At first, she was too busy juggling her class load at the City College of New York while she learned the ins and outs of her chosen profession. Now she had her economics degree in hand, but she was too busy keeping up with the steadily growing demand to have time for a social life. Not tonight, though. Tonight, she was taking some much needed downtime.

"You're meeting someone like who?" Lillie asked.

"A friend of a friend." Lillie's eyes lit up, but Grace tried to temper her obvious excitement. "Don't get too worked up. It's just drinks. If it turns into something more, I'll tell you all about it. If it doesn't, you were better off not knowing in the first place."

And, by extension, the whole neighborhood. Lillie was a valued employee and an even dearer friend, but she couldn't keep a secret if her life depended on it. Grace wasn't in the closet by any means, but she didn't want Lillie spreading the news about her and whoever Lynette had dug up for her until she knew there was something to tell.

When the downstairs buzzer sounded, Grace walked over to the intercom mounted on the wall and pressed the speaker button. "Yes?"

"Hi, it's Dakota Lane. I have an appointment with Grace Henderson."

"Finally," Grace said under her breath.

"I'm sorry I'm late. I had a problem at work."

"A problem at work?" Lillie said. "Did she forget how to smile or something?"

Grace hastily pulled her hand away from the speaker button. "Shh. She might hear you."

Lillie furrowed her brow. "A few minutes ago, you wanted to wring her neck. Now you're acting like she's your best friend."

Grace wouldn't go that far, but she had to admit Dakota sounded stressed. And sexy as hell. Her voice was like a cat's purr— low-pitched and comforting. At the moment, however, she sounded as if she needed to receive some TLC rather than dish it out. Grace leaned toward the speaker. "I'll buzz you up."

"Thank you."

"Where is she from?" Lillie asked as Grace pressed the button that disengaged the downstairs lock. "She sounds like she's from down South. She even remembered to say thank you, so she definitely ain't from around here."

Grace returned to the cutting table while she listened for the service elevator. "I think she's from Savannah."

"You *think* or you *know*?"

"I'm ninety-nine percent sure I read it somewhere." In the vast selection of articles Grace had come across while she prepared for today's meeting, the interviewers had done their best to drag details out of Dakota to no avail. "She doesn't seem to like talking about herself or her family."

"Good," Lillie said decisively. "I can't stand people who put their business in the streets. I don't want to know what somebody had for breakfast this morning or who they slept with last night unless I'm sitting across the table from them or lying in bed next to them."

As she reached for a notebook and pen, Grace tried to scrub the images Lillie's comment had evoked from her mind. She had seen Dakota's name in the gossip columns more than once, but she didn't know if those mentions were by accident or design. Publicists often fabricated stories in order to garner attention for their clients. Perhaps Dakota's were no different. If so, they might want to rethink their strategy because it often seemed as if they were taking the old adage about there being no such thing as bad publicity too much to heart. If the gossip columnists were to be believed, Dakota was a train wreck waiting to happen. Each time she picked up a newspaper or tabloid that featured a mention of Dakota within its pages, Grace mentally braced herself for the collision.

Her breath hitched in anticipation when she heard the freight elevator rattle to a stop. The building was almost a hundred years old and the elevator was nearly as ancient. Both added character to a neighborhood that was historic in some areas and thoroughly modern in others. To many, Williamsburg, Brooklyn, was the hipster capital of New York if not the world. To Grace, it was simply the area she and her family had always called home. But with increasing gentrification, home might not feel that way for much longer.

Her father owned the building they worked in, and the brownstone they lived in was rent-controlled. Many of their friends and business associates, however, were slowly being priced out of the neighborhood. At times, Grace felt like she and her father were the last ones standing. How long would he hold out before he pulled up stakes, too?

She had been in charge of the company's day-to-day operations for years now. Her father made an appearance a few times a week to serve the handful of clients who felt more comfortable having a male rather than a female tailor. He had vowed to pass the business on to her when he finally retired in a couple of years, but would he keep his promise if a real estate developer made him an offer too lucrative to pass up? Each time she finished a design, Grace felt like she was continuing a family legacy. She hoped she would have an opportunity to uphold the traditions that had been established decades ago.

Business was steady, but it wasn't growing as fast as it had in the past. She and her father had lost some of their professional football clientele to younger, more aggressive tailors who sent representatives to pre-draft workouts to dole out business cards and offer discount packages to promising players. Grace's father didn't believe in chasing business. He preferred to allow it to come to him. The philosophy had worked so far. She prayed it would continue to pay off. If the company went out of business, everything she had been striving for would vanish, and she would have to start from scratch—after she figured out what she wanted to be when she grew up. She had longed to become a tailor since the first time she picked up a needle and thread. If she couldn't pursue her dream, her life could become a nightmare.

Grace tightened her grip on her notebook when she heard the elevator doors slide open, then slam shut. She didn't usually get nervous before she met with clients for the first time, but neither this meeting nor this particular client were like any she'd ever had. She wanted to make a good impression. Too bad her tardy client didn't seem to feel the same way. A few seconds later, the office door creaked open and Dakota Lane poked her head inside.

Dakota was tall—six feet, if she was an inch—long limbed, and gifted with broad shoulders that tapered to a narrow waist. A suit would hang wonderfully on her, whether tailor-made or off-the-rack. She was working as a bike messenger when a scout for one of the leading modeling agencies saw her parked at a traffic light one afternoon. The scout liked what he saw, ordered his cabbie to follow her to the site of her next delivery, and offered her a contract on the spot. She had been working steadily as a model ever since, but she evidently hadn't given up her day job because she was dressed head to toe in cycling gear and had the mangled remains of a lightweight road bike draped over one shoulder.

"Am I in the right place?" Dakota removed her bicycle helmet and tucked it under one smoothly muscled arm. The muscles in her corded thighs and cut calves were even more well defined. Grace dragged her gaze away from the view as Dakota continued speaking. "I emailed a few days ago to schedule an appointment for a fitting. I got a reply directing me to come today at five thirty."

Grace pressed her lips together to prevent herself from pointing out that five thirty had come and gone. "Yes, you've come to the right place. I'm Grace Henderson and this is Lillie Washington, our best seamstress." Dakota reached to shake her hand, but Grace left her hanging when she noticed the large scrape on Dakota's right knee and the trickle of blood sliding down her shin. "Are you all right?"

Dakota looked down, apparently unfazed by the sight of blood pooling in her expensive-looking cycling shoe. "I'm fine."

"What happened?"

"A cab driver sideswiped me while I was making my last delivery."

"Did you call the police, baby?" Lillie asked.

"No, ma'am." Dakota pulled off her padded cycling gloves like a boxer waiting to hear the decision after a fight. "The driver didn't stick around long enough for me to get his name. He was probably afraid I'd kick his ass, which I was sorely tempted to do, believe me."

Lillie punched the air. "Good for you. Most cabbies drive like the rules of the road don't apply to them. You take your life into your hands each time you flag one down."

"You can leave your bike in the hall," Grace said, trying to steer the conversation back to where it belonged. "It'll be safe out there. In the meantime, I'll grab the first aid kit so we can take care of your leg."

"It's just a scratch," Dakota said. "I get them all the time. Most drivers view cyclists as nuisances and treat us as such. Sometimes, the feeling is mutual." She put the bicycle down and wheeled it—or tried to—into the hall. The front tire was flat, the frame was bent, and several spokes were missing. She had apparently been lucky to wind up with only a scraped knee. From the looks of her bike, her injuries could have been much worse.

"Mmm, mmm, mmm." Lillie slowly shook her head. "I don't know what you were trying to deliver, child, but let FedEx handle it next time. Ain't no package worth getting killed for."

Dakota shrugged. "It's one of the risks of the job."

"And you're still willing to take that risk, considering everything you have at stake?" Grace asked.

Her heart skipped a beat when Dakota turned to look at her. Dakota's eyes were arresting. One of her eyes was brown and the other was blue. Both seemed to peer past Grace's exterior into her soul. Dakota's features were angular, accentuated by a strong jaw and an aquiline nose. Her breasts were small, her lips full. Her short, dark brown hair was styled into a pompadour fade. Cut low on the sides, but with enough height on top to make Elvis—or his modern equivalent—proud.

"Despite what you might have heard," Dakota said, "I'm more than just a pretty face."

Grace wouldn't call her pretty. Handsome was the adjective that came more readily to mind. And Dakota certainly was that, but her appeal was lost on Grace. Grace preferred more feminine women. After dealing with men and their hard, straight lines all day, she looked forward to going home with someone soft. Someone with curves. The only curves Dakota Lane had were on the wrecked bicycle in the hall.

And the irresponsible way Dakota had handled their appointment stuck in Grace's craw. The accident didn't sound like it had been Dakota's fault, but Grace was miffed Dakota hadn't had the decency to give her a call to explain the delay. Dakota's apology sounded sincere, if a bit practiced. Like she was accustomed to using her good looks and obvious charm to get her out of a jam. Sharks had pretty smiles, too, but their bite was nothing to play with.

"Let's get you patched up." Grace pulled a tube of disinfectant, a pack of gauze, and a small roll of medical tape from the first aid kit.

"That's okay. I can do it." Dakota plucked the items from

Grace's hands, took a seat on the bench in front of the worktable that doubled as Grace's desk, and began dabbing at the blood on her leg. She looked up as she applied disinfectant gel to the scrape on her knee. "Are there any questions you need to ask me before you whip out the measuring tape?"

"Several."

"Then let's get started." Dakota placed a square of gauze on her knee and carefully taped it in place. Then she rubbed antibacterial cleanser on her hands and flashed another one of those killer smiles. "I've already kept you waiting long enough, don't you think?"

"Yes, you certainly have."

Even though Grace had the theme song from *Jaws* running through her head, she couldn't help wondering how long she would have to wait before she saw Dakota Lane again.

CHAPTER TWO

Grace's questions were obviously designed to help her craft the perfect suit to fit her customers' needs, but they were so probing Dakota couldn't help feeling defensive. More than that. She felt exposed. Like Grace was slowly peeling back the layers to get to her core. Did Grace like what she saw? Because Dakota certainly did.

Grace's skin and eyes were a rich dark chocolate. Her hair was long and thick. As luxurious as the gentle swell of her hips. Her breasts were full, straining the buttons of her black blouse. Her heels were stylish but sensible, lessening the chance she would wind up with aching feet at the end of the workday. The houndstooth skirt she was wearing came to rest just above her knees, giving Dakota an unobstructed view of her shapely legs under the picnic-style table that served as her desk.

The instant Dakota laid eyes on her, one word had come immediately to mind: ripe. Dakota longed to taste the expected sweetness, but she could tell the chances of that happening were somewhere between slim and none. Despite Dakota's apology, Grace had seemed none too pleased by her late arrival. Grace had acted momentarily concerned when she caught a glimpse of Dakota's scraped knee, but she had been all business ever since Dakota tended the wound.

It was just as well, Dakota thought. Her friends called her the one-hit wonder because she rarely if ever took a woman on a second date. With so many women in the world, why should she limit herself to just one? Successful, beautiful, and obviously intelligent, Grace Henderson was the kind of woman who might tempt her to change her philosophy. But her way of life had worked out well so far. Why should she change now?

Grace glanced at her handwritten notes. "I asked you to collect pictures of suits you like so I can get an idea of your design aesthetic. Did you remember to bring them?"

Dakota felt color rise in her cheeks. She hadn't blushed in years. Why was she acting like a bashful schoolgirl now? "Yes and no." She reached into the pocket built into the back of her cycling jersey and pulled out her waterlogged phone. "I saved the pictures on this, but it ended up in the gutter after my accident. It won't be good to anyone until it's been sitting in a box of rice for at least twenty-four hours."

Grace's hard expression softened, and the crease between her eyebrows slowly faded from view. "That explains why you didn't call."

"Pardon?" Grace waved off Dakota's question, making Dakota even more anxious to please her. "I have my portfolio in my messenger bag. Would that work?"

"I'm afraid not. While I'm sure the suits in the pictures are quite stylish, I don't want to see someone else's idea of you. I want to see yours." Grace scribbled something in her notebook and underlined it three times, making Dakota wish she could read upside down. She'd give anything to know what required that much emphasis. "Are you making the purchase for a special occasion, or are you simply looking to expand your wardrobe?"

Finally a question Dakota could answer.

"My sister's getting married in June and I need a suit to wear to the wedding. Most of the ones in my closet are black, dark blue, or charcoal gray. They would be much too funereal for what's supposed to be a joyous occasion. And late spring in south Georgia is almost as bad as the middle of summer here. I don't want to roast while I'm waiting for Brooke and her intended to say 'I do.'"

Grace nodded and jotted another note. "Then I suggest a

lightweight material. Something breathable. Are you going to be a member of the wedding party?"

"No," Dakota said quickly so she wouldn't have to spend too much time rehashing that conversation in her mind. Her family disapproved of most things she did. Being passed over for maid of honor or even bridesmaid in her sister's wedding only reinforced the fact. Even though she would have balked at wearing a dress, she thought she could have pulled off the rest of the required duties without much effort. "My official duties are limited to attending the ceremony and making a toast at the reception."

"I see. That means you're free to choose any color you like. Do you have any preferences?"

Dakota rubbed her chin as she considered the question. "I know what I don't want. I don't want to wear white because I don't want to risk upstaging the bride. I don't want to wear yellow because I don't want to end up looking like Big Bird. And red's out, too, because I don't want to look like a pimp."

Grace reached for a selection of fabric swatches and slid it into the space between them. "How about salmon?"

Dakota leaned toward her. "Do I strike you as someone whose design aesthetic is geared toward the pink section of the color wheel?"

A corner of Grace's mouth quirked up into a smile. "No, you don't." She looked through the swatches until she found one that caught her eye. "How about this one?"

Dakota peered at the sample Grace had selected. The swatch was a gorgeous robin's-egg blue, though the fabric didn't appear to be wool. According to the company website, Henderson Custom Suits used some of the highest quality wools on the market. Why was Grace offering her something else? Dakota rubbed the swatch between her fingers to feel the material. "Is this linen?"

"Yes. Most of the suits we make are wool, but I think linen— no pun intended—would better suit your needs. It's light and comfortable and works really well as a summer suit. With the proper care, the material will prove just as durable as wool. Pair it with a white dress shirt and matching pocket square, and you'll be all set."

Dakota imagined the finished product. She had a white leather belt and a pair of white canvas tennis shoes that would provide the perfect accessories. "I like it. Let's go with that."

"Excellent." Grace made a few more notes and reached for a roll of measuring tape. "After I take your measurements, we can wrap things up."

Dakota reached into her messenger bag. "No need. I brought my own."

Grace frowned as she examined the numbers printed on the piece of paper Dakota handed her. "When did you have these taken?"

"Before Fashion Week in January. Why?"

Grace glanced at the numbers again. "No offense, but I think these might no longer be accurate."

"Is that a diplomatic way of saying I should lay off the craft beer and all-you-can-eat hot wings?"

"No, it's my way of guaranteeing I have a satisfied customer." Grace set the paper aside, draped the measuring tape across her shoulders, and rose from her seat. "Shall we?"

"Do you want me to strip down, or am I fine as is?"

"There's no need for nudity just yet."

"But you'll be sure to let me know if something changes, won't you?"

Dakota thought the line was pretty good, but it didn't elicit a smile, let alone a verbal response. Grace simply spread the measuring tape across Dakota's shoulders and went to work taking the thirty measurements she and her team needed to tailor a suit.

I must be losing my touch, Dakota thought as Grace called out a series of numbers and Lillie carefully recorded them. Grace's tone was businesslike, but her touch was light. Dakota felt a shiver run down her spine each time Grace repositioned her hands.

"Flex your arm for me."

Dakota did as requested when Grace stood behind her and wrapped the measuring tape around her bicep. "Welcome to the gun show." She turned to gauge Grace's reaction to her quip. "I'll bet you've heard that joke a time or two."

"You might say that."

Her beautiful face a blank mask, Grace called out a number for Lillie to record, then measured the length of Dakota's arms. She paused while Lillie added the new number to the growing list. Dakota enjoyed the respite. She could feel the heat of Grace's body, and it was all she could do not to press herself against her.

"Now I'm going to measure the fullest part of your chest," Grace said, giving her fair warning. "Do you want the suit to play up or deemphasize your bust?"

Dakota tried to formulate a response, but she couldn't think straight with Grace's arms wrapped around her and the tape pressing against her breasts. She felt her nipples press against her cycling jersey. The form-fitting material did little to hide her growing arousal. Grace was behind her so she couldn't see the effect her actions were having on her. Lillie, however, was perfectly positioned to see everything.

"This building gets kind of drafty during the winter," Lillie said with a teasing smile. "If it's too cold in here for you, I could ask Grace to turn up the heat."

"No, thanks. I'll be fine." And, without even realizing it, Grace was doing just fine ratcheting up the heat on her own. "We're almost done, aren't we?"

Lillie's smile grew broader. "Honey, we've barely begun. She hasn't even started measuring you for the pants yet."

Dakota's body temperature spiked a few degrees when she considered the effect that endeavor might have on her. If this process went on much longer, she thought she might spontaneously combust.

Grace dropped to one knee. Dakota looked away so she wouldn't be tempted to treat herself to an eyeful of Grace's glorious cleavage. "Do you dress left or right?"

"Pardon?" Dakota asked, unsure she had heard correctly.

"I know it's an unusual question—"

"Believe me, I understand the question. I model men's clothes for a living." Dakota didn't mention she had been known to rock a dildo in public from time to time because Grace already seemed to be very much aware of the fact. Otherwise, why would the subject come up? "But I'm not planning on packing at my sister's wedding." She was used to receiving attention, both positive and negative, but she didn't want to be responsible for drawing any of the focus from Brooke on a day when the spotlight was supposed to be on her.

"The accessories you choose to wear to your sister's nuptials are entirely up to you, but if you plan on wearing the suit on less-formal occasions, I thought it would be easier if I made the appropriate adjustments to the design now so you won't have to make a return trip. My mission is to give you what you want, but I can't give that to you unless you tell me what that is."

Grace's smile was like catnip. Earthy, yet intoxicating. Even though Dakota had just met her, Grace's opinion of her mattered. She wanted to please her. Impress her. Win her over.

"The wedding and reception will last a few hours," Grace said. "The suit you're asking me to make will be meant to last much longer than that. And most importantly, it will be made according to your specifications. With that being said, would you like me to leave a bit of extra room along the inseam?"

Some women Dakota had come across thought toys should only be worn in the privacy of the bedroom. Nothing in Grace's cool, professional demeanor made her feelings on the matter clear, but Dakota longed to know where she stood. And to slowly slip inside her while she was wearing the "accessory" both of them had referred to but neither had named. "Yes."

"Which one?" Grace prompted. "The left or the right?"

"The left."

"There. That wasn't so hard, was it?"

You have no idea, Dakota thought as Grace pressed the tape against the inside of her left leg. While Grace got the measurements she needed, Dakota's clit throbbed so insistently she could feel the pounding in her temples. She and Grace hadn't discussed the final price yet, but whatever the suit wound up costing, it had better be worth the torture she had to endure to get it made.

She mentally recited the alphabet backward to distract herself from the sensation of Grace's hands sliding down her thighs and circling her hips. The first few letters came easily, but when Grace's fingers fluttered against her overheated flesh, the only ones she could come up with were O, M, and G.

Lillie chuckled. "I don't know about you, child, but I could use a cigarette."

"So could I," Dakota said. "And I don't even smoke."

❖

Grace could tell Dakota was turned on. Hell, she would have to be blind not to. All the classic signs were there. From the color in Dakota's cheeks to her rapid breathing to her hard nipples to—Well, the less she thought about the rest, the better.

Dakota wasn't the first client who had gotten stirred up while their measurements were being taken, but she was the first whose excitement had seeped into Grace as well. It had taken every ounce of her concentration for her to remain professional as she gathered the information she needed.

While Dakota and Lillie made jokes about Dakota's condition, Grace had been fighting a battle of her own. When she had inhaled the musky scent of Dakota's arousal, she had wanted to immerse herself in it like she was bathing in a river.

"And we're done," Lillie said after she recorded the final set of measurements. She gathered her belongings and headed for the door. "I'll let you two take it from here."

"It was nice meeting you," Dakota said.

"You, too, honey. Good luck. I think you're gonna need it."

Grace used Lillie's departure as an opportunity to pull herself together. When she went over the final details with Dakota, she wanted to make sure her voice wasn't husky with desire.

"What's next?" Dakota asked, shifting uncomfortably in her seat. Grace knew the feeling.

"Let me run the numbers." Grace factored in labor and the cost of materials to arrive at an estimate for the final price for the suit and dress shirt Dakota had commissioned. She wrote the number on a cost sheet and turned the paper around so Dakota could see both her calculations and the expected price for the completed outfit. "Does that work for you?"

"It looks perfect."

"Let me print you a copy of the cost sheet, and you can be on your way. I'll draft a design and contact you for final approval. After that, the work begins in earnest."

"When do you think you'll be done?"

"I'll start working on the design right away and email you for approval when I'm done, but construction won't begin right away. There's a backlog ahead of you."

"How much of a backlog?"

Grace consulted the list of outstanding orders. It was only April, so she felt certain she would be able to meet Dakota's June deadline, but if adjustments needed to be made to the preliminary version of the suit, they might be cutting it close. May meant NBA playoffs and June meant draft night. During that two-month span, their clients who were already in the league and the ones who hoped to join them would be lined up outside the door. Her sisters would be right behind them, everyone hoping to score in one way or another.

"We should be done in six weeks at the outside," she said, "but I'll try to shoot for five. I'll contact you when construction is complete so you can come in and try your suit on for size. If you're not happy with the fit, we can make changes and have the final version ready for you about a week after that."

"Sounds good."

"Do you have any other questions?"

"Just one." Dakota placed the customer copy of the cost sheet in her messenger bag. "May I take you to dinner tonight? I'd like to make it up to you for being late."

"Thank you, but that won't be necessary. Plus I've already made plans for the evening."

"Oh." Dakota's expressive face fell. "I didn't mean to overstep. Are you seeing someone?"

"No, tonight's a first date." Grace folded her hands on her desk to stop them from shaking. Adrenaline was coursing through her and she couldn't keep still. She was now free to start focusing on the date Lynette had set up for her and she didn't know whether she should be excited or terrified.

"I know I'm supposed to say I hope everything works out between you, but I'm not going to."

"Because?"

"I would love a chance to make a good second impression on you since I blew the first in rather spectacular fashion."

Grace pressed her lips together to keep from saying the wrong thing. Dakota's confidence bordered on cockiness, a trait Grace usually considered a turnoff. Usually. On Dakota, confidence looked good. It looked *really* good.

"I make it a rule to keep my business and personal relationships separate," she said diplomatically. Seeing the disappointment etched on Dakota's face, however, she was almost tempted to muddy the waters. Almost.

"No worries. Thanks for letting me know." Dakota's smile seemed half-hearted as she reached across the desk to shake her hand. "I look forward to hearing from you."

Grace began to second-guess herself the second Dakota closed the door behind her. Was her excitement due to the woman she had yet to meet, or the one who had just walked out the door?

CHAPTER THREE

Dakota had been told no before, but she couldn't figure out why Grace's refusal of her dinner invitation stuck in her craw. She didn't have time to worry about it now, though. She had things to do and places to be.

Her friend Josefina "Joey" Palallos owned a bike shop slash dive bar a few blocks away from Grace's office building. The bike shop closed at eight and the bar at ten. Dakota had only a few minutes to get over there before the shop shut down and the drinks started flowing in earnest.

She had a feeling her bike was beyond repair, but Joey had worked miracles before. Perhaps she had another one up her tattooed sleeves. If not, Dakota would have to fork over the money for a new set of wheels before she reported to work on Monday. She had been wanting to upgrade her cheap aluminum frame for a more expensive carbon fiber one for a few years now but hadn't been able to convince herself to pull the trigger on the extra expense. Perhaps now was finally the time she dipped into some of the money she had been saving instead of hoarding it for a rainy day.

She held on to her day job because she was well aware her shelf life as a model was limited. Styles changed every season, and the roster of people showing them off for the buying public often turned over just as quickly. She needed to make as much money as she could while she could before agents, designers, and bookers turned their attention to the next hot new face waiting to be discovered.

The best-paid female supermodels routinely raked in tens of millions each year. Only a select few male models were lucky to crack seven figures. Because she was a woman who modeled menswear, she was paid more like Tyson Beckford at his peak than Heidi Klum at hers. Even though the money wasn't as good as it could have been if she modeled bikinis and wedding dresses instead of board shorts and tuxedoes, she wasn't willing to compromise her identity in order to pad her bank account. She didn't like attaching labels to herself or anyone else. As a result, she had been blurring the lines between male and female for as long as she could remember. Getting paid to do so was an added bonus.

When Grace had asked her to describe her design aesthetic, she hadn't known what to say. Just because she worked in the fashion industry didn't mean she kept up with the latest trends. She just knew what she liked.

When she was doing print ads or walking the runway, designers dressed her in a wide variety of suits from traditional to contemporary to avant-garde. Once the cameras were off, however, she felt most comfortable in jeans, tennis shoes, a hoodie, and a backward baseball cap. Joey called her a frat boy in training, but Joey was a fine one to talk, considering they had the same taste in clothes. And more often than not, in women as well.

People had been confusing her for a boy since she was a six-year-old girl running around in her brother's hand-me-down jeans and faded R.E.M. T-shirts instead of the closetful of floral-print dresses and pastel ruffled skirts her mother kept trying to force on her. Now she was able to make a living being who she had always tried to be: herself. If her family could accept her as she was instead of stubbornly trying to change her into someone else, everything would be right with the world.

She wasn't holding out hope, but perhaps a change was in the air. Her sister Brooke had invited her to her wedding and, surprisingly, had even suggested she should bring a date. Dakota didn't plan on subjecting anyone to the stresses of a Lane family get-together, but it was good to know the option was open if she decided to change her mind.

When Dakota had come out to her parents and siblings, Brooke had taken the news the hardest. The baby of the family, Brooke was thirteen at the time. She was just becoming interested in the opposite sex and was worried about how Dakota's revelation might change her schoolmates' perception of her. She had locked herself in her room, complaining she would not only be friendless but dateless as well. Dakota's brother, on the other hand, hadn't batted an eye. Probably because the two of them had been competing for the same girls' attention since Townsend was fourteen and she was twelve.

Their parents, on the other hand, had had plenty to say. None of it positive.

Dakota's hometown was twenty-five minutes from Savannah and half an hour from Fort Stewart, the army base in Hinesville. Growing up so close to a military installation had its good points and its bad ones. Being surrounded by hundreds of women in uniform was very good. Being bombarded by conservative ideas about gender roles? Not so much.

In her father's eyes, girls were girls and boys were boys. There was no in-between. No matter how many times—or how loudly—he tried to make his point, Dakota couldn't be swayed to accept his line of thinking.

Her mother had opted to take a quieter approach. She started by reciting the usual tired quotes from the Bible and ended by resorting to her favorite criticism: "Would it kill you to put on a dress and wear a little makeup from time to time?"

Dakota wore makeup for every fashion show and photo shoot, but she hadn't donned anything close to a dress since she had reluctantly sported a kilt for one of Marc Jacobs's shows.

She was tempted to ask Richmond Hill, her roommate and best friend, to accompany her to the wedding in full drag, but he had a scheduling conflict. Even if his calendar was clear, she doubted he would agree to the idea. She went home every Thanksgiving out of guilt, family loyalty, or both, but Rich hadn't returned to the small Savannah suburb he had co-opted as his drag name since they moved to New York six years ago. She couldn't blame him. His parents had been even less accepting than hers. Why put up with the drama when you didn't have to?

"Like the old saying goes," she said as she waited for a traffic light to change from red to green, "you can choose your friends, but you can't choose your family."

And her family of friends was one she wouldn't trade for anything in the world. They kept her ego in check when her head threatened to get too big, and they were there for her whenever she needed them. Day or night. What more could she ask for?

Having Grace Henderson tell her yes instead of no would be a good place to start.

"Dude, what the fuck happened to you?" Joey said when Dakota walked into the Broken Spoke.

Joey's family had emigrated from Manila twelve years ago when Joey was fifteen. Her mother made the best chicken adobo Dakota had ever eaten. Mrs. Palallos's generous portion sizes were probably one of the main contributing factors to the recent expansion in Dakota's waistline.

"I had a close encounter with a cab driver on Fifth Avenue. I had right of way, but he didn't seem to agree because he tried to run over me instead of waiting for me to cross the street."

Joey nodded in solidarity. "Been there, done that."

"Do you think the bike can be saved?"

Joey frowned. "I don't know, bro. Let me see." She came around the counter to take a closer look.

The Broken Spoke was one of many specialty establishments that had popped up in Williamsburg over the past few years. Instead of selling homemade artisan ice cream or vintage clothing, Joey repaired bikes on one side of the building while her girlfriend Whitney hawked imported beer and upscale bar food on the other.

Dakota lived in Greenwich Village, but she made the trek to Brooklyn to visit the Broken Spoke every few weeks or so. She did it because she liked supporting a friend. But even more than that, the venue was an awesome place to hang out. The theme was cool, the vibe was chill, and although the food and drink selections were limited, the quality of both was out of this world.

"Would you like your usual?" Whitney asked as she poured a couple of PBRs for a pair of bearded hipsters in skinny jeans and nearly identical plaid flannel shirts.

Dakota's favorite beer was a French brand she had discovered while waiting for a flight at Charles de Gaulle Airport several years ago. Whitney always made sure to keep it in stock so Dakota could have one when she dropped by.

"Give her something stronger than Kronenbourg," Joey said. "She's going to need it."

Whitney reached for a squat bottle on the top shelf behind the bar. "One tequila shot coming up."

"Is it really that bad?" Dakota asked.

Joey wiped her hands on a grease-stained towel. "Let me put it this way. I could fix it, but between the parts and the labor, it would cost you just as much as buying a new one."

"I was afraid you were going to say that."

"So what do you want to do?" Joey removed the cycling cap she wore to keep sweat out of her eyes and ran a hand over her close-cropped hair. "Do you want me to fix it, do you want to replace it with a similar model, or are you finally ready to buy the one you drool over every time you walk through the door?"

Dakota looked at the two-thousand-dollar cycle hanging on the wall like a fine piece of art. Then she downed the tequila shot in one swallow to numb the pain before she reached for her credit card. Even though she could afford the expense, that didn't mean she liked taking it on. "Let's do it."

"Cha-ching!" Joey pumped her fist and began to ring up the sale. "Are you hanging out tonight, or do you have someplace to be?"

Dakota sat on a stationary bike hooked to a simulator projecting images from a past leg of the Tour de France. "The first thing I need to do is go home and take a shower, but I haven't decided what I'm going to do afterward. Rich is having a going-away party at the Stonewall Inn tomorrow night. I'll attend that, for sure."

Joey handed Dakota the receipt so she could sign it and finalize the sale. "How long is he going to be on the road?"

"From May to September."

"Four months?" Joey placed the signed receipt in the register and closed the drawer. "Damn, that's a long time."

"I know, but I'm happy for him. He's been dreaming about this since we were kids."

Rich had been working as a professional drag queen since he was nineteen. Using a fake ID card, he had honed his skills five nights a week at several gay clubs in and around Savannah for two years before he decided to take on a larger market. He and Dakota had moved to New York when they were twenty-one so he could pursue his dreams. For the first few years, both had struggled to make ends meet. Then she had signed her first modeling contract, lifting the burden of deciding which bills to pay and which ones to let roll over for another month.

Rich was understandably frustrated back then, but he never got down on himself or gave up hope. Now things were finally going his way. After he sent in an audition tape for the most recent season of a popular televised drag competition, he made the cut, flew to California to film the episodes, and wound up finishing third in the contest. In a few weeks, he and a dozen other former contestants from the show would embark on a sixty-city international tour. When they finally returned to the States, Rich was supposed to record an album of dance music. Dakota hoped the producers had invested in Auto-Tune because although Rich was a world-class lip syncer, singing was definitely not one of his strengths.

"The party's not until tomorrow," Joey said. "What are your plans for tonight?"

Dakota ran her hands through her hair in a useless attempt to clear her head. She had been in a fog for the past few hours, and visibility wasn't getting any better. "I think I'll stay in tonight. It's been a long day."

Joey removed Dakota's new bike from the wall mount, checked the tires to see if they needed air, and adjusted the seat to Dakota's preferred height. "Do you have a photo shoot coming up or something?"

"Not for a couple of weeks."

Joey locked the bike's seat in place and turned her attention to the handlebars, making sure they were set at the proper angle. "Then why are you staying home on a Friday night?"

"Because I don't have a reason not to."

Joey tucked her wrench in the back pocket of her jeans and pressed the back of her hand against Dakota's forehead.

"What are you doing?" Dakota asked.

"Checking your temperature. I thought I heard you say you aren't going out tonight. I wanted to see if you've finally gotten over your wicked case of FOMO."

"You're such an asshole. And I don't have a fear of missing out."

Joey scooted out of reach after Dakota took a playful swipe at her leg. "I might be an asshole, but it's not like you to take a pass on an opportunity to meet someone new."

Dakota's smile faded as she turned back to the images of the French countryside flashing across the simulator. "I think I already did."

"Yeah? Tell me all about her."

"How much time do you have?"

Joey turned off the neon Open sign in the bike shop window. "Loads."

Dakota glanced at the chalkboard menu above the bar. "I'll have a bottle of Kronenbourg and a plate of buffalo wings, Whit. This could take a while."

Grace and her date had agreed to meet at the Tea Room, a gay bar within walking distance of both Grace's office and her house. Grace had hoped to get to the bar early so she could scope things out while she waited, but Dakota's late arrival had thrown her off schedule. She hated being late. Even if, as in this case, she was technically still on time.

She walked into the Tea Room and paused to get her bearings.

Most of the usual suspects were in attendance, but she did spot a few unfamiliar faces. Which one was she supposed to be looking for? Lynette hadn't shown her a picture of the woman she was meeting tonight. She had only said her name was Renee, she was twenty-eight years old, and she was a personal trainer based out of one of the most exclusive gyms in Manhattan.

Once she started searching in earnest, Grace spotted Renee right away. And wished almost as quickly that she hadn't let Lynette talk her into this.

Renee was standing in front of the crowded bar staring at her reflection in the mirror behind it like Narcissus falling in love with his own image. She had a gorgeous body and she obviously knew it. Despite the unseasonably cool temperatures outside, she was wearing a barely-there tank top that showed off the muscles in her impressive arms, shoulders, and upper back. Her jeans fit more like tights, hugging her round butt and flared thighs like spandex instead of denim.

"I should have known Lynette couldn't be trusted."

Grace had been friends with Lynette Walker since junior high school. They knew each other better than they knew themselves. And Grace knew Lynette well enough to know that if Renee was as great a catch as Lynette had made her out to be, she wouldn't need help finding dates.

Grace felt like she had gotten played. But she wasn't about to get played for a fool. After spending a few minutes watching Renee practically make love to her reflection, she turned to leave. She thought better of it before she reached the door. Though her first impressions were normally spot-on, perhaps she was seeing what she wanted to see instead of what was actually there. Deciding to give Renee a second chance, she forced herself to stay. She made her way through the growing crowd and over to the bar.

"Renee?"

Renee turned away from the mirror, set her drink down, and fixed Grace with a lingering look that was naked in its appraisal. She nodded as if to say, "I can work with that," then stuck out her hand. "You must be Grace." She indicated a pair of empty bar stools nearby. "Have a seat and tell me what you're drinking. The first round's on me."

The *first* round? She must have liked what she had seen during her thorough visual inspection. Grace's spirits lifted. Perhaps she had passed judgment too soon. She climbed on a bar stool and ordered a tequila sunrise.

Renee made a face. "Are you sure that's what you want?"

"Why?" Grace asked, shrugging off her coat. She had been looking forward to the drink all afternoon. Longer than that, really. She abstained from alcohol during the week so she could keep her head clear for work. The sacrifice often made the first drink of the weekend feel like a celebration. After the long week she'd had, she could use some good cheer. "Do you know something I don't? There hasn't been another produce recall for *E. coli*, has there?"

"Not that I know of. Between the grenadine and the orange juice, that's way more sugar than you should ingest in one sitting. One of the rules I teach my clients is you should eat your fruit, not drink your fruit. A glass of bottled orange juice contains more sugar and calories than a can of soda."

Grace thought she had agreed to a blind date, not a lecture.

"What'll it be?" the bartender asked.

Grace opened her mouth to speak, but Renee responded before she could. "She'll have a skinny margarita." She turned to Grace after the bartender left to gather the ingredients he needed to prepare the drink. "You can thank me later."

Grace wasn't so sure about that, but she didn't feel like arguing. "How long have you been a personal trainer?"

"Five years. I started out small. Now I have a roster of about a dozen clients. That's not counting the various celebrities I train on the side. I would tell you their names, but most of them have asked me to sign confidentiality agreements in order to maintain their privacy. For the amount of money they pay me to get them in shape for their next movie, TV show, or concert tour, I'm willing to sign anything they want." Renee took a sip of her drink. Something see-through and probably sugar-free. "How much do you weigh?"

"Excuse me?" Apparently, no one had told Renee it wasn't polite to ask such questions in general, let alone on a first date.

"You look like you're somewhere between a size eight and a size ten." Renee slipped two fingers in her back pocket, pulled out a business card, and slid the card toward Grace. Grace glanced at the card but didn't reach for it. "I could get you down to a size six in no time. A four if you're really dedicated."

"And have me looking like a balloon-headed stick figure like Oprah did when she lost sixty-seven pounds and traipsed across the stage in skintight jeans? No, thanks. I'm fine the way I am."

Renee frowned in disapproval. "I've always been health-conscious. I expect any woman I date to be as well."

Grace didn't appreciate Renee's condescending attitude. "How do you know I'm not health-conscious? Just because my body doesn't have zero percent fat doesn't mean I don't care what goes into it."

"Perhaps, but I see definite room for improvement. Don't you want to be the best version of yourself that you can be?"

"Of course, and that version includes exercising three times a week, eating in moderation, and splurging on the occasional piece of cheesecake, not giving in to body shamers who want me to starve myself in an attempt to achieve their ideal of beauty. Could I stand to lose a few pounds? Certainly. Who couldn't? But if you can't see and appreciate the woman I am instead of the one you want me to be, that's your loss."

The bartender placed Grace's drink in front of her. She took a sip and found it was not only lacking in sugar and calories. It was also lacking in taste.

"I think we got off on the wrong foot," Renee said. "Do you want to start over?"

"No, I think we should call it a night. Thanks for the drink."

Grace grabbed her coat and walked out. She wanted to kick herself for going against her own instincts. If she had followed her gut, she could have avoided this tedious—and testy—encounter. Outside, she pulled her cell phone out of her purse and called Lynette.

"What did you think of Renee?" Lynette asked without bothering to say hello.

"Beautiful body, ugly personality."

"She just takes some getting used to, that's all. She's direct. Straight to the point."

"She's also rude, obnoxious, and stuck on herself." Grace decided to walk instead of hailing a cab to give herself time to calm down before she got home.

"Okay, yeah, she is, but did you see her arms? They're to-die-for. Anyway, since Renee didn't work out, I know someone else you might like. Her name's Karin and she's—"

Grace cut in before Lynette could finish making her pitch. "I've had enough of your matchmaking for one night, Nettie. I'll call you tomorrow."

She ended the call and shoved her hands in her coat pockets as she continued on her way. When she made it to the corner, she saw Dakota speeding along the cross street. Dakota had ditched her mangled bicycle in favor of one that looked as fast and as sleek as a greyhound. When Grace raised a hand in greeting, Dakota must have thought she was trying to flag her down because she braked to a stop and joined her on the sidewalk.

"Where did you get the new wheels?" Grace asked.

"A friend of mine owns a shop not too far from here. She sold me this bike after we put my old one out to pasture. Where are you headed?"

"Home. My date didn't go as well as planned."

"I'm sorry to hear that."

"That's not what you said earlier."

Even by the soft glow of the streetlight, Grace could see color rise in Dakota's cheeks.

"Yeah, well, I've been told I have a knack for saying all the things that are often best left unsaid. How far is your place?"

"It's about a five-minute walk," Grace said warily. She hoped Dakota didn't expect her to invite her in for a nightcap because she wasn't in the mood to play happy hostess. Or anything else, for that matter.

Dakota seemed nice enough, but based on the articles Grace had read about her, everything was a joke to her. She didn't seem to take anything seriously, especially relationships. Why would any woman want to trust her heart to someone like that?

"Would you like a ride?" Dakota asked. "You can be my first passenger."

Grace took a long look at the bike's skinny tires. "Those don't look substantial enough for one person, let alone two."

"You never know until you give it a try." Dakota climbed off the bike and moved closer. "Hop on," she said, patting the handlebars.

Grace let out a nervous giggle. "I haven't ridden that way since I was a kid. The last time I did, I fell off and nearly broke my neck."

"So is that a no?"

Grace thought it over. The idea that a grown-ass woman—in a skirt and heels, no less—would pass up traditional methods of transportation in order to climb on a relative stranger's handlebars seemed abjectly ludicrous on one hand and delightfully frivolous on the other.

"If you're worried," Dakota said, "I'll let you borrow my helmet."

"I'm not worried."

"Then what are you waiting for? I won't let you fall, Grace. I promise."

Dakota unbuckled her chin strap, pulled off her helmet, and held it out. To Grace, the move felt like a challenge. Logic said she should have shrunk from it, but Dakota's promise made her feel like nothing could go wrong.

Grace grabbed the helmet and cinched it into place. "What's the worst that could happen?"

❖

Dakota had offered to be Grace's ersatz Uber driver on a whim. Now she had to figure out how to make the idea work. She held the bike steady and offered her shoulder for support while Grace tried to climb on the handlebars.

Grace let out a squeal of alarm when she slipped and nearly fell. The death grip she held on Dakota's arm nearly took them both down. Bracing her legs, Dakota wrapped an arm around Grace's waist until she regained her balance. The helmet she had loaned Grace drooped over one of her eyes like Veronica Lake's famous peekaboo curls. Dakota used the tip of her finger to nudge the helmet back into its proper position.

"Are you okay?"

When Grace met her gaze, she looked both determined and adorable. "Take two." Grace hitched up her skirt and tried again. Her second attempt was touch-and-go for a while but ultimately proved successful. "I did it." She sounded surprised—and a little pleased with herself.

Dakota took a second to savor the sight of Grace perched on her handlebars like a queen on a throne. "Hang on. Here we go."

She walked the bike forward a few steps to gain some momentum, then started pumping the pedals as hard as she could to make sure she didn't lose it. She wobbled a time or two as she struggled to get up to speed, but it was smooth sailing once she found her rhythm.

Grace's scent—light and citrusy like a summer day—made Dakota feel homesick. She wanted to take her to Georgia and get to know her while they sat in a porch swing and shared a pitcher of sweet tea.

A honking car horn snapped Dakota out of her reverie. "Where to?" she asked, swerving to avoid a pothole almost as deep as the Grand Canyon.

"Take a right at the next corner. I'm two blocks down on the left."

Dakota made the turn and let the bike coast on the slight downhill slope. She didn't want to build up too much speed because if she had to hit the brakes in a hurry, Grace might go flying off. The ride was going well so far. She didn't want to be responsible for dredging up bad memories.

"Over there." Grace let go of the handlebars long enough to point out a set of three-story brownstone row houses. Each house was painted a different color. Some were a muted gray or conservative off-white while others were as bright as Easter eggs.

"Which one's yours?"

"The sepia one with the pot of begonias on the stoop."

Dakota crossed the street and gently squeezed the brakes to slow their speed. "Those are pretty. Do you like plants?"

"My mother does."

"Oh, your mother lives with you?"

"My whole family does. My parents live on the first floor, my sisters are on the second, and I'm on the third."

"How did you get lucky enough to have a floor of your own?"

"The third floor is the hottest one in the house. No one else wanted it, so I called dibs."

Dakota stopped in front of the sepia brownstone, then offered Grace her hand to help her climb down. "What's wrong?" she asked after Grace gingerly stepped on the sidewalk.

Grace grimaced as she placed her hands on her butt. "It looks so romantic when couples do that in the movies, but no one ever mentions how painful it can be to sit on an unpadded metal bar."

Dakota couldn't hold back the laugh that erupted from her. Nor did she want to. "I would offer to rub out the kinks, but I'm afraid you might take it the wrong way."

Grace unbuckled the helmet and tossed it to Dakota. "Is there any other way to take a comment like that?"

"I could think of several," Dakota said with a grin. "In case you're wondering, unless it's an incredibly hot day, getting caught in the rain is overrated, too."

"I'll keep that in mind the next time the weatherman says I should grab an umbrella on my way out the door."

"You do that." A slight movement over Grace's shoulder caught Dakota's eye. She looked up to see someone peeking out the front window. "I think we have company."

When Grace turned around, the figure let the curtain fall and quickly moved away from the window.

"That would be my nosy sister checking to see if I got lucky tonight."

"Did you?" Dakota asked before she could stop herself.

"In a way," Grace said mysteriously as she climbed the steps.

When Grace reached the top of the stoop, Dakota felt like Romeo staring up at Juliet on her balcony. *A rose by any other name.*

"Thanks for the ride," Grace said.

"Anytime."

Dakota waited until Grace was safely inside before she began to make her way home. She secured her helmet, then turned her bike toward the nearest subway station so she could take the train back to Greenwich Village. She told herself not to turn around, but she couldn't help herself. She had to have one last look.

When she sneaked a peek at Grace's brownstone, someone was looking out the window again. Except this time it wasn't Grace's sister staring at her. This time, it was Grace.

❖

"Oops." Grace closed the curtains and backed away from the window. Dakota had turned around unexpectedly and had nearly caught her staring. "That was close."

She turned to head upstairs, but her sister Faith was standing in her way, a half-empty plate of food in her hands. "You certainly changed your tune in a hurry."

Grace knew exactly what Faith was referring to, but she tried to play it cool. "Where is everyone?"

"Mommy and Daddy are at church and Hope is on a date." Faith sat on the couch and propped her feet on the coffee table, a sure sign that their mother wasn't home. If she had been, she would have been yelling at Faith to get her feet off the furniture. Charity Henderson was a firm proponent of the notion that a lady should keep one foot on the floor at all times, whether in mixed company or not. "Don't try to change the subject. That was Dakota Lane you were talking to, wasn't it?"

"Yeah. So?"

"You've always said you don't find her attractive because she looks too much like a boy." Faith speared green beans with her fork and waved them in the air as she made her point. "A very pretty boy, but a boy nevertheless."

Grace grabbed a piece of baked chicken from Faith's plate. "I never said she wasn't attractive," she said, going back for more. "When have you ever seen a model who wasn't gorgeous? But that doesn't mean I'm attracted to her."

Faith stabbed at Grace's fingers to prevent her from pinching a piece of corn bread. "That's not what Lillie said."

"Oh, God." Grace got a sinking feeling in the pit of her stomach. "What rumor is she spreading now?"

Faith's eyes twinkled the way they always did when she had a juicy secret she wanted to spill. "It's not a rumor if there's truth behind it."

Grace sighed in exasperation as she headed to the kitchen to fix herself a plate of leftovers for dinner. "Just tell me what she said."

"That you and your new client were so busy making googly eyes at each other you could barely get her measurements right."

Grace lifted the lids to see what was in each pot. "Mom never cooks this much on a Friday night. What gives?"

Faith came in the kitchen and leaned against the doorjamb. "Stop beating around the bush and answer the question."

Grace turned to face her. "When have you ever known me to let a client get under my skin?"

"Never," Faith said, joining her by the stove. "But what I want to know is if you plan on letting this one get into your pants."

"What I plan to do, little sister, is make her a suit. Nothing more." Grace grabbed a fork from the utensil drawer and nudged the drawer closed with her hip. "So don't go running that mouth of yours any more than you already have."

Faith held up her hands in mock surrender. "Fine. I won't say anything to anyone. But you'd better make sure you tell Lillie the same thing you just told me."

"Don't worry. I intend to have a come-to-Jesus meeting with her first thing Monday morning."

Grace picked up her plate and headed out of the kitchen. She replayed the events of the day as she climbed the stairs. She couldn't deny the charged tension that had coursed between her and Dakota that afternoon, but she had dismissed it as a fluke. Now she wasn't so sure. How had one bike ride managed to change her perspective? Perhaps it wasn't the ride itself but the woman behind the wheel.

Grace made clothes that drew attention, but she preferred to fit in rather than stand out. Everywhere she went, Dakota drew stares. Not because of what she was wearing but because of the way she looked. Grace had seen it firsthand tonight from people they had passed on the street. Sometimes the looks were of admiration, sometimes of scorn.

Grace didn't want that kind of scrutiny. She didn't want a woman like Dakota.

After she reached her room, she closed the door behind her, pulled out her cell phone, and called Lynette.

"Okay, I'm listening," she said after Lynette picked up. "Tell me about Karin."

Chapter Four

Dakota squirted styling gel into her palm, rubbed her hands together, and worked the gel into her damp hair with her fingers. "What are you smiling at?" she asked as Rich stood in the doorway and watched her get ready.

Rich folded his arms across his chest. He was wearing penny loafers, hot pink capri pants, a dark blue cardigan, and a scoop-neck white T-shirt that hugged his narrow frame. He was nearly half a foot shorter than she was and so thin one might be tempted to refer to him as delicate. Dakota knew from experience, however, that he was stronger than he looked. She had witnessed both his mental and physical toughness over the years as he used his quick wit to shrug off taunts from bullies and disapproving family members alike. She had known him since she was three and she felt privileged to be able to call him her friend.

The tiny bathroom in the apartment they shared was barely large enough for one person. Two crammed into the same space felt crowded, even if Rich was pocket-sized. He draped his arm across her shoulders after he joined her in front of the mirror. "If you had a penis, I'd fuck you."

She straightened the plastic tiara perched haphazardly on his head. "I've got one in the nightstand next to my bed. Will that do?"

"If I don't meet any cute guys tonight, I might ask you to pull it out." He rested his head against her like he needed a shoulder to cry on. "How did we get here?"

"By 'here,' I take it you don't mean this apartment."

She and Rich lived in a third-floor walkup around the corner from the Stonewall Inn, the iconic tavern often referred to as the birthplace of the gay rights movement. The bar and the park across the street from it were two of their favorite places to meet up with friends. Thanks to the Stonewall's history and symbolism, Dakota couldn't think of a better venue for Rich's going-away party. Its proximity was a motivating factor as well. Since their destination was close enough to walk to, they wouldn't need to hail a cab or depend on a designated driver when the time came for them to stumble home. Dakota didn't plan on getting too wasted tonight, but she couldn't let an occasion this momentous go by without toasting it with a drink or three. And toasting with water was allegedly bad luck, so why take the chance?

"No, I mean how did we get *here*?" Rich said. "On the verge of everything we've ever wanted." He wrapped his arms around her, his green eyes wet with tears. He cried at the drop of a hat. He always had. Sappy commercials that left her doubled over with laughter made him bawl like a baby. Lately, though, he needed even less reason than normal to start the waterworks. "We're just a couple of small-town kids from south Georgia. How did we get all the way to New York City?"

"We dreamed big, then we worked our asses off to make those dreams come true." In school, she had been his de facto bodyguard. Though he no longer needed protecting, she still felt responsible for keeping him safe. "Be careful, okay?"

"Don't worry. I packed so many condoms, each of Trojan's stockholders should send me a handwritten thank-you note."

She wrapped her arms around his as he continued to hold on to her. "That's not what I mean."

Ever since the mass shooting at the Pulse nightclub in Orlando, Dakota had held her breath when Rich went to work at Mainline or made a guest appearance at another venue. She didn't live her life in fear—neither of them did—but she was much more cautious than she had been before the night domestic terrorism hit the heart of their community. She held her friends even closer than she had before. And she told them she loved them every day, whether they wanted to hear it or not.

"I know it isn't," Rich said, giving her a squeeze, "but everything's going to be fine. And on the off chance that I'm wrong, just think of the millions you stand to inherit."

She laughed at the absurdity of his comment and turned to face him. "I've seen your bank statements. At the moment, the only things I stand to inherit are your overdraft balances. And what's with all the condoms? I thought you and Aaron were getting serious."

Rich lowered his eyes. "We were."

"But?"

"I'm going to be on the road for four months, sixty cities, and twelve countries. That's a lot of miles and a lot of men. You know me. I can resist anything except temptation. And when I'm hungry, nothing beats a good sampler platter." He put his hands on his slim hips. "Don't give me that look."

"What look?"

"The one that says you think I've chosen to do something I might end up regretting. Why are you lecturing me anyway? You pick up someone new every time you go out. Do you expect me to believe you don't hook up when you head to some exotic locale for a photo shoot?"

"That's not true."

"Which part?"

"I don't hook up *every* time I go out."

"No? When was the last time you went clubbing and didn't get laid?"

"Probably junior high school."

"Ha!"

"Don't *ha* me. I'm single."

"So am I."

"Since when?"

"Since about six hours ago."

"Rich—"

"Stop. I know what you're going to say. I whined about not having a boyfriend, then I found one and kicked him to the curb the first chance I got. Aaron will still be here when I get back. If he wants to pick up where we left off, fine. If he doesn't, I'll deal. Don't look so worried. I got this, girlfriend."

Like a boxer with great defense, Rich had learned to roll with the punches. Dakota, on the other hand, usually ended up taking most blows on the chin. Thankfully, she didn't have a glass jaw.

She buttoned her French blue oxford shirt and tucked the hem into her jeans. Then she buckled her belt, took one last look in the mirror, and reached for her jacket. "Ready?"

Rich sat on the couch instead of heading for the door. "Let's wait a few minutes. I want to be fashionably late." He pointed to his new fashion accessory. "This tiara means I'm queen for the day."

"I thought that was every day."

"Bitch." He tossed a throw pillow at her and missed by a mile. "I heard Sophie moved to town. Is that true?"

"Sophie Mestach?" Dakota picked up the throw pillow and returned it to its place on the couch. "Where did you hear that?"

"Luke and I had brunch this afternoon. You know clients tell their hairdressers everything. One of Luke's best customers is an editor who was going on and on about a photo shoot her magazine has planned with Sophie for an upcoming issue."

Thanks to the bombshell Rich had just dropped on her, Dakota no longer felt like celebrating. Sophie Mestach, a former Olympic swimmer from Belgium, was her main rival in a competitive niche market. With her broad shoulders and blond hair, Sophie looked like a surfer waiting for the next big wave. Despite—or perhaps because of—her all-American looks, she worked primarily in Europe. Dakota had lost out on more than one well-paying gig in that market because the designers or photographers had chosen to go with Sophie instead. If Sophie had relocated to New York, that meant they would be competing for jobs stateside as well.

Fewer gigs meant less money. And with Rich not around to kick in his half of the rent for the next four months, less money was not an option.

"Remind me to call my agent tomorrow. He and I have some things we need to discuss."

"And in the meantime?"
"Let's go get laid."

❖

Grace always woke up on Sunday mornings feeling inspired. With good reason. Ever since she was a little girl, Sunday meant getting dressed up, walking to church with her family, and heading to their favorite local restaurant for a leisurely brunch after services. The day usually started early when Grace's mother woke around six a.m. to have a cup of coffee and watch the sun rise through the kitchen window. To put everyone in the proper mood, she tuned the radio in the living room to a gospel station and cranked the volume up loud. That meant Grace woke to the rousing sound of soaring vocals drifting from one floor to the next as they made their way to the heavens.

This Sunday morning was different. This Sunday she didn't wake up with thoughts of salvation or soul food on her mind. She woke thinking of Dakota Lane. More precisely, the suit she had been asked to craft for her. She had a design idea in mind, and she wanted to get the images on paper while they were still fresh.

She tossed her bed covers aside and padded barefoot across the cold hardwood floor. Then she grabbed her sketchbook and drawing pencils off her bureau and returned to bed. After she propped her pillow against the headboard and rested the sketchbook against her bent knees, she went to work.

She started on the dress shirt first. Instead of the classic or button-down collar, she decided to go with the semi-spread to give the shirt a slightly different look. She used the same approach on the cuffs, ditching the traditional one-button square cuff in favor of a three-button angle cuff. The rest of the shirt was easy. Roomy through the chest and shoulders but tight to the body, giving the finished product a tapered look that would perfectly mimic Dakota's silhouette.

After she completed the design for the shirt, Grace flipped to a new page so she could start on the preliminary sketches for the suit.

She tapped her pencil against her chin as she debated the proper cut. There were three to choose from, and she needed to make sure she chose wisely. Otherwise, she would have to start from scratch. Thanks to the tight schedule they were on, she didn't have time for do-overs.

She decided against the American Cut, which was designed for comfort rather than style. People in the industry didn't call it the sack suit without reason. Its moderately padded shoulders, single vent, roomy waist, and overall boxy look were ideal for clients with wide middles. Dakota might have been slightly larger in the waist than her last set of official measurements, but she was still a long way away from having to shop in the plus size department.

That narrowed Grace's choices down to two. Should she go with the English Cut or the Italian? The English Cut was the traditional choice for men's suits. It featured flap pockets, tapered sides at the waist, and little to no padding in the shoulders. The dual vents in the back of the coat came from the days of horseback riding since the vents made the jacket set better at the waist while the owner was astride his steed. Now the vents were used to make the wearer look taller and thinner. Dakota didn't need any help in that regard.

By process of elimination, that meant Grace had only one choice.

The Italian Cut played off the client's small waist to create an inverted triangle. Slash pockets added to the streamlined silhouette. The look was highly fashionable, giving off an air of power and authority. The lack of vents meant less mobility, but Grace didn't see that as too much of a drawback. Unless Dakota planned to breakdance at her sister's wedding, she should be fine.

Grace drew a notch collar and designed the coat around it. The ideas were flowing so freely the whole process took only a matter of minutes. The sketch for the pants came together just as quickly. The traditional four-pocket design with cuffed hems and a flat-front waist.

She made a few tweaks to the final image and leaned back to take a look at what she had done.

She tried to make each suit she designed unique to the client's personality. The questions she asked during the interview sessions before and after the initial fitting helped her get an idea of what the clients wanted and what they were about.

As she looked at the sketches, she thought she had captured Dakota's personality on paper. Vibrant, playful, and far from traditional. She hoped Dakota would be pleased with her designs, but she wouldn't know for sure until she got to the office on Monday, added fabric swatches to her sketches to offer a frame of reference, and emailed the completed presentation to Dakota for final approval.

Grace was tempted to ask Dakota to come into the office so she could watch her react to the designs in person, but that wasn't how she normally operated. She always sent an email or fax and waited for her clients to reply in similar fashion. Why was she tempted to change her M.O. now? Why did Dakota's opinion of her work—and, by extension, of her—matter so much? Granted, Dakota wasn't like the rest of her clients, but was that the only reason she was treating her differently?

"Of course it is," she told herself as she stood in front of her closet and searched for a dress to wear. "What other reason could there be?"

After she showered and dressed, she joined her family downstairs for the five-block walk to church. Services began at eleven and, unless the pastor was long-winded, were usually over by noon. Brunch, thankfully, didn't have a time limit. It could last anywhere from a couple of hours to the rest of the afternoon, depending on how in-depth the conversation got between courses. If the topic was juicy enough, brunch sometimes segued into dinner.

Grace loved Sundays. They afforded her an opportunity to spend time with her family and play catch-up. Even though they lived in the same house, they didn't get many chances to see each other during the week. Her parents were semiretired, but they were active in the church and the community. Her older sister Hope was a home health care aide who ping-ponged between day and night shifts, depending on her clients' needs. And Faith was in her sophomore year at NYU. Her heavy class load didn't give her many chances to socialize. Grace's schedule was equally crazy since some clients treated the official business hours as little more than suggestions. When she left for work each morning, she never knew what time she would make it home. Yet another reason she had such a hard time establishing, let alone maintaining relationships.

One day, she thought as she slowly walked along the tree-lined streets leading to Bethlehem AME Zion Church. *One day, all the sacrifices I've made will be worth it.*

But would she have someone to share her accomplishments with, or would she be forced to enjoy them on her own?

"I heard you had a date Friday night," her father said as he and her mother walked arm in arm at the front of the pack. "How did things go?"

"Fine," Grace said noncommittally.

Her family had always been outwardly accepting of her sexuality, but she sometimes sensed a subtle air of disapproval if a woman she was seeing didn't meet their exacting standards.

Her father obsessed over even the slightest imperfection in a piece of fabric. He was just as demanding when it came to his daughters' suitors, Grace's included. Except the bar he set for her sisters' potential partners seemed even higher for hers. Hope and Faith eventually stopped bringing their boyfriends to the house because their father always managed to find fault with them. Faith once complained he wanted them to be single for the rest of their lives because he was too stingy to pay for three weddings. Grace thought his reasons had more to do with heart strings than purse strings.

"I want you to do what makes you happy," he'd told her after she came out to him, "but I don't want to see you hurt. Any woman who breaks your heart will have to answer to me."

Fortunately, that day hadn't yet arrived. Grace had been in her fair share of relationships, but she'd never been so head over heels in love that she'd been heartbroken when the unions came to an end. She was starting to wonder if she ever would. Perhaps some of her exes were right. Perhaps she put so much of her energy into her job and her family that she didn't have any left for anything—or anyone—else.

"Are you planning to see her again?"

Her mother's question drew Grace out of her own head and back to the conversation at hand.

"No," Faith said with a mischievous grin. "She already has her eye on someone else."

Grace tried to dig an elbow into Faith's ribs, but Faith danced out of the way before she could make contact.

"Oh?" her mother said. "Do I know her?"

"No, but you've seen her," Faith said. "Her picture's all over Times Square."

"What?" her mother asked, frowning. "She's not wanted or anything, is she, Grace? You know your father and I don't approve of you and your sisters getting mixed up with someone with a criminal background. It wouldn't reflect well on the business or our family."

Grace had heard this speech so many times she could quote it from memory. Her father was an important member of the community. His was one of the few black-owned businesses outside of Harlem that had managed to maintain a consistent level of success. And so on. And so on.

She would never do anything that might tarnish her father's legacy or negatively affect her future. Hadn't she proved that time and time again? "Pay no attention to Faith. She doesn't know what she's talking about."

"Does Lillie?" her father asked. "Because she certainly had plenty to say when she called the house Friday night." He looked back at Grace to make sure she was paying attention. "She said you and one of your clients were having a hard time keeping your hands to yourselves."

"I wouldn't put it that way."

"Then how would you put it? You know how I feel about mixing business with pleasure."

"Yes, Dad, I do. I feel the same way."

"You don't want to get with Dakota Lane, anyway," Hope said.

Grace wasn't sure she wanted to hear the reasons behind Hope's statement, but she asked the question nevertheless. "Why not?"

"She's too mannish. The women you normally date look like

women, not imitation men. What's the point of being a lesbian if you're going to date a woman who looks like a dude?"

"Because underneath it all, she's still a woman, isn't she?"

"*Way* underneath."

Grace felt offended. On her behalf or Dakota's, she wasn't sure. Butch women might not be her cup of tea, but they deserved to be able to express themselves in any way they chose. In the immortal words of the famed philosopher RuPaul, everyone's born naked and the rest was drag. Hope threw her shoulders back as if she didn't expect Grace to challenge either her statements or her attitude, but Grace decided to push the issue rather than letting it drop. "Perhaps I had a change of heart."

Hope stopped in her tracks. "You? Get real. You're so set in your ways you won't even change your hairstyle, let alone your dating patterns. You grew up with posters of Janet Jackson and Whitney Houston on your wall. You're not about to start dating k.d. lang."

"How do you know?" Grace asked defensively. What Hope referred to as being set in her ways, others might call being stuck in a rut. Neither situation felt like one Grace wanted to be in. "I might surprise all of you one day."

"Dream on, sis," Hope said with a caustic laugh. "The day you sleep with a woman who doesn't look like *Jet* magazine's Beauty of the Week is the day I finally walk down the aisle with Idris Elba. And the day you bring Dakota Lane home is the same day you get cut out of the will."

"Why are you so dead set against her? You don't even know her."

"I know what I've seen. And since she doesn't seem to know the meaning of the word *discreet*, I've seen plenty. She reminds me of that guy who was kicked off of a reality show on MTV years ago. The guy who used to dip the same finger he picked his nose with into the communal jar of peanut butter."

"Ew." Faith wrinkled her nose in distaste. "Gross."

Since Dakota wasn't around to defend herself, Grace felt

compelled to do it for her. "She wasn't like that when I met her. She was friendly, respectful, and well-mannered. Lillie even remarked on the fact that she said 'please' and 'thank you' and called her 'ma'am.'"

"She sounds like the perfect gentleman," Hope said sarcastically. "Did she pull Lillie's chair out for her, too?"

"The opportunity didn't present itself."

"That's too bad. For Lillie, I mean." Hope examined Grace's face as if she were trying to gauge her level of interest in Dakota. She narrowed her eyes after she seemed to reach her conclusion. "You know who we're talking about, don't you, Daddy?" She performed an image search on her phone and pulled up several unflattering photos of Dakota and a series of women in various stages of undress, as well as sobriety.

Grace's father glanced at the photos but quickly averted his eyes. "Put that away. That's not something any of us should be seeing on a Sunday morning."

"Or any other morning, for that matter," Grace's mother said. "Shameful. Or should I say shame*less*?"

Grace's mother made the word sound pejorative, but Grace considered it a compliment. Dakota lived her life on her own terms without caring who was watching or what they had to say about the way she looked, dressed, or acted. The only person's approval she sought was her own. Grace wished she could say the same.

"Do her parents know what she's up to?" her mother asked.

"They should," Hope said. "She's in the tabloids all the time."

"And we all know tabloids never manufacture stories or headlines in order to sell magazines."

"Does this look made up to you?" Hope showed Grace a picture of two people crammed into what looked like a bathroom stall. Dakota's face was visible only in profile. Her companion's visage, however, was plain to see as she paused to document the moment with a well-timed selfie.

Grace shrank from the picture—and the hint of cruelty in her sister's gleeful smile.

"I trust you won't find yourself in similar circumstances," Hope said. "Unless having sex in a nightclub bathroom is your idea of a good time."

"Not hardly." Grace wasn't into excessive public displays of affection. A kiss or two were okay as long as the busses remained relatively chaste. The images Hope was thrusting in her face, however, seemed like stills from a porn film.

"I didn't think so."

Grace's father turned to face her. "We've serviced controversial customers before. I suppose it won't hurt our bottom line to be associated with this Dakota person professionally. But given the photographic evidence Hope just produced, is she someone you think you'd like to spend time with on a personal basis?"

Grace didn't know Dakota well enough to be able to separate fantasy from reality. Logic said she should keep her distance, but curiosity tempted her to take a peek behind the curtain. One thing stopped her: she didn't like being the center of attention, and Dakota couldn't seem to get enough. "No, Dad, she's just a client."

"Good. Make sure that's all she remains."

Her father nodded as if the matter had been put to rest, but Grace felt unsettled. As she continued the trek to church, she wondered who she was trying to please in her thus far futile search for love: her family or herself.

Chapter Five

Dakota completed her last morning delivery, then made an unscheduled stop after she clocked out for lunch. She was under contract with Whitaker Models, one of the most prestigious modeling agencies in New York City. Laird Jennings was her agent. He was supposed to be at her beck and call twenty-four hours a day, but she hadn't been able to get him on the phone since she dug her cell out of the bowl of uncooked rice it had been sitting in all weekend while she waited for it to dry out.

Laird usually returned her calls right away, but she hadn't heard from him despite the four voice mails she had left asking him to call her as soon as he got her message. She needed to know how Sophie Mestach's arrival on the scene would affect her standing in the industry. Had she gone out of style like last year's fashions, or was she still on trend? Laird's uncharacteristic silence was increasing her anxiety.

She hadn't seen any press releases about Sophie signing with a New York–based agency. Was Whitaker planning to make a run at her? If so, the competition between them was about to get even more heated.

"Mr. Jennings has been in meetings all morning," Laird's personal assistant said as Dakota waited for him outside his office. "I told him you're here. He'll try to squeeze you in as soon as he can."

Dakota picked up a two-month-old magazine and flipped through the pages. "I've got nothing but time."

That wasn't entirely true. She had a pickup scheduled for one o'clock and she needed to get back on her bike in plenty of time for her to get there. And as for her second career, she was starting to feel like her time was running out. She'd had a good run, but she wasn't ready for it to be over. She was having too much fun to jump off the merry-go-round now.

Her phone chimed while she waited for Laird to wrap things up with whoever was in his office. She dug her phone out of her messenger bag and checked the display. An email from Grace was sitting in her in-box. Technically, the email had come from Henderson Custom Suits since the company's official email address was listed as the sender, but Grace was undoubtedly the author.

Dakota didn't expect the email to be personal in nature since Grace had taken great pains to keep her distance thus far, so she wasn't surprised to see the content was purely business-related. Grace had completed her design for the suit Dakota had commissioned and she needed approval before she could proceed to the next phase.

Dakota tossed the out-of-date magazine aside and opened the email attachment so she could take a look at the design. What she saw blew her away. Even though Grace's sketches weren't three-dimensional, they seemed to leap off the screen. Dakota could sense both the energy behind the drawings and the passion Grace had obviously put into them.

The suit was perfect. Every detail was one Dakota would have selected herself. She couldn't believe Grace had been able to capture exactly what she wanted when she hadn't been able to put it into words. She couldn't wait to see the finished product—and to have Grace see her in it. She had modeled for thousands of people over the years. At the moment, she wanted to strut her stuff for an audience of one.

She hit the Reply button and typed her response.

I love it. Don't change a thing.

She heard Laird's door open right after she hit Send. She looked up to see Laird shaking hands with Sophie Mestach and her husband Ruben, an attorney who also served as her business manager.

"I look forward to working with you, Sophie," Laird said. "I think we can do great things together."

"I agree. I can't wait to get started." Sophie's enthusiasm appeared to wane a bit when she turned and spotted Dakota sitting in the waiting area. She quickly plastered on a smile that seemed decidedly less than genuine. "Dakota, it's a pleasure seeing you again."

Sophie spread her arms and offered her cheeks to be kissed. Dakota obliged, bussing the air next to Sophie's face. She didn't have to force herself to make small talk because Ruben took Sophie by the arm and drew her away before she could say much more than hello.

"I have someplace I need to be," Sophie said, "but let's have lunch sometime. You pick the place and I'll pick up the tab as long as you promise to be a cheap date."

As Sophie and Ruben headed to the elevator, Dakota tried to gauge Laird's reaction. He looked like he'd rather be somewhere else.

"I wasn't expecting to see you today." He shoved his hands in his pockets as if he didn't know what else to do with them. "What's with the surprise visit?"

"Didn't you get my voice mails?"

"Yes, but I've been in meetings all morning."

"So I see." Dakota let her gaze drift to the elevator. The doors had just closed and the car was starting to make its descent to the ground floor.

"Come in and have a seat." Laird steered her into his office and grabbed a bottle of mineral water from the stocked mini-bar. The thing looked like something out of *Mad Men*, the classic television show about boozing New York ad execs. Don Draper, the main character, would have been proud. "Would you like something to drink?"

"No, but I'd appreciate some answers."

"I'm sure you would." Laird sat on a corner of his desk. A pose he always took on when he was trying to seem personable rather than aloof. "I know what you're thinking, but you don't have anything to worry about."

"So you didn't sign Sophie as backup because you're worried I'll become a cautionary tale like Gia Carangi?"

Gia Carangi was considered to be the first supermodel. Before Naomi, Elle, Helena, Kate, and Christy, there was Gia. The Philadelphia native was known for her meteoric rise to fame and the heroin addiction that helped bring both her career and life to premature ends. Dakota liked to live close to the edge, but she always remained in control of herself and the situation. She had no intention of following Gia's self-destructive path, but perhaps Laird and the rest of the executives at Whitaker thought she was already on her way to doing just that.

"Everyone at the agency is very happy with you and your work," Laird said. "We aren't looking to replace you. What we're trying to do is shore up the team so we can corner the market. Demand for you and your peers is increasing, but you can't be everywhere at once. That's where Sophie comes in. With her on the roster, we'll have two of the most sought-after models in the industry. Don't look at her as your competition. Those days are over. From now on, she's your ally. If everything works out, it could result in twice the bookings, which means more exposure for you and more money for everyone."

"And if it doesn't?"

He leaned back as if he had expected her to accept his proposal without raising any objections. "You're seeing the glass as half-empty rather than half-full."

"Wouldn't you if you were in my position?" She took in his expensive clothes and accessories and looked around his well-appointed office. The room, filled with trappings of his success, was larger than her apartment. She was proud of the money she had made over the years, but it was chump change compared to what Laird pulled in. "You'll get paid whether your little experiment succeeds or fails. I, on the other hand, might not."

"You're flying to Belize in two weeks for a photo shoot, you have shows scheduled throughout Fashion Week, and your face is going to be all over *Vogue*'s September issue," he said, ticking off each point on his fingers. "Your calendar's full, Dakota. Bringing Sophie into the fold isn't going to change that."

"But what about—"

Laird held out his hands in a placating gesture. "You're not going anywhere. You have my word on that. You're under contract for three more years and we aren't looking for a loophole to spring you from it. I hope you aren't either."

Even if she found a way to break free, she wouldn't be allowed to sign with another agency until her contract with Whitaker expired. Like it or not, she was stuck. If she wanted to keep working as a model, she had to do it for Whitaker. And she had to do it with Sophie Mestach.

Laird looked up when his assistant poked her head in the room to remind him he had a twelve thirty reservation at a high-end seafood restaurant run by a famed French chef with three Michelin stars under his toque. "I'm on my way." He turned back to Dakota. "I hate to cut this short, but I've got to go. If I keep Anna Wintour waiting, she might decide to bump you from the cover. The September *Vogue* is the biggest and most important magazine publication of the year. Do you realize how much exposure you'd miss out on if the issue hits the stands with someone else on the front?"

"Yes," Dakota said wearily.

"So are we cool?"

"Yeah, we're cool."

"Good." He offered her one last bit of reassurance as he walked her to the door. "Relax, Dakota. You're part of the family."

She might have found comfort in his words if she hadn't seen firsthand how easily family could turn their backs on her.

❖

Grace picked up a bolt of charcoal gray pinstripe wool and rolled it out on the cutting table, where she pinned a series of paper sewing patterns to the material. She had always viewed putting a custom suit together like assembling a jigsaw puzzle. Each piece of cloth had to be precisely cut and placed in the correct position in order to form a cohesive whole. If even one measurement was slightly off, it threw everything else out of kilter.

"Have you seen all the requests for fittings that have come into the website today?" her father asked as she carefully traced the outlines of the patterns with her sewing scissors.

Grace waited until she had completed her task before she answered the question. She needed to make sure she didn't cut too close to the paper or the seamstress assigned to the job wouldn't have enough material to assemble a jacket based on the measurements she had taken during the fitting. The client was a seven-foot NBA center. When he tried on the coat, Grace didn't want it to look like it had been made for a six-foot point guard.

"No," she said as she gathered the assembled pieces of cloth into a pile and began to lay out the pattern for a pair of pants to match the jacket she had just finished working on. "I've been too busy trying to clear the backlog of orders to check on potential new ones."

"We average two requests a day if we're lucky, but we've had ten since Saturday night."

"For real?" Business didn't pick up that much unless Easter Sunday, All-Star weekend, or draft night were on the horizon. Two of those events had already passed, and they were currently working through the onslaught of orders for the third. "Who are the messages from?"

Her father reached for his reading glasses and moved closer to the monitor. The specs were his only concession to getting older. At sixty-six, he stood as straight and tall as ever, his face was wrinkle-free, and his close-cropped hair bore only a light dusting of gray. He looked a good ten years younger than his actual age, and he had the energy to match. She hoped she had inherited his genes as well as his business sense. "None of these emails are from our regulars. They all seem to be from new customers."

Grace plucked a pin from the cushion strapped to her wrist and used it to affix the pattern to the wool. "The interview you did on *Good Morning, New York* must have captured people's attention."

Her father scowled at the computer screen. "I don't think so." "Why do you say that?" "I appeared on the show to talk about the suit we made for LeBron James to wear to the awards presentation if he beats out Steph Curry and Kevin Durant for league MVP this year. These requests aren't from other NBA players. They're from women."

Grace set her sewing scissors down and flexed her fingers to prevent her hand from cramping. "All of them?" The company's roster of female customers was so limited she sometimes felt she could count them on one hand and still have fingers to spare. Now they had ten new ones? It didn't make sense.

"Well, the majority are women. Two are from men who say they used to be women, and one woman who's now a man."

Grace had serviced a wide variety of clients over the years, but she couldn't remember having a transgender customer visit the shop. She was excited by the opportunity. And, to be honest, a bit nervous. Most trans consumers had a hard time buying clothes off the rack because mass market designs weren't made to suit their unique dimensions. If they were reaching out to Henderson Custom Suits for help, she wanted to make sure she and her father gave them what they had been searching for but hadn't been able to find.

Her father printed the emails and set them next to her. He traditionally worked with the people who indicated they felt more comfortable being measured by a male tailor. All the new clients must have asked for a female tailor because her father walked away from the cutting table empty-handed. She could see the disappointment on his face and in his body language. Though he had promised the business would be hers one day, he obviously wasn't ready to pass the torch just yet. Neither was she. He still had plenty to teach her and she was more than willing to learn.

"Your friend Dakota must be singing your praises because each potential client said she recommended them to us," her father said as he inspected the lining on a three-piece suit Lillie's granddaughter had just finished sewing. Tracy wasn't quite as skilled a seamstress as her grandmother yet, but she was catching up fast. "Good job." Grace's father gave Tracy a pat on the shoulder before he rejoined

Grace at the cutting table. "Did you promise Dakota some kind of discount if she talked us up to her friends?"

"No, our meeting was straightforward. I picked her brain about what she wanted, took her measurements, gave her a quote, and told her I'd get in touch with her when we were done. That's it. There was never any mention of quid pro quo."

Her father looked perplexed. "In that case, I don't know whether to thank her or ask her to cease and desist."

"Do you want to ignore ten potential orders simply because they came from a segment of society we haven't done business with before?"

"Of course not, but are you sure this is a direction you want to go in?"

"What do you mean?" Her father had never been hesitant about taking on new business before, so she didn't know why he seemed to be dragging his feet now.

He pulled off his glasses and rubbed the bridge of his nose. "You know as well as I do that we have a conservative clientele, Grace. Some of our established customers might have an issue if this influx of orders proves to be more than a one-time thing."

Grace felt her temper flare. "If they have a problem with us doing business with gay, lesbian, or trans clients, I don't want to have them as customers."

"I wouldn't be too hasty if I were you. Ideals are good to have, but they don't put food on the table. Think of the commissions we might miss out on if some of the professional athletes we service decide to take their business elsewhere because they don't want to tarnish their images by being associated with us."

"Tarnish?"

"Forgive my choice of words, but you know what I mean. Some of these guys take the locker room mentality with them wherever they go. They might not be as open-minded as you want them to be."

"I know, but I think it's a better idea for us to diversify our roster of clients than depend on the largesse of a select few. Most athletes are fickle, Dad. They jump from one trend to another. You can't depend on them to have brand loyalty unless there's a sponsorship deal involved. If they don't want to do business with us, fine. We can replace them with other clients. The newcomers might not be as high-profile, but that shouldn't matter as long as we get paid." She picked up the emails he had printed. "There's obviously an untapped market here waiting to be serviced. The numbers may be small now, but that doesn't mean they're destined to remain that way. Ten requests from one referral? That's some seriously effective word of mouth." Her father still didn't look convinced. "These people reached out to us. We need to treat their requests with the respect they deserve, no matter what our other clients might think. Sometimes the old saying is wrong. The customer isn't always right."

"I don't think I've ever seen you get this fired up about something. I can tell how much it means to you."

"But?"

Her father was quiet for a moment. "Fine," he said at length. "I'll let you take the lead on this one. Just make sure you don't lead us off a cliff while you're at it."

"Yes, sir."

Even though she had just been issued a not-so-subtle ultimatum, Grace couldn't stop smiling. Her father always consulted with her on business decisions, but if they had a difference of opinion, he had final say. This was the first time he had chosen to follow her recommendation instead of his own. Now she had to make sure the company didn't lose business while she attempted to help it grow.

"I'm going home for lunch," her father said, putting on his coat. "I think there are some pork chops left from last night. Do you want me to ask Charity to fix you a plate?"

"No, I need to get out of here for a while to force myself to take a break. If I eat at my desk, I'll try to keep going until all the orders are caught up, even though I know there's no way that can happen in one day." She massaged her lower back with both hands. The muscles ached from the hours she had spent bending over the cutting table. If she didn't stop soon, she'd be paying the price for hours to come. "I'll head to the deli up the street in a little while and grab a turkey sandwich or something."

"Make sure you do. You're losing weight, and your mama thinks it's my fault because she says I'm working you too hard." He shook his head. "You're working hard, and I'm hardly working. Maybe somebody's trying to tell me something."

She couldn't tell if he was fishing for a compliment or complaining about his light workload. "Tell Mama I'm the same size I've been since my senior year of college. And no one's trying to tell you anything. You're still the man and you know it."

He flashed a wistful smile. "I always knew you were my favorite for a reason." He put on his hat and gave her a kiss on the cheek.

"What was that for?"

"I'm proud of you, baby. I just felt like showing it, that's all. Are you sure you don't want me to bring you a plate?"

"I'm sure."

"Then I'll see you in a little bit."

"Your family is far less dysfunctional than mine," Tracy said after Grace's father left. "Watching your father dote on you, your mother, and your sisters the way he does makes me cry every time." She dabbed at her streaming eyes. "I need to go fix my face. I've got makeup running everywhere." She grabbed her purse, pushed herself away from the sewing table, and headed to the bathroom down the hall.

Blessed with some much-needed time alone, Grace picked up her phone and called Dakota. "I don't know what you said or did to make my family's company so popular," she said when Dakota picked up, "but I wanted to call and thank you. Our in-box is flooded with emails, and I'm told you're responsible."

Dakota's low-pitched chuckle was nearly drowned out by the sounds of revving engines, honking horns, and curses hurled in a half dozen languages. She sounded like she was in the middle of a huge traffic jam. Otherwise known as a typical day in downtown Manhattan. "I may have talked you up at a party I went to Saturday night. If my comments inspired people to want to do business with you, that's a good thing, isn't it?"

Grace wished she could have been a fly on the wall at the party

Dakota had referenced so she could understand why she had become a topic of conversation with a bunch of people she had never met. "It's great for my bottom line, but why did you do it?"

"Why wouldn't I?"

"I haven't finished your suit yet. It might not turn out how you want it to. If you're disappointed in the final result, your friends might not be so eager to place their own orders."

"I doubt it. If the suit you end up making is half as good as the sketches you sent me today, you'll have a customer for life. I'm sure my friends will tell you the same thing after you meet with them."

"Thank you, Dakota. I can't begin to tell you how grateful my father and I are for the opportunity you've afforded us. Are you free for lunch?"

"Unfortunately, no. I'm actually heading back to work as we speak. I have just enough time to pick up a bite to eat on the way."

"I see." Grace tried to keep her disappointment from seeping into her voice. She hadn't made the call intending to invite Dakota to lunch. Getting turned down had unexpected sting.

"Could I have a rain check, though?" Dakota asked with puppyish enthusiasm. Grace found her eagerness endearing. "During the week isn't good for me because my schedule changes so constantly I never know where I'm going to be from one day to the next. Or from one hour to the next, for that matter."

"Believe me, I know the feeling."

"We could get together this weekend if you're not doing anything."

Grace was supposed to contact Lynette's friend Karin so she could arrange a meeting to see if they might be compatible, but after her disastrous outing with Renee, she hadn't been able to summon the energy to take a chance on another blind date. Dakota offered a relatively safe alternative. She was someone Grace could spend time with without stressing over whether they would fall into bed at the end of the night. Dakota was a client. Nothing more.

"I'll call you Friday afternoon," she said.

"I'm looking forward to it."

And so, Grace realized with a start, was she.

CHAPTER SIX

Dakota had been hitting the gym every night for the past week
to prepare for her upcoming photo shoot in Belize. Once she
arrived on the beaches of the picturesque Central American country,
she would be modeling beachwear for one designer and formal
attire for another. Based on past experience, both photography
crews would want her to show plenty of skin. She wouldn't have
to get completely nude—fashion photographers liked keeping her
gender as much of a mystery as she did—but she knew she could
count on having to be shirtless in several shots. That was more than
enough incentive for her to cut the fun stuff from her diet and try to
get into the best shape she could before her plane landed in Belize
City on Thursday. Having Sophie Mestach nipping at her heels also
offered plenty of motivation to stay on top of her game.

In addition to increasing the duration and intensity of her
workouts, she eschewed her favorite dinner staples of hot wings and
beer in favor of grilled chicken and mineral water. Good-bye, spare
tire. Good to see you again, abs.

When she walked into East River State Park on Saturday and
was inundated by the mouthwatering aromas wafting from the giant
food market Grace had invited her to, she felt certain her newfound
resolve was about to be sorely tested.

"What would you like?" Grace asked as they slowly walked
past dozens of vendors hawking Dakota's favorite carb-loaded
meals: pizza, burritos, mozzarella sticks, Louisiana-style po' boys,
and fish and chips, to name a few.

"One of everything." Dakota barely resisted the siren call of the ramen burgers calling her name, and her stomach growled when she and Grace neared a seafood stand that sold what was advertised as the best lobster rolls outside of New England.

"I know what you mean." Grace pointed to two vendors located next to each other. "I could eat a gallon of their bourbon brickle ice cream. And don't let me anywhere near those *arepas* or I won't come up for air for the next two hours."

"Got it." Dakota wrapped her arm around Grace's and led her away from temptation. "What's over here?"

"More of the same." Grace pointed out various vendors and described what they sold. "No matter what you're looking for, I'd be willing to bet you can find it here. Brooklyn Flea launched Smorgasburg in 2011, and they operate year-round. A hundred local and regional vendors show up each weekend to sell their wares."

"Is the market held here both days?"

"No, it sets up here on Saturdays and at Breeze Hill in Prospect Park on Sundays. It's held outdoors most of the year, but there's an indoor venue set aside for the winter months. I prefer this location, though."

"Why?"

"Few things say spring and summer in New York like walking in the park with a hot dog in your hand and the sun on your face."

Dakota loved listening to Grace play tour guide, but she liked the feel of Grace's hand on her arm even more. Grace's touch was casual, not possessive. It felt natural. It felt like it belonged. For one of the few times in her life, Dakota felt the same way.

"How about some Japanese food?" she asked as they neared a yakitori stand serving skewers of grilled beef, chicken, fish, vegetables, and deep-fried tofu.

"Meat on a stick always works for me."

Grace ordered chicken and mushrooms while Dakota opted for asparagus wrapped in thinly sliced pork. Dakota offered to pay, but Grace wouldn't hear of it.

"It's my treat," Grace said after she plucked a piece of chicken off her skewer and licked the salty-sweet *tare* sauce off her fingers. "I invited you, remember?"

"So you did." Dakota looked around the busy market, which teemed with vendors and customers alike. "I wonder if Whit knows about this."

"Who's Whit?"

"Remember when I said I had a friend who owns a bicycle shop a few blocks from your office?"

"How could I forget?" Grace rubbed her bottom like she had the previous week when riding on Dakota's handlebars had left her with a sore rear end.

"Joey Palallos owns the bike shop. Her girlfriend Whitney Robbins runs a small gastropub in the same space. The menu is somewhat limited, but the food is amazing. If the vendor fees aren't too steep, Whit could probably make a killing out here."

Grace nudged Dakota with her elbow. "If I rack up nine more referrals like that, then we'll be even."

"To paraphrase one of my favorite movies, this could be the beginning of a beautiful friendship." Grace laughed at Dakota's impersonation of Humphrey Bogart. "It wasn't that bad, was it?"

"I give you bonus points for effort."

"My very first participation trophy. Is that like an honorary Oscar?"

"Not quite. Are you a movie buff?"

"I wouldn't call myself a film geek, if that's what you're asking." Dakota wiped her hands on her napkin and tossed the napkin and her empty skewer in a nearby trash can. Grace followed suit. "I take my portable DVD player with me when I have to take a long trip because the in-flight movie selections usually suck, but that's just something I do to help pass the time so I don't get too bored going from Point A to Point B."

"In that case, what do you do for fun?"

"That depends on where I am. When I'm home, I like to crank up my all-terrain vehicle and find a good place to go off-roading. The muddier the spot, the better."

"And what about when you're here?"

"I like hanging out with my friends, I love dancing—even though I have more enthusiasm than skill—and I love watching my roommate Rich perform his drag act. His performances always blow me away. I don't have the time or the inclination for much more than that."

"Is that why you're always seen with a different woman on your arm?" Grace put a hand over her mouth as if she couldn't believe she had asked the question. "Wait. You don't have to answer that. That's entirely too personal."

"No, it's fine." Dakota always deflected intrusive questions when interviewers tried to dig into her personal life, but she liked the idea of Grace wanting to know more about her. "I have what some might call an active social life. I like to go out and have fun, but I'm not looking for a relationship, serious or otherwise."

"Because you're too busy or you're not interested?"

"Because I've never met anyone who makes me want to come back for more."

She was only twenty-seven years old. Why should she get tied down with one woman when there were so many she hadn't met yet? She made sure the women she slept with knew what was up before she took them to bed, but she had a feeling Grace was different. Grace wouldn't be down for a one-night stand. She'd want something meant to last. Dakota wasn't ready to make that kind of commitment. But there was something about Grace she found impossible to resist.

She had a hunch she wasn't what Grace was looking for, but that didn't stop her from wanting to change Grace's mind. In fact, it made her even more determined to convince her to give her a chance.

"Don't you want to meet someone who sweeps you off your feet?" Grace asked.

Dakota felt like she already had. She felt unsteady when she was around Grace. Like her world had shifted on its axis. She was seeing things from a different perspective. And the funny thing was she was starting to like the view. "When I see the kind of relationship my parents have with each other, the one my brother has with his wife, and the one my sister is committing to with her fiancé, I wonder how it would feel to experience the same thing."

"But?"

Dakota wanted to give Grace's question the answer it deserved, but the issues the query raised were too deep for a casual conversation. Resorting to a tried-and-true defense mechanism, she resorted to humor to deflect attention. "It looks like a lot of work and I'm inherently lazy." Grace didn't look satisfied with the answer, but Dakota changed the focus of the conversation before Grace could press her for a more in-depth response. "What about you? With your workload, I doubt you have much time for a personal life."

"That's one of the reasons the last woman I was dating cited when she broke up with me. She said she came a distant third on my list of priorities because I put my family and business responsibilities first. She wanted to be the center of my attention, not an afterthought. I wish I could say she was wrong, but I can't. She deserved better," Grace said, a hint of sadness in her voice. "We both did."

"Do you miss being part of a couple?"

"At times. I miss having that one person you can't wait to call when you want to share good news or you need help dealing with bad news. Don't get me wrong. I love my family and I adore my friends, but experiencing things with them isn't the same as sharing my life with someone. I don't want to miss out on that. My friend Lynette keeps trying to set me up with women she knows, but her attempts keep missing the mark. The last woman I went out with started the date by making unwanted comments about my weight. The rest of the night went downhill from there. The current woman Lynette has in mind for me sounds good on paper, but I'm not holding out hope that she's the woman of my dreams."

"Who is? I mean, what kind of woman are you looking for?"

"Obviously the kind I haven't been able to find," Grace said with a rueful laugh.

"I'm sure she's out there somewhere. What kind of woman are you attracted to?"

"When I was younger, I used to have a huge crush on Janet Jackson. She first caught my eye when she played Penny on *Good*

Times and she held my interest throughout her music career. She lost me during her so-called 'wardrobe malfunction' at halftime of the Super Bowl because it seemed intentional rather than accidental, but I'd discovered Halle Berry, Gabrielle Union, and Angela Bassett by then, so it was all good."

Dakota noted that all the women Grace listed were beautiful, glamorous, and feminine. Three words she would never use to describe herself. Were they the only type of women Grace was attracted to, or could she see herself with someone else? Someone who preferred leather to lace and lip balm to lipstick. In other words, someone like her.

"What about you?" Grace asked. "Who's your celebrity crush?"

"I have two. When I was younger, I wanted to be as badass as Jenny Shimizu when I grew up, and I wanted to have a torrid affair with Jodie Foster."

"You're doing a fine job at the former, but I'm afraid Jodie's spoken for."

"I know. Her wife got to her before I could plead my case. I guess I'll have to shift my focus to someone more attainable. Any suggestions?"

"As I said, you seem to be doing just fine on your own. You don't need any help from me. This has been fun." Grace sounded almost surprised. Dakota was definitely surprised when Grace asked, "Do you want to do it again sometime?"

"I'd love to. I have to go to Belize next week, but I'll give you a call when I get back in town."

"Sounds like a plan. Do you want to split a small order of oysters before we go?"

"Aren't oysters supposed to be an aphrodisiac?"

Grace placed her hand on Dakota's arm. This time of her own volition. "I won't tell if you won't."

Dakota ran her fingers over her mouth. "My lips are sealed."

But she hoped they wouldn't have to remain that way for long.

❖

Grace hated Mondays for two reasons: their arrival meant that her brief weekend respite was over, and they served as a tangible reminder of how much work needed to be done before she would be able to take another break. Mondays made her envy her sisters, who were able to cash in on the prestige of the family name without having to be burdened by the shackles of the day-to-day responsibility that went into maintaining the cachet that had been built up over the years. This Monday, however, wasn't like the others. This Monday, she didn't wake up with the usual sense of déjà vu. This Monday, she woke up refreshed and ready to tackle whatever came her way.

She began the day bright and early. After she downed a cup of coffee and an English muffin topped with a liberal helping of strawberry preserves, she got to the office an hour before opening time so she could properly prepare for the fitting she had scheduled with one of the referrals Dakota had sent her way.

First, she checked her notes to make sure she was familiar with her client's story. According to the email he had sent to the company website, Austin Lawrence was a student at Vanderbilt University Law School who needed a suit to wear to job interviews. That sounded simple enough, but the story turned out to be much more complicated than it appeared at first glance.

Despite his stellar grades and impressive résumé, Austin was having a hard time getting his foot in the door because the law firms that had agreed to meet with him were reluctant to hire someone who identified as transgender.

Grace considered herself lucky. She had been working for her father off and on since she was a teenager. Whether she was an unpaid intern or a full-time employee, her father had always trusted her to fulfill their clients' needs, even when their vision—and hers—differed from his. She couldn't imagine subjecting her dreams and aspirations to someone else's limitations.

She doubted a bespoke suit would completely resolve Austin's issues finding a job, but perhaps wearing it could provide him with the confidence boost he needed to convince some law firm's search committee to give him a contract offer rather than a cursory interview.

Grace felt the heavy weight of expectation settle on her shoulders. Even though Austin wasn't a famous actor or athlete with millions of followers keeping track of his latest fashion exploits on social media, the meeting they were about to have seemed like the most important of Grace's career.

Lillie took a pointed look at her watch when she arrived a few minutes before nine. "What are you doing here so early? I'm usually the first one in the office, especially on Mondays."

"Today's different."

"How so?" Lillie asked, hanging up her coat.

"Because today's a brand-new day."

"Mmm-hmm. Tracy told me about all those emails you got last week." Lillie folded her arms across her chest. "Is today a new day for the company or a new day for you?"

"Both."

"Go 'head, girl. It's about time we got some new blood up in here. I'm tired of dealing with the same people all the time. That gets old fast."

"I wish Dad felt the same way."

"Like most men, he doesn't like change. He'll come around. Just give him time."

Austin's appointment was set for nine thirty. He arrived ten minutes early.

"Prompt," Lillie said as Grace buzzed Austin upstairs. "I like this one already."

In her mind, Grace had pictured Austin as a slightly younger version of Dakota. When they finally met face-to-face, Grace was surprised to discover Dakota and Austin were nothing alike. Dakota was tall and thin. Austin was relatively short—five foot six at the most—and sturdily built. Almost stocky. And while Dakota exuded confidence, Austin seemed almost painfully shy.

"Would you like something to drink?" Grace asked after she showed him to his seat. "Coffee? Soda?"

Austin wiped his palms on his jeans as his eyes darted around the room. "Bottled water if you have it. I don't do caffeine, and I try to avoid added processed sugar as much as possible."

"Then how do you expect to stay awake for all those late-night study sessions when you try to pass the bar?" Lillie asked.

Austin let out a nervous laugh. "Willpower, I guess."

"I don't have either one, baby," Lillie said, pouring herself a cup of coffee. "The will or the power."

Austin laughed again, his tension seeming to dissipate. Once again, Grace felt indebted to Lillie for her effortless ability to set customers at ease. "Here you are." She handed Austin a bottle of water from the mini-fridge and took a seat opposite him. "I normally begin the interview session by asking clients how they heard about the company. In your case, I already know the answer. How long have you known Dakota?"

Austin ran a hand through his short brown hair. His blue eyes were slightly magnified by the thick lenses of his horn-rimmed glasses. "About five years, give or take. During my freshman year of college, my roommate and I decided to go to Savannah for Saint Patrick's Day. Growing up, I'd always heard how wild River Street could be on that day, and I wanted to experience it for myself. Dakota happened to be in town at the same time, and even though we were surrounded by thousands of people, I recognized a kindred spirit."

"Is she always the life of the party, or does it just seem that way?"

"She draws a lot of attention, that's for sure. She doesn't ask for it. It just happens. But you've seen her, so I'm sure you understand why."

It didn't take much more than a fleeting glance to see why Dakota turned heads, but Grace planned to keep hers on straight.

"She bought me a drink—nonalcoholic, of course, since I wasn't twenty-one yet," Austin said. "We chatted for a while and exchanged phone numbers so we could keep in touch. We've been friends ever since. She calls me the little brother she never had. I don't know how accurate that is, but I do know I can talk to her about anything at any time. No matter where she is or what she has going on, I can count on her to be there for me. That's huge for me. I don't make friends easily because I'm...different, but Dakota is definitely one of them. She remembers every birthday, every anniversary, every special occasion. No matter where she is or what she's got going on, you can count on receiving a card, a text, or a phone call." His cheeks colored. "That's a whole lot more information than you asked me for, isn't it?"

"Everything you say helps me get to know you." Thanks to Austin's story, she felt like she'd gotten to know Dakota a bit better, too. Dakota was much more substantial than her slight frame and jovial attitude made her appear. She had to be if she inspired such loyalty in her friends. What else was she hiding under that striking androgynous exterior? "Since you'll be wearing the suit to job interviews, I assume you're in the market for something conservative."

Austin nodded. "The firms I've sat down with have pretty strict dress codes. No surprise, given they're all in the Deep South. They insist on skirts, dresses, and heels for the women, and suits and ties for the men. I don't want one of those flashy get-ups you see lawyers wearing when their trials are televised, but I don't want to look like I'm going to a funeral either. I want a suit that commands respect when I walk into a courtroom."

"I think I know what you're looking for." Grace flipped through fabric swatches until she found a dark blue sample with a subtle gray pinstripe. "How about this one?"

Austin's eyes widened. "I love it," he said, fingering the small square piece of cloth, "but it's wool, isn't it? It looks really expensive. It feels that way, too. I'm a broke college student, remember?"

"Don't worry. This sample is from our line of budget-friendly fabrics."

"Seriously? Then, yeah, that one will be perfect."

"Would you need a dress shirt as well?"

"No, I can go to any clothing store and find shirts and jeans that fit. When I try to buy anything else, though, I always end up looking like I'm playing dress-up with clothes from my father's closet. That's why I came to you. Dakota said you could give me the silhouette I see in my head instead of the one I see in the mirror."

Grace set her pen down and looked Austin in the eye. "When I'm done, I promise you those images will be one and the same."

"Thank you."

Austin's chin trembled as he fought back tears. Grace had never received that kind of reaction during a fitting. Then again, she'd never had an appointment like this one. Part business meeting, part therapy session.

"Are you okay, baby?" Lillie asked gently.

"I'm fine. Thank you, ma'am." Austin sipped his water and took a few moments to get his emotions under control. "Before we continue, I'd like to make a suggestion if I may."

"Of course," Grace said. "This is a collaborative process. Your input is vital."

"Actually, my issue isn't with the process. It's with your website."

"The website? What's wrong with it?" Until now, she had heard nothing but praise for its clean look, professional design, and ease of use.

"When I drafted my email, I noticed you have a dropdown box that lists the four basic salutations we've all grown accustomed to, and there's even a box to check to indicate if a client would prefer to be measured by a male or female tailor, but there's one thing missing."

"What might that be?" Grace and the web designer had worked hand in hand for months prior to the site's launch. She couldn't think of anything they might have left out.

"If you're going to be working with trans clients," Austin said, "it would be a good idea to add a field to your site where those clients can indicate their preferred pronoun. Most cisgender people think the choices are limited to him or her, he or she, and what's often termed the ungrammatical 'they.' Believe me, there are a hell of a lot more options than those five. It would save you some time and, perhaps, spare you from embarrassment if you give your clients a chance to tell you how they see themselves instead of waiting for you to try to guess."

Grace stared at him, open-mouthed. She couldn't believe the transformation from the shy wallflower who had walked into the office a few minutes ago into the assertive, confident young man sitting before her now.

"Did I say something to offend you?" Austin asked.

"No, but you have given me a lot to think about. I'm ashamed to say it had never occurred to me that my father and I might not be meeting all of our clients' needs. When you and I are done with your fitting, I'll call the webmaster and have her make the necessary changes."

"Awesome." Austin beamed as if he'd just won his first case.

Grace could tell he would make a great lawyer one day. When they shook hands at the door, she made sure to tell him so.

"I'll remember that when I'm trying to pass the bar exam," he said with a self-deprecating smile. "Thanks for meeting with me. I look forward to hearing from you."

"Out of the mouths of babes," Lillie said after Austin left. "He certainly taught you a thing or two."

Before today, Grace had thought she knew everything she needed to know about what it was like to be lesbian, gay, bi, or trans since she was a card-carrying member of the community. Meeting Austin—and Dakota—had exposed her shortcomings. She realized there was a lot more she needed to learn.

"I hope I'm a quick study. If not, I might be about to get in over my head."

CHAPTER SEVEN

Dorothy Parker was a poet and author known more for what she said during her lifetime than what she wrote. Of the many witty quotes attributed to the charter member of the infamous Algonquin Round Table, Dakota's favorite was: "I hate writing. I love having written." She felt the same way about traveling. She loved exploring various parts of the world so she could experience different cultures and ways of life, but she hated the act of getting from one place to another.

The long lines in Customs tested her patience each time she traveled internationally, and making her way through the security checkpoints was usually a pain in the ass. Every time she whipped out her boarding pass and photo ID, she seemed to get stuck with a TSA officer who thought the *F* printed in the gender section of her driver's license or passport was a typo. She had been subjected to enhanced security screenings so many times she was starting to wonder if her name had been placed on some super-secret government list.

She didn't mind the pat-downs. Most of the time. If the TSA officer was cute and didn't get too handsy during the search, she was willing to stand in the security line for hours if she had to. Then there were times like today. Times that made her wonder why she had to continuously jump through hoops in order to be true to who she was.

After she sent her shoes, watch, belt, cell phone, and carry-on bag through the X-ray machine, she held her hands over her head and stepped into the full-body scanner. The machine whirred as its oversized camera circled her body. When the scanners were first introduced, some people had claimed that the machines invaded their privacy because the images they took revealed what people in them looked like under their clothes.

Dakota was on the fence about the issue. She didn't like the idea of someone she didn't know being aware of what she looked like naked, but if it kept someone from taking over a flight she had booked passage on, she was willing to live with the intrusion.

The balding male TSA officer on the other side of the scanner held up a hand to prevent her from stepping out of the machine. The laminated tag clipped to his royal blue uniform shirt indicated his name was Officer Frank Warren.

"Wait one moment," Officer Warren said, peering at the monitor that displayed the results of the scan. He frowned, then waved her forward. "Step to the side, please."

Dakota knew from experience what was coming next. She was wearing baggy jeans and a loose-fitting sweatshirt so she could be comfortable on the plane. She wished she had ditched the sweatshirt in favor of the tight T-shirt she was wearing underneath so the TSA officers in the security area would have fewer reasons to give her the quizzical looks they were hitting her with now. With a weary sigh, she hitched up her jeans, stepped out of the scanner, and headed to the area reserved for enhanced searches.

Officer Warren pressed a switch on the two-way radio strapped to the epaulet on his shirt and said, "I need a female agent to perform a passenger pat-down."

Dakota glanced at the clock on a nearby wall. She had arrived at the airport three hours early so she would have plenty of time to navigate the security checkpoint before she made her way to her gate. She would rather while away the hours between now and her scheduled flight time reading a book while she grabbed a bite to eat than getting felt up by a complete stranger.

A few minutes later, a middle-aged woman with a large mustard stain on her black uniform pants and a good two inches of gray roots peeking out of the part in her dyed-orange hair sauntered over. The last name on her name tag wasn't visible, but Dakota could see her first name was Evelyn. Evelyn glanced at her, looked past her, and turned back to Officer Warren. "You called for a female passenger pat-down? Where is she?"

Officer Warren jerked his head in Dakota's direction.

"You're kidding, right?" Evelyn looked Dakota up and down. "Come here for a second, Frank."

Evelyn walked a few feet away and waited for Officer Warren to follow her. After he joined her, they began a heated but whispered discussion. Dakota knew she could defuse the situation by saying something to one of the officers so they could hear her voice and realize she truly was biologically female, but she wasn't in the mood to let either of them off the hook.

"Fine," Evelyn said, throwing her hands in the air. "If that's what the ID says, I guess we have to go with it." Walking toward Dakota, she snapped the latex gloves on her hands like a proctologist about to perform an exam. "Miss Lane?" She glanced at Dakota's passport for confirmation. "The scanner indicated an anomaly in your, uh, genital area so I've been asked to perform a manual screening. Is that okay with you, or would you prefer a male agent?"

The passengers who had successfully completed their security screenings stared openly before they made their way to their gates. Most seemed curious, some empathetic, others almost contemptuous. Dakota had grown accustomed to receiving those looks, but she had never learned to like it.

She wordlessly extended her arms as Evelyn ran the back of a gloved hand up her legs, over her hips, and across her chest. Each time she moved to a different area of Dakota's body, Evelyn eyed her crotch as if checking to see if she had managed to get a literal rise out of her.

"Sorry," Dakota said when she'd had about all she could take, "but you're not my type."

Evelyn pursed her lips and returned Dakota's ID. "Have a safe flight, ma'am," she said through clenched teeth. "Next time you have a situation like this, Frank, handle it yourself."

Dakota gathered her belongings and headed to the international terminal. Though she had managed to walk away from the uncomfortable encounter with most of her dignity intact, she felt far from triumphant. Such run-ins always left her feeling frustrated. Why did she keep having to prove herself to people? Why couldn't they accept her for who she—and her ID—said she was and leave it at that?

After she located her gate, she headed to the bar a few feet away and ordered a vodka tonic. She had vowed to refrain from alcohol until she finished her photo shoot so she wouldn't undermine all the hard work she had put in at the gym, but she needed something stronger than mineral water to take the edge off.

"How much do I owe you?" she asked after the bartender placed her drink in front of her.

"Don't sweat it. It's already paid for, compliments of the dude over there."

Dakota turned to see Sophie raising a toast in her direction. Sophie was wearing a white oxford shirt under a light gray cashmere sweater. Her sleeves were rolled up, revealing the colorful Olympic rings tattooed on the outside of her right wrist. Dressed the way she was with her hair cut even shorter than normal, she could have easily been mistaken for a butch lesbian or a metrosexual man. The bartender had obviously chosen to go with the latter assumption.

Dakota grabbed her glass, picked up her carry-on, and joined Sophie on the other end of the bar. "Thanks for the drink."

"You looked like you could use it." Sophie took a sip of her martini and carefully set her glass on the granite bar top. "The incident I witnessed at security. Does that happen to you often?"

"You saw what went down?"

Dakota hadn't seen Sophie in the security area while she was being searched. Seeing someone who could relate to what she was experiencing might have made the situation easier to deal with, but Sophie had an out she didn't have. Sophie dressed the way she did because she was being paid a great deal of money to do it. Dakota did it not because the money was good but because it felt right.

"I was a few people behind you in line," Sophie said. "I started to intervene after the agent I was dealing with waved me through, but I was afraid I would end up doing more harm than good."

"That kind of thing never happens to you when you fly?"

"Occasionally, but not often. It helps having Ruben around to vouch for me. Swimmer's shoulders or not, no one assumes I'm a man when I'm standing next to one."

"Lucky you." Dakota looked around the bar but didn't see Sophie's omnipresent other half anywhere. "Where's Ruben now?"

"Home packing his bags. This trip was last-minute, so he wasn't able to book a seat on the same flight. He's catching the red-eye tomorrow morning and will be joining us in Belize around noon."

"Us?" Dakota almost choked on her drink. She thought she had this gig to herself.

"Yes. Laird didn't tell you we're going to be working the same photo shoots this week?"

"No, he conveniently forgot to mention it to me."

Sophie shrugged. "Everything happened so fast he probably didn't have time. He gave me a call last night and asked me to fill in for Hunter."

"Wait. Hunter has been looking forward to this trip for months. There's no way he would have dropped out voluntarily. Did he get sick or something?"

"He probably wishes he had come down with something. Saying he had a bad case of stomach flu would be far less embarrassing than telling the truth."

"Which is?"

"I'm not sure whether to call it dumb luck or a freak accident, but he walked into a utility pole while playing Pokémon Go and broke his nose. Unless you're doing an ad for boxing gear, no one wants to hire a model with two black eyes. So it looks like you're stuck with me for the next four days."

"I'm looking forward to it."

"I'm sure you are," Sophie said after she ordered another martini.

"What do you mean?"

Sophie turned to face her. "Be honest, Dakota. I know you view me as competition."

"Of course I do. That's only natural, considering we're often up for the same jobs, but that doesn't mean I dislike you. To be perfectly honest, I thought you were the one who had an issue with me."

"I've always been cordial to you, haven't I?"

"If by cordial, you mean frosty, yes, you have."

Sophie flashed a crooked grin that made her look like Brad Pitt during his *Thelma and Louise* heyday. "I've always admired your work. I'm sorry if our relationship hasn't been as warm as you might like. Perhaps we could remedy that this week."

"What do you have in mind?" Dakota asked warily. Sophie was obviously working up to something, but she seemed to have much more in mind than the lunch they had promised to have and had yet to take.

Sophie slid a pimento-stuffed olive off a swizzle stick with her teeth. "It's actually Ruben's idea," she said between bites. "He's the marketing genius in our household. He's come up with a wonderful way to garner both of us some free publicity. All we have to do is upload a few social media posts that make it seem like you and I are sleeping with each other. The media will eat it up. They've been painting us as rivals for years and you've obviously bought into it as well. This is the perfect way to bury the hatchet, don't you think?"

"By pretending to be lovers?"

"It happens all the time in Hollywood. Most of the great celebrity romances are created in a publicist's office. Ask Tom Cruise. On second thought, don't. He might sue you for defamation. I hear he's good at that."

"He's had lots of practice. But in case you haven't noticed, we're not in Hollywood. And you say this was Ruben's idea?"

In Dakota's opinion, Ruben seemed to view Sophie as something of a pet project. An object of beauty to be sculpted and admired but not necessarily loved. Their partnership often seemed more like a business arrangement than a marriage. Dakota hadn't been around them often enough to classify their union as devoid of passion, but she didn't feel much heat emanating from them. As Sophie's manager, Ruben had a financial stake in her success. Was that the reason he had concocted such a harebrained scheme to gain attention for his client/wife? It had to be. No other explanation made sense. Because if she loved someone enough to marry her, she wouldn't be trying to convince her to climb in bed with someone else. Figuratively speaking or not.

"He knows what people will say if the story gains traction," Sophie said, "but he's secure enough with himself and our marriage to be able to tune those things out. What do you say? Are you in?"

"No, count me out."

"Why? You're single, aren't you?"

"Yes."

"Then what's the problem? I'm not asking you to sleep with me."

"Just make it seem like I am."

"Exactly. All we have to do is take a few selfies, write a few cleverly worded posts, and wait for everyone to pick up on the hints we drop. The Twitterverse will explode. Think of the attention we'll receive."

"I'm actually thinking of the phone call I'll get from my parents when they stand in the checkout line at the grocery store and see my face on the cover of some tabloid underneath a headline that says I'm sleeping with someone who's off-limits. That's not the kind of attention I want."

"You're an adult, Dakota, not a child. Does your parents' opinion matter so much to you that you're unwilling to take a step that might advance your career? If we leverage this the right way, we could wind up with our own reality show."

"Are you trying to offer me more incentive or less? Because the idea of having my life documented for public consumption holds zero appeal to me. And the idea of pretending to have an affair with a married woman holds even less."

"Any married woman, or just me?"

"I'd do you in a heartbeat if you were single."

Both of them had strong personalities and even stronger drives to be the best. Trying to top each other would be a serious turn-on. Sleeping with the enemy always was. But bedding Sophie was one thrill Dakota would rather not seek. Not as long as Sophie sported a wedding ring.

"With your reputation, I wouldn't have thought you'd be such a prude," Sophie said.

"Just because my parents and I don't see eye to eye on some things doesn't mean I don't try to live my life in a way that would make them proud of me."

"Were they proud when you were photographed boning some random woman in the bathroom of a crowded bar?"

That hadn't been one of Dakota's finest moments. She had been too caught up in the excitement of the moment to pump the brakes when she should have. She didn't regret that it had happened. Her only regret was that the woman she was with that night had seemed to be more interested in becoming the next Kim Kardashian than she was in her. The sex was memorable, but Dakota could have done without the ensuing fallout. The kind of fallout she could avoid by choosing not to participate in Sophie and Ruben's ridiculous ruse. "I've fought too hard to be true to who I am to jeopardize that now."

"But your whole life is based on an illusion. What's so different about what I'm asking you to do?" Sophie looked at Dakota out of the corner of her eye. "Perhaps you're not as comfortable with yourself as you pretend to be."

Dakota forced herself to appear calm even though she could feel her blood boiling. The last thing she wanted was for someone to whip out their cell phone, record her kicking Sophie's ass, and sell the footage to TMZ. If she didn't control her temper, she would give Sophie everything she wanted—and lose everything she had worked so hard to achieve.

"Unlike you," she said, struggling to keep her voice even, "I'm not pretending to be someone else. When you look at me, what you see isn't an illusion. It's who I am. Thanks for thinking of me, but

I'm not willing to compromise my principles for you or anyone else."

Sophie held up her hands in surrender. "I didn't mean to offend you. It's just the gin talking. I've never been able to hold my liquor."

"Then do yourself a favor." Dakota pushed Sophie's half-empty glass away from her. "Switch to water. You're far less likely to end up with your foot in your mouth."

❖

Grace returned from lunch on Friday to find a bright yellow Post-it Note affixed to her computer monitor. She read the note three times, but she couldn't figure out what it said because Lillie's handwriting was worse than a doctor's. Grace's father had never felt the need to hire a full-time receptionist, so Lillie and Tracy took turns manning the phones. Grace waited for Lillie to finish her current call before she held up the note and said, "What's happening at two o'clock?"

"Hart Stephens has to go out of town to host a beauty pageant, so he needs to reschedule his appointment. He called to see if he could come in a day early," Lillie said as she scribbled something in the appointment book. "I told him you had an opening at two."

Hart Stephens was a popular comedian and talk show host who was almost as famous for his flashy suits as he was for his off-color jokes. He didn't come into the shop often, but when he did it was all hands on deck. Hart was a clotheshorse of the highest order. Even if Grace and her father lost every other client on their roster, Hart's order alone would be enough to keep the company solvent.

"Dad's his regular tailor, but he's still at the distributor's checking out fabric samples. Did you let him know Hart's on the way?"

"I called him, but there isn't anything he can do. Even if he'd left the warehouse as soon as I got him on the phone, he wouldn't have been able to make it back here in time. That means you're it."

Grace glanced at her watch. "I have half an hour to prepare to meet with one of the company's most lucrative clients. No pressure."

"Think of it as practice for when you're in charge for real instead of in name only."

Grace logged into her computer and accessed Hart's file. "This is still Dad's company, Lillie, not mine."

"Maybe, but who's bringing in most of the business and doing the majority of the work?"

Lillie had a point, but Grace didn't feel the need to belabor it. She didn't have time to point out the obvious. She needed every possible second to prepare for Hart Stephens's arrival. "Who was that on the phone?" she asked as she gathered the information she needed for her upcoming meeting.

"A nice little old lady from Queens."

Grace smiled despite her mounting stress. Though she looked a good ten years younger, Lillie was almost seventy. Her definition of "old" changed by the minute. In Lillie's world, the term could be applied to anyone who was over fifty but less than one hundred. To hear her tell it, anyone who was older than that was already dead; they just didn't know it yet.

"Her name's Ruth Goldstein and she wants to buy her grandson a suit to wear to his bar mitzvah," Lillie continued. "I told her your father would be happy to meet with them in the morning, but she said she needed to meet with you instead. You know what that means, don't you?"

Grace walked over to Lillie's desk so she could check out the entry in the appointment book. The grandson's name was either Jonah or Joshua. Grace couldn't tell which. Lillie had written "transgender boy" next to his name, penciled him in for ten a.m., and entered Dakota's name in the referral slot.

"Dakota's in Belize until Sunday," Grace said. "Unless she's working her friends list between photo shoots, I doubt she's responsible for Mrs. Goldstein's call."

Lillie looked up at her. "Do you keep track of every client's schedule, or just the ones you think are cute?"

"I never said I thought Dakota was—"

"Belize, huh?" Lillie said, not giving Grace a chance to finish her sentence. "Where's that?"

"In Central America. It's a small country bordering Mexico and Guatemala. It's popular with wedding planners because of its picturesque beaches and relatively low costs."

"It sounds pretty."

"It is. Check this out. Dakota texted me this last night." Grace grabbed her phone off her desk and showed Lillie a picture of a pair of palm trees silhouetted against a pastel-colored sky as the bright orange sun slowly sank into the crystal-clear waters of the Caribbean Sea.

"'The view from my hotel,'" Lillie said, slowly reading the caption beneath the picture. "'Don't you wish you were here?'"

Each time she looked at the picture, which was often, Grace could almost feel the ocean breeze blowing against her skin. She could practically see herself sipping a piña colada while she lay on a chaise longue and worked on her tan. Hell, yes, she wished she was there. She didn't know if she wanted to be there with Dakota—they barely knew each other—but traveling with a friend was always more fun than going it alone. What better way to get to know someone than by spending time with them in a country neither of you called home? By the time the trip was over, your friendship would be either cemented or ruined, the resulting memories guaranteed to last a lifetime.

"It's pretty, all right," Lillie said, "but that's way more water than I can swallow. It sure makes a nice picture, though." She pulled off her reading glasses and allowed them to dangle from the braided gold chain around her neck. "I had set my mind to retiring at the end of the year, but I might have to stick around for a while. Lately, you never know who's going to walk through the door next. And I certainly want to be a fly on the wall when your father finds out what you're up to."

"What am I up to?" Grace asked. Lillie made it seem like she was planning a hostile takeover. The new clients had reached out to her, not the other way around.

"You and Dakota seem to be spending a lot of time together. You went to Smorgasbord last week—"

"Smorgas*burg*."

"Whatever the name of the place is, you two went out together last week and now you're sexting each other on your phones."

"I think you mean texting."

"I know exactly what I mean, but do you?"

"What are you getting at?"

"You've always said you'd never date a client—"

"Dakota and I aren't dating. I took her to lunch to thank her for the business she sent my way and we exchanged a few text messages after I reached out to her to let her know the fabric for her suit has been ordered. That's all there is to it."

Lillie reached for the ringing telephone. "If it walks like a duck and quacks like a duck," she said before she answered the incoming call, "I'm going to slap a sailor shirt on it and call it Donald. Thank you for calling Henderson Custom Suits. How may I help you?"

While Grace waited for Hart Stephens to arrive, she tried to figure out why she had grown so defensive when Lillie accused her of dating Dakota. Accused. That was too strong a word for what had taken place, yet it was the only one that seemed to fit.

What was it about being romantically linked to Dakota that put her so on edge? Dakota liked women; so did she. What was the problem? Simple. Because Dakota wasn't like any woman she had ever met. And she was definitely nothing like the women she had chosen to date.

Grace had told Lynette she was looking for someone real. Dakota felt—and looked—more like a fantasy.

"Someone else's fantasy because she certainly isn't mine."

Lynette's friend Karin taught music at a public high school in the Bronx. Not the sexiest job in the world, but it was one Grace could relate to. Perhaps it was time to find out if she could relate to Karin as well.

She picked up her phone and looked up the number Lynette had given her weeks ago but she had never bothered to use.

"Hello, this is Karin Oliveira."

Grace's breath caught. Karin's voice was melodic, apropos of her profession. "Hi, it's Grace Henderson."

"Lynette's friend? I think she said you were a tailor or something like that."

"I am, yes." Grace detected a slight accent. She couldn't tell what kind, but she definitely wanted to hear more. "As you probably know, Lynette thinks you and I should meet. If you feel the same way, I'd love to buy you a cup of coffee sometime."

Whether the response took a few seconds or a few minutes, waiting for a woman to respond to a question as fraught with potential heartache as "Will you go out with me?" always seemed to take forever.

"I'm busy tonight," Karin said, "but how about tomorrow? My niece has a soccer game in Seton Park at ten a.m. She's only seven years old, so she and her teammates don't do much scoring, but they're a lot of fun to watch."

"I'll bet." Grace never thought she'd willingly spend a Saturday morning watching a bunch of little kids running around a soccer field, but she thought it seemed appropriate. She had been running in circles for years. It would be nice to watch someone else do it for a while.

"I'll bring the coffee if you bring the doughnuts."

"I think that can be arranged."

"Great," Karin said with what sounded like genuine enthusiasm. "I'll see you tomorrow."

"How will I recognize you?"

"Just look for the crazy Brazilian in the Neymar jersey yelling at the referees for missing what she thinks are obvious calls. That would be my sister. I'll be the one sitting next to her holding two cups of coffee. How do you like yours? Black or with a touch of cream and sugar?"

"Are we still talking about coffee?"

When Karin laughed, she sounded like a singer running the scales. "I like you already."

Grace felt the same way. If the date went as well as the phone call, her dry spell might be coming to an end.

"I'll be damned," she said to herself after she ended the call. "I think Lynette finally got it right."

CHAPTER EIGHT

Dakota had sand in places she wished she didn't. After she finished the second and final day of her swimwear shoot, she gingerly made her way across the beach and stepped into the outdoor shower. The water was cold, the spray stinging, but it got the job done. As the photographer's assistants held up towels to protect her privacy from the gawkers lining the beach, she stripped off her clothes and tried to rid herself of all the beach sand that had managed to find its way inside her dirt-caked board shorts and surf shirt. All the clothes she wore during photo shoots were comped, which meant they went home with her instead of the designer at the end of the day. High-end was always better than off-the-rack, and it was infinitely more so when it was free.

Mike Burnett, one of Dakota's favorite photographers, sauntered over to her after she turned off the shower. "You've really been on top of your game this week. I got some really incredible shots of you. I think the client is going to love what we've captured."

"I hope so." She sluiced water from her hair, grabbed a beach towel from one of Mike's assistants, and wrapped the towel around her to ward off the chill. Despite the warm temperatures, goose bumps had formed on her skin. Why, she often wondered, was the water at the beach always colder than it was anywhere else? "I'd hate to think we did all this work for nothing."

"Not a chance," Mike said. "I'm really looking forward to the wedding shoot tomorrow. Laird threw out an idea that has me intrigued. It would mean twice as much work, but it would also result in twice the exposure."

"Laird usually lets the creative team do its own thing. Why is he offering his opinion now?"

Mike glanced toward the water, where Sophie and Ruben were reenacting the famous kiss between Burt Lancaster and Deborah Kerr in *From Here to Eternity*. Like most remakes, it paled in comparison to the original. Probably because it seemed more like a planned publicity stunt than a spontaneous act. "I think she might have put a bug in his ear."

Dakota had figured as much. "What did she suggest?"

"It's borderline genius, if you ask me. Most wedding shoots focus on the bride because the women who buy the magazines like to fantasize about wearing those gorgeous dresses. Since same-sex marriage is legal in the US now, it makes perfect sense to focus on a gay couple as well as a straight one. We could do one layout with you and Gisele as the featured couple and one layout with you and Sophie walking down the aisle. In tuxes, of course. I wouldn't dream of asking either one of you to break out the taffeta."

Dakota had to admit the idea was a good one, even if Sophie had come up with it. "Have you pitched the new scenario to the client?" she asked as Sophie signed autographs for the gathered onlookers.

"Laird did first thing this morning."

"And?"

"They flipped for it. They pride themselves on being ahead of the game, and this layout will fit in perfectly with their brand. Everyone else is on board. What do you say? Are you in or out?"

Dakota didn't want to do twice the work for half the pay. "Would it mean more money?"

"Naturally. Laird's in the process of negotiating the fees right now."

"Then count me in."

"You two are going to look so hot together," Mike said after Sophie joined them. "I can't wait to capture your heat on camera. I'll see you tomorrow at the location."

"So this was your idea?" Dakota asked Sophie after Mike left to oversee the packing of his camera equipment and Ruben went to check on the status of the upgrade he had requested for a larger room. As if the spacious suite he and Sophie currently occupied wasn't big enough. Dakota wasn't a size queen. As long as the bed was comfortable, her room could have the surface area of a postage stamp and she wouldn't care. Sophie and Ruben obviously didn't share her point of view. Or was Sophie throwing her weight around to see how much leverage she had with her new agency?

"It was one of my better ones, don't you think? I knew I'd get you in bed one way or another. Metaphorically speaking, of course."

Sophie moved closer, infringing on Dakota's personal space. Dakota was tempted to take a step back, but she refused to give ground. Literally and figuratively. "Just remember one thing: I get to be on top."

"For now," Sophie said. "For now."

On Saturday morning, Grace tried to feign enthusiasm as she watched the tiny members of two ten-and-under girls' soccer teams fight for possession of the ball in the second half of a scoreless contest. The players were enthusiastic but not very skilled. Neither team's goalie had faced any serious pressure from the opposition all day. The real action was taking place on the sidelines rather than the field as overenthusiastic parents tried to live vicariously through their offspring. Grace might have found the scene amusing if it weren't quite so sad.

"Are you having fun?" Karin asked.

Grace didn't want to lie, but being truthful could prove problematic. Even though the chances of her and Karin seeing each other again after today were mediocre at best, she didn't want to hurt Karin's feelings.

At first glance, Karin seemed perfect for her. She was gainfully employed, smart, funny, and drop-dead gorgeous. But her sharp wit, self-deprecating sense of humor, long black hair, dark brown eyes, tawny skin, and dazzling smile couldn't make up for the fact that she hadn't stopped talking about her ex since Grace had claimed the seat next to her in the crowded bleachers. If Grace downed a shot every time Karin said her former lover's name, she would have been wasted well before halftime.

"I kept trying to convince Antonia to come to the games," Karin said, reaching for another doughnut hole Grace had bought from a bakery on nearby Riverdale Avenue, "but she always found something else to do."

Karin's sister, Mariana, stopped haranguing the game officials long enough to turn her vitriol on Karin. "You and Antonia broke up because she's a crazy bitch who can't be trusted. And you're still too hung up on her psycho ass to let go. Was the sex that good or what?"

Grace sipped her cold coffee and tried to make herself invisible as Karin and Mariana's assorted friends and family members who were sitting within earshot whooped like a modern-day Greek chorus. Grace hadn't experienced anything remotely like it since high school when crowds of bored teenagers hungry for excitement would surround a pair of reluctant combatants and egg them on to fight. She cast a quick sideways glance at Karin to gauge her reaction to Mariana's comments. Karin looked as mortified as Grace felt.

"Watch your language, Mari." Karin pointed to the team bench located a few feet away. "The kids can hear you."

Mariana clicked her tongue against her teeth. "My kids are the ones who taught me to curse in the first place. You're just mad because you know what I'm saying is true. Are you going to spend time with the woman sitting next to you, or are you going to keep talking about the one who dumped you? For someone with a college degree, you can be really stupid sometimes." She turned back to the game. "That was a hard foul, ref! That kid deserves a red card, not a yellow! Throw her out!"

"I'm sorry you had to hear that," Karin said. "Mari means well, but she gets a little carried away sometimes. Antonia shares the same trait. She and Mari are too much alike. That's one of the reasons they never got along. I know how to handle them, though, because I deal with hotheaded students every day. Is your family as passionate as mine?"

"My sisters and I used to get into some knock-down, drag-out fights when we were younger, but we grew out of it. As Desmond Tutu once said, 'Don't raise your voice. Improve your argument.'"

"That's a good saying. Antonia collects inspirational quotes, but I don't think she has that one. Let me text her and see."

"The two of you are still in touch?"

"Oh, yes," Karin said, typing a long message into her cell phone. "As a matter of fact, we talk more now than we did when we were together. I can't wait to introduce you to her. I think she'll like you as much as I do. We should have dinner sometime. What are you doing next Friday night?"

"Um, I'll check my calendar and get back to you."

If she didn't have anything else planned, she'd make sure to come up with something. This date was even more disastrous than the last one she'd gone on. And that was saying something.

She tried to find an escape route, but all the exits seemed to be blocked. Whenever she'd found herself in this situation in the past, she would text Lynette and ask her to call her on her cell phone so she could make an excuse to leave. That tactic wouldn't work this time because Lynette was the one who'd gotten her into this mess in the first place. She couldn't ask her sisters either because neither Hope nor Faith would ever let her live it down. Lillie and her parents were off-limits for the same reasons—because she wanted them to think she had enough on the ball to be able to solve her own problems.

Only one name came to mind. It was a long shot, but she was fresh out of options.

As Karin launched into a long-winded story about her and Antonia's most memorable date, Grace slipped her phone from her pocket, texted *Please call me ASAP*, and fervently hoped her message would not only be received but heeded.

CHAPTER NINE

Dakota yawned as she waited for Mike to finish uploading that morning's photos from the memory card in his digital camera to his computer.

"Late night?" he asked as the progress bar slowly scrolled across the screen.

"Early morning."

She had been awake since the ass crack of dawn because Mike wanted to take advantage of the morning light for the first set of shots. She was never up that early unless she was just heading home after a fantastic night out on the town, but she was following someone else's schedule this week, not her own.

She had caught a quick nap after she stumbled from her hotel room to one of the two courtesy vans waiting to take everyone to the luxury resort that had been selected to provide the backdrop for this morning's photo shoot. After a bumpy ride across town, she had fallen asleep again after she settled into the makeup chair. The makeup artist in charge of perfecting her look had smeared what felt like half a tube of Preparation H on the bags under her eyes before he finally pronounced her camera ready. She had been on the go ever since.

She wanted to crawl back into bed and spend the rest of the day making up for the three hours of sleep she had missed out on, but she had another photo shoot scheduled for this afternoon. Fortunately, Sophie had more than enough energy for both of them. Sophie picked her up whenever she started to drag. Sometimes literally.

Dakota and Sophie had shared the same runway before, but they had never teamed up for a print layout. Despite Dakota's initial misgivings, she thought the morning's shoot was turning out well. Instead of jockeying for prime position like she was prone to do at fashion shows, Sophie was behaving like a consummate professional in front of the camera.

Dakota had expected Sophie to try to make herself the center of attention since the storyline behind the shoot was her idea, but her poses accentuated Dakota's rather than overshadowing them. Mike had made suggestions from time to time, but he hadn't needed to say much. Dakota called it being in the zone. When one move flowed effortlessly into the next with no hesitation in between. And Sophie was right there with her, playing off her last pose and anticipating the next one.

"Come take a look at these," Mike said after the upload was complete. "I knew you guys would be hot together, but these pictures are practically melting my monitor."

Dakota looked at the screen. Even in their unpolished state, she could tell the photos were some of the best she had ever taken. "What can I say? You bring out the best in me, Mike."

"No, I think it's pretty obvious you bring out the best in each other. I was just there to capture it for posterity."

"See?" Sophie said. "There's enough room for both of us at the same agency after all."

"Perhaps," Ruben said, looking over Sophie's shoulder to peer at the screen, "but there's room for only one at the top."

And despite Sophie's assurances that she was a team player, Dakota knew her rival wouldn't be satisfied until she was the last one standing.

"Wardrobe has your next set of outfits ready," Mike said. "Get changed, and I'll see you in thirty."

Sophie, with Ruben in tow, headed to one dressing room. Dakota headed to another. Her phone buzzed as a flock of wardrobe assistants helped her exchange one designer tuxedo for another. She knitted her brow in confusion as she read Grace's text. *Please call me ASAP.* What did that mean?

If there was a problem with the fabric Grace had ordered for her suit, they might have to start from scratch. Unless Grace put a rush on the next order, there was no way she'd be able to make a suit in time for Dakota to wear it to Brooke's wedding.

"Give me a minute, guys. I need to make a phone call."

"But—"

"I'll make it quick. I promise."

She ushered everyone out and closed the door so she could talk in private. Grace answered on the first ring.

"Hallelujah," Grace said with almost palpable relief before her voice took on a more businesslike tone. "I mean, this is Grace Henderson. How may I help you?"

Dakota felt like she was missing something. "It's Dakota. You texted me and asked me to call you, remember?"

The phone rustled. When Grace spoke again, Dakota wasn't entirely sure she was talking to her. "I'm so sorry, but I have to leave. I have a situation at work that requires my immediate attention. No, it can't wait. It was a pleasure meeting you, though."

Dakota heard a voice she didn't recognize. A woman's voice. "Thanks for coming today," the voice said faintly. "What did you decide about dinner next Friday?"

"I'll get back to you," Grace said.

Dakota smiled to herself as she slowly realized what was going on. "Did you just use me as your emergency bailout to extricate you from a bad date?"

"Guilty as charged. Thank you for calling me so fast. I was this close to gnawing off my arm in order to get away."

"Was it that bad?"

"I've been out with women who were hung up on their old girlfriends before, but this one tops them all."

"How so?"

"She and her ex aren't a couple anymore, but they're locked in a weird codependent relationship. Get this. She wanted the three of us to get together next week so the ex could meet me."

"Maybe she was trying to make the ex jealous to see if there's still a chance they could pick up where they left off."

"Good point. I hadn't thought about it like that. I was so busy trying to figure out how I could leave without being rude. Oh, God, I just realized what time it is. It's almost noon here, but Belize is two hours behind New York. I didn't wake you, did I?"

"I wish. I've been up since five."

"That means you're probably working. I didn't mean to interrupt you."

"You're not," Dakota said hurriedly so Grace wouldn't end the call. "I'm in the middle of a wardrobe change. I have twenty more minutes before I have to be anywhere."

"In that case, do you want to keep me company on my cab ride back to Brooklyn?"

"I'd love to." Dakota longed to grab a seat and make herself comfortable while she and Grace talked, but if she wrinkled her suit, it might result in a delay she couldn't afford. Not with only an hour between the scheduled end of this photo shoot and the beginning of the next one. She leaned against the wall as she listened to Grace hail a taxi and give the cabbie her address. "Did you know your date was a walking caution sign before you agreed to go out with her or after?" she asked after she heard the cab door close.

"She's a teacher, so I assumed—incorrectly, it turns out—that I wouldn't have anything to worry about in that regard. She didn't raise any red flags when we talked on the phone yesterday. If I'd known it was all an act, I never would have agreed to meet her in the first place."

"Perhaps you should find someone else to play matchmaker for you. I'm starting to detect a theme."

"So am I," Grace said with a sexy chuckle that made Dakota's stomach turn flips. "But you have to kiss a lot of frogs before you find your princess, right? I have the warts to show for it." She groaned. "That sounded a lot better in my head than it did when it came out of my mouth."

"It's okay," Dakota said. "I know what you mean."

"May I ask you a question? A personal question."

"Uh-oh. That can't be good."

"Not necessarily. It's just—I had a conversation recently that made me realize I've been making an assumption about you that might not be accurate, and I want to make sure I get it right."

Grace sounded so serious Dakota couldn't tell which direction she was trying to steer the conversation. "What do you want to know?" she asked, pushing herself upright.

"Of the myriad available pronouns, which one do you prefer to be called?"

Dakota's mounting sense of dread evaporated. "Ah, you've been talking to Austin, I see. He called me after your meeting and told me he persuaded you to update your website. Thank you for following through on your promise instead of simply offering lip service to appease a customer." She had checked the site after she ended the call with Austin and was surprised to see the changes Austin had suggested had already been implemented. Talk about a rapid response time. "To answer your question, I'm not into labels. Designer or otherwise. I'm just Dakota."

Grace was quiet for a moment as if she were trying to absorb what Dakota had said. "If you're not into labels, what are you into?"

Dakota heard what sounded like a flirtatious note in Grace's voice. "That's not a question I can answer in twenty minutes or less," she said, responding in kind. "Do you like baseball?"

"That's a random question."

"Not really. I ask because a very beautiful woman once told me nothing says spring and summer in New York like walking in the park with a hot dog in your hand and the sun on your face. Grabbing a dog at a baseball game comes a close second. I have to throw out the first pitch at the Mets game Friday night. It's my agent's idea of good publicity, but he doesn't seem to realize the person making the pitch never gets any media coverage unless the throw goes wrong."

"Maybe he's secretly hoping you'll roll the ball into the plate or uncork a wild pitch that beans an unsuspecting fan in the stands."

"I wouldn't put it past him to root for either scenario. That's why I could use some moral support. Can I count on you?"

"After the situation you just bailed me out of, there's no way I can say no, is there?"

"You don't have to say yes out of obligation." Dakota didn't quite manage to keep the disappointment out of her voice. She didn't want Grace to accompany her to the game because she felt like she had to but because she wanted to. "You don't owe me anything. I was happy to help. If baseball isn't your thing, then—"

"Dakota, I was kidding. I would love to go to the game with you."

Dakota felt like a kid who had gotten every gift she'd included on her Christmas list when she'd expected to receive only socks and underwear. "Really?"

"Yes, really. Just let me know the details, and I'll be there."

"Awesome." Mike stuck his head in the door and tapped on his watch. Dakota nodded to let him know she was on her way. "I've got to go back to work, but tell me something first."

"What?"

"Out of all the people you could have asked to give you a helping hand today, why did you choose me? Because you don't know me well or because you'd like to get to know me better?"

"I don't know." Grace sounded as if the admission came at a cost. A steep one. "I haven't been able to stop thinking about you since we met, but I don't know why."

"That's okay," Dakota said, feeling almost giddy with anticipation. "We can figure it out together."

❖

Since Grace had used work as an excuse to bring her calamitous date with Karin to a premature end, she decided it might be good karma if she headed to the office and got some actual work done. When she reached the building, she disabled the alarm, locked the door behind her, and headed upstairs.

The building was quiet, devoid of its usual hustle and bustle. Despite the encroachment into her scheduled downtime, the solitude was Grace's favorite part of working weekends. She could concentrate on one task at a time instead of trying to put out fifty fires at once.

She familiarized herself with the design she had drawn for the suit she was due to craft next, then headed to the fabric room to retrieve the heavy bolt of cloth that matched the swatch the client had selected. She dropped the bolt on the cutting table and went to work, humming to herself as she made slow but steady progress.

"This morning might have been a bust, but at least I'm managing to get something accomplished today."

After the company was officially hers, days like this would either become more frequent or increasingly rare. There were only twenty-four hours in a day and seven days in a week. As much as she might like to, she couldn't add more time to either. She needed to find a way to strike the perfect work balance so she could give both the operational and creative sides of the business equal attention without burning herself out in the process. Sometimes she put one side on the back burner in order to concentrate on the other. She wouldn't be able to do that when her father wasn't around to pick up the slack.

She could always hire another full-time employee. If she went that route, she needed to find someone now so they'd be up to speed when she needed to rely on them. Bringing in a partner was another possible solution, though an unlikely one. Henderson Custom Suits had always been a family business. That's what it was always meant to be. Selling a portion of the company to an outsider was out of the question. Her job—among many—was to keep the company intact until she entrusted it to the next generation. Whether the kids turned out to be hers or her sisters' remained to be seen. But one thing was clear: she needed to start figuring things out now before her father put his measuring tape down for good. Otherwise, the only place she'd be running the family business was into the ground.

She sighed and stepped back from the table to take a hard look at what she had accomplished so far. "I'll start making plans soon, but not today."

Today, she was finding it hard to concentrate on the backlog of orders, the future of the company, or anything else work-related. Today, all she could think about was Dakota Lane.

"We'll figure it out together," Dakota had said after Grace voiced her doubts about embarking on any kind of relationship with

Dakota except a professional one. But what was there to figure out? Attending a baseball game together as friends was one thing, but starting a relationship with her was a line she couldn't cross.

As much as she wanted to, she couldn't deny she was attracted to Dakota. But what was she supposed to do about it? Ignoring the attraction felt like a copout. Giving in to it to see where it might lead felt like a challenge. A challenge she wasn't sure she was willing to accept.

She had never denied being a lesbian, but she had never advertised it either. In some settings, it was safer to blend in than stand out. Being with Dakota would be like coming out all over again. Not just to her friends and family, but to everyone they came across. She didn't want to walk around with a target on her back. She just wanted to live her life. And since Dakota Lane had walked into it, her life had become a lot more interesting. And complicated.

What had she been thinking when she had agreed to go out with Dakota Friday night? Not only was it a conflict of interest, but Dakota wasn't even her type.

"Tell that to my hormones."

The little buggers started surging whenever she thought about Dakota. And when she talked to her on the phone or saw her in person, she could barely hold back the tide. If she didn't get a grip soon, she was in danger of being swept away.

She set her scissors down because her hands were shaking too badly to perform a precise cut. Then the downstairs buzzer rang, preventing her from doing any serious damage to her work in progress.

"Who is it?" she asked cautiously. She wasn't expecting a customer or a delivery, which meant she had little incentive to let anyone inside.

"It's me."

Lynette's voice was as familiar to Grace as her own. "I didn't know you were in the market for a suit."

"I'm not, smart-ass," Lynette said. "Karin called me after you hightailed it from her niece's soccer game. I'm here to find out what went wrong this morning."

"Seriously? You dragged yourself all the way from the Bronx to ask me why I bailed on a bad date?"

"Surely you're not surprised. I've traveled longer distances for less. Now are you going to let me in, or are you going to make me stand on the street, dishing the details of your love life for every Tom, Dick, and Harry passing by?"

Grace pressed the lock release long enough for Lynette to enter the building. After the elevator rattled to a stop, she heard Lynette's heavy footsteps echoing in the tiled hallway. Lynette entered the room as she did most things: at full speed.

Lynette was of average height, but everything else about her was extraordinary. From her passion for old-school hip-hop to her unwavering devotion to her friends. She had a degree in social work and had been toiling in the trying field for several years. Unlike some of her jaded coworkers, who left their cases at the office, she often took her job home with her. If she had her way, she would probably adopt most of the kids in her care rather than allow them to remain in the foster system, but her partner Monica wasn't having it. Monica, a corrections officer at Rikers Island, had borne witness to so many examples of both the foster and justice systems' failures that she was reluctant to take a child into her home—or her heart. Lynette kept trying to convince her to change her mind, but Monica was standing firm.

Grace didn't know if Lynette would eventually get her way, but she knew from experience that Lynette wouldn't stop trying. Lynette was like a mama bird in many ways, but with one big difference: once she took you under her wing, she didn't try to kick you out of the nest.

Lynette glanced at the various pieces of cloth scattered across the cutting table. "You really are working." She came over for a closer inspection. "Looks like a regular suit to me. What's so important about the order that it couldn't wait? Karin was beside herself when she called. She thinks she might have done or said something to drive you away."

"She did."

Lynette put her hands on her hips and spread her legs like she was preparing to mete out a little discipline on one of her wayward charges. "What did she do?"

"She's fixated on her ex."

Lynette's bluster faded like a balloon that had sprung a leak. "Oh, that."

"Is that really all you have to say? You could have given me a heads-up about that, you know. Or were you waiting for me to discover that juicy little nugget of information on my own?"

Lynette set her purse down. "You're not making it easy for me to find someone for you, Grace. I'm running out of options. You haven't given anyone I've tried to hook you up with a second chance. I was starting to think you'd already found someone and were trying to keep it on the down low. Then I come here and find you working on a Saturday. That shoots my theory all to hell."

"If I were seeing someone, you'd be the first to know."

Lynette picked up a fabric remnant, gave it a quick once-over, and set it aside. "Fat chance of that happening if the only places you go are work and church. You're not interested in any of the ballers that come through here. That leaves the holy rollers, and I can't see you hooking up with any of them unless you're looking to get saved instead of laid."

Grace nearly told her about her plans to accompany Dakota to the Mets game Friday night. At the last possible second, she decided to keep the news to herself. If she didn't call it a date, maybe the night wouldn't end up going sideways like all the others that had preceded it. "I'll be fine, Lynette."

"Are you sure? I thought you said you were tired of waking up alone."

"I am, but I'm not going to fall into bed with the next woman who crosses my path just so I can have company when I open my eyes the next day."

"Girl, you need to lower your standards and your drawers. How will you know when the right woman comes along if you keep telling everyone no?"

"Because when I finally meet her, I firmly believe my heart won't allow me to say anything but yes."

CHAPTER TEN

The Mets comped Dakota four tickets for Friday night's game and left them for her at the Will Call window. They were great seats, too. In the front row right behind the home team's dugout. There was only one problem. Like most kids in Georgia, Dakota had grown up a Braves fan. Even though she was a transplanted New Yorker and the Braves were one of the worst teams in the major leagues, she still held a special place in her heart for the Atlanta-based team.

She felt like a traitor after she stopped by the Mets' public relations office to pick up a fitted team cap and commemorative jersey with her last name stitched on the back. When she was younger, her favorite baseball player was Chipper Jones, the left fielder who spent his entire nineteen-year career in Atlanta and was known for his success against the Mets. Now she was wearing the opposition's team colors. Seeing the Braves position players stretching in the outfield and the starting pitcher warming up in the bullpen made the betrayal complete. If her brother and parents were watching the game, which they most likely were, they would never let her hear the end of it.

"All set?" Joey asked after Dakota joined her, Whitney, and Grace in the tunnel under the stands in Citi Field.

Dakota had given one of her three spare tickets to Grace. She had given the other two to Joey and Whitney in the hopes that their presence would make tonight seem more like a group outing and less like a date. Grace was obviously freaked out about the idea of going out with her in an official capacity, so she wanted to make sure Grace felt as comfortable as possible while she got used to the idea.

Usually when Dakota met someone she was attracted to, the race to bed began as soon as she said hello. She didn't feel that same sense of urgency with Grace. In fact, she was enjoying taking it slow. The thrill of pursuit, she now realized, was magnified when the object of her affection proved harder to catch. Grace could take all the time she needed. Dakota suspected she was worth the wait.

"Almost," Dakota said. "I need to warm up my pitching arm first so I don't end up looking like a complete idiot out there. You guys can grab your seats if you like. I'll join you as soon as I can."

"Good luck, dude. Go out there and represent." Joey gave her a high five. "Just don't embarrass me, okay?"

"Babe, cut it out." Whitney smacked Joey on her arm. "Can't you see she's already nervous as it is?" She gave Dakota a much-needed hug. "Don't let her psych you out, D. You got this."

"Thanks, Whit. You're a good friend."

In more ways than one. Whitney had closed the bar tonight in order to come to the game, which meant she was losing money by being here to support Dakota in her time of need. To show her appreciation, Dakota had offered to pay the vendor fee for Whitney to take part in Smorgasburg, but Whitney said she'd take care of the expense herself. In her eyes, the chance to spend some quality time with Joey without having to worry about tending to customers more than made up for the lost revenue.

"Are you coming, Grace?" Joey asked.

Grace looked at Dakota and frowned as if she didn't like what she saw. "Go ahead. I think I'll stay here for a while."

"Cool. We'll see you in a bit."

"Are you okay?" Grace asked after Joey and Whitney left.

"No, I feel like I'm about to throw up." Dakota bent and put her hands on her knees. "Why did I agree to do this?"

"Because you knew you could handle it." Grace rubbed Dakota's back. The gentle, smooth strokes made Dakota feel less nauseous, but her nerves were still getting the best of her. "Come here." Grace tugged on her shoulders and forced her to stand. "Look at me."

Dakota's head swam when Grace cradled her face in her hands. Then she looked into Grace's warm brown eyes and the rest of the world fell away. Making a fool of herself in front of tens of thousands of people seemed inconsequential. The only things that mattered were the feel of Grace's hands on her skin, the reassuring sound of Grace's voice, and the tender expression on her face.

"Go out there and pretend no one's watching," Grace said. "It's just you and the catcher. You're in your backyard tossing the ball back and forth. There's no one in the stands. There's no one in the dugout. There's no one in the bullpen. There's no one in the press box. It's just you."

The butterflies in Dakota's stomach stilled, but her heart took flight.

"Better?" Grace asked.

Dakota nodded because she couldn't trust herself to speak. She didn't want to say something stupid and ruin the moment. She simply wanted to savor it for as long as it lasted. Forever was a pretty nice place to start.

"Good." Grace seemed so into her role Dakota half expected her to conclude her pep talk by smacking her on the ass and shouting, "Play ball!" Instead, she held out her hand for a fist bump. "Go get 'em."

"You got it, coach."

Grace felt nervous as she settled into her seat. The task Dakota had been asked to perform was purely ceremonial, but she was taking it as seriously as if she had been picked to be the starting pitcher in the seventh game of the World Series. Grace liked that about her. She liked when people owned up to their responsibilities rather than shirking them. But her yearning to see Dakota do well wasn't what had her feeling anxious. It was her yearning for Dakota.

When she had taken Dakota's face into her hands a few minutes ago and Dakota had looked deep into her eyes, Grace had felt a connection unlike any she had experienced before. She couldn't remember half the things she had said to Dakota as she tried to talk her through her sudden bout of nerves, but she vividly remembered all the things she had felt. All the things she was still feeling. Fondness. Curiosity. Fascination. And above all, desire.

She was pretty certain Dakota felt the same way about her. Now, like it or not, they were locked in a dance where Dakota seemed perfectly willing to take the lead if only Grace would accept the invitation. Thanks to the influx of new business, Grace could handle losing Dakota as a client. But was she willing to accept her as a lover?

Joey raised her hand to draw the attention of a roaming vendor. "Would you like something, Grace?" she asked after she ordered two cups of beer and a large bag of popcorn.

"I'll wait until the game starts, thanks."

"It's a good idea to pace yourself. Whenever I go to a game, I always end up ordering one of everything."

"Then she spends the rest of the night complaining about how much her stomach hurts," Whitney said.

"Careful, honey," Joey said. "We're supposed to be trying to make a good impression. If you keep saying things like that, Grace will think I have impulse control issues."

"That's because you do."

Grace laughed at Joey and Whitney's teasing banter. They seemed to be polar opposites. Joey was short and Whitney was tall. Joey was dark and Whitney was fair. Joey's look veered toward the butch end of the spectrum while Whitney's was undeniably femme. Despite their differences, they had one very important thing in common. Every look, every touch, and every word that passed between them demonstrated how much they loved each other.

"How long have you been together?" Grace asked.

"Five years," Joey said.

"How did you meet?"

Whitney smiled as she rubbed Joey's jeans-covered thigh. "Do you want to tell her, or shall I?"

"You tell the story a lot better than I do," Joey said, giving Whitney a kiss on the cheek. "Go for it."

"Dakota's roommate Rich is one of the featured performers at Mainline," Whitney said. "I don't think you've met him yet, but you will if you stick around long enough. Anyway, Joey and I ran into each other at Mainline one night. Purely coincidence. We were both out with friends and happened to end up at the same place at the same time. We noticed each other immediately and flirted from afar for a while, but neither of us made a move right away. After about an hour of smiling and making eye contact, Joey came over and asked me to dance. Even though the dance floor was empty, I said yes because I thought she was cute—duh—and because my favorite song was playing. It turned out there was a very good reason no one was dancing. The two of us had been paying so much attention to each other we had missed the announcer introducing the next performer."

Joey laughed, apparently anticipating the punch line.

"Rich, who was doing his Lady Gaga impersonation that night, signaled for the DJ to cut the music. Then he grabbed a microphone and said—I do a really bad Southern accent, but I'm going to try anyway. He said, 'I've been known to share many things, but a stage ain't one of them, so get off of mine and find your own.' Joey and I slunk away with our tails tucked between our legs."

"We've been together ever since." Joey wove her fingers through Whitney's.

"How do you manage to work together without having it affect your relationship?"

"If we worked together all day, it might be a problem, but our schedules overlap only a few hours a night," Whitney said. "I get to have me-time when she's running the shop, and she gets downtime when I'm behind the bar."

"That way, we don't get too sick of each other."

Whitney playfully smacked Joey on the arm. "Speak for yourself."

Grace looked back and forth between them. "You guys are a lot of fun. I can see why Dakota likes you."

Joey grabbed a fistful of popcorn. "I could say the same about you."

"Me? Fun? My sisters might beg to differ. They're always saying I'm too serious."

"Ignore them," Whitney said. "I can see why Dakota thinks so highly of you."

"Yeah," Joey added, "you're a classy lady."

Grace couldn't think of a higher compliment. Her mother had raised her and her sisters to comport themselves with class. She was glad to hear the lessons had paid off.

"Ladies and gentlemen, welcome to Citi Field," the public address announcer said. "Tonight's game features the Atlanta Braves and the New York Mets." The large crowd cheered at the mention of the home team. "Please direct your attention to the infield."

Heeding the public address announcer's suggestion, Grace turned to see Dakota approaching the mound with a baseball in her hand and three photographers at her heels.

"Please give a warm welcome to Dakota Lane," the PA announcer continued, "here to throw out the first pitch."

Dakota doffed her cap and saluted the crowd. Though the cheers she received weren't as deafening as they were bound to be for the players once the game was under way, they were loud enough to give Grace goose bumps. Dakota seemed so down-to-earth it was easy to forget she was on the fast track to becoming a household name.

Dakota toed the rubber after the Mets backup catcher crouched behind home plate. Grace held her breath when Dakota, looking as serious as a closer brought in to protect a slim lead in the bottom of the ninth, settled into her stance. Technically, the pitch didn't mean anything—it wouldn't affect the outcome of tonight's game in any way—yet it meant so much.

Dakota wound up and threw the ball toward home plate. Grace thought she heard a faint grunt of effort as the ball left Dakota's hand. The pitch landed in the catcher's mitt with a loud smack. A perfect strike right down the middle.

"Yes!" Grace jumped out of her seat and cheered as if the game was over instead of about to begin.

On the mound, Dakota saluted the crowd again and strode toward the catcher, who was jogging toward her to present her with a souvenir baseball. Dakota held the ball aloft as she met Grace's eye. "Thank you," she mouthed.

"You're welcome," Grace mouthed back.

Joey reached for her beer. "I'd have to take a look at the speed gun before I offered her a contract, but that was pretty impressive."

"Yes," Grace said, watching Dakota give an on-field interview to a reporter from the Mets' cable network, "she certainly is."

CHAPTER ELEVEN

Dakota's feet were on the ground, but she felt like she was walking on air. She had forced herself to keep her expectations low so she wouldn't make the rookie mistake of trying too hard. Tonight wasn't make-or-break, she had told herself. It wasn't about pitching her case or trying to bully Grace into putting her concerns aside and fall into bed with her. Tonight, she simply wanted to show Grace a good time and, if she was lucky, lay the appropriate groundwork for a second date. So far, she seemed to be doing just that.

Inviting Joey and Whitney to accompany her and Grace to the game had accomplished exactly what she had hoped it would: it had helped to break the ice. Grace was relaxed, smiling, and receptive. She was laughing at all of her jokes—even the bad ones—and she was getting along so well with Joey and Whitney they already seemed like fast friends.

Dakota wasn't completely surprised by the latter development. Whitney always managed to find some good in everyone she met; Joey was harder to impress. So when Joey caught her eye during the seventh-inning stretch, nodded at Grace, and flashed a surreptitious thumbs-up, Dakota grinned at the unexpected seal of approval.

She sang along with the crowd when the PA system blasted "Take Me Out to the Ball Game," but fell silent when local staple "Lazy Mary" started up. Grace tried to teach her the words, but Dakota couldn't master the intricate Italian lyrics. She laughed at her increasingly comical attempts.

"Sorry. My Southern tongue doesn't work that fast."

"You might want to address that deficiency before you start receiving complaints about your performance," Grace said with a wink.

"I'll keep that in mind." Ignoring the thought of how much she wanted to show Grace she wasn't entirely lacking in skills in the bedroom, Dakota pointed to the scoreboard, which showed the Mets leading 11–2. "Do you want to get out of here? Unless the Braves find their missing offense and mount a miraculous comeback over the next two innings, I think the Mets have this game in hand." She wasn't ready for the night to end, but she didn't want to press her luck by suggesting they head somewhere else after they left the stadium.

"Do you want to grab something more substantial than a hot dog?" Grace asked. "Since Whitney's place is closed tonight, there's a new Honduran restaurant in Williamsburg I'd love to try."

"I know the place you're talking about. La Tigra on Melrose Avenue."

"Yeah, that's the one."

"I'm up for it." Dakota turned to Joey and Whitney. "What about you guys?"

Joey and Whitney exchanged a look. "You two have fun," Joey said after they came to a silent decision.

"You're going to love it," Whitney added. "If you like tripe, make sure to try the *mondongo* soup. It's ah-may-zing."

Joey made a face. "Do yourself a favor and stick with the *catrachitas*. Deep-fried tortilla strips, mashed refried beans, melted cheese, and tons of hot sauce. My four favorite foods on one plate."

"They both sound so good I don't think I could go wrong with either choice." Grace tossed her purse strap over her shoulder as they headed for the nearest exit. "I appreciate the recommendations, but you're coming with us, aren't you?"

Joey shook her head. "We'll ride the train to Williamsburg with you, but we'll let you take it from there."

"Bailing so soon?" Dakota asked after they reached the top of the stairs. "It's not even ten o'clock yet."

"Running two businesses simultaneously means we don't get

to have date night often." Joey wrapped her arm around Whitney's waist as they walked toward the subway station that provided direct service to the stadium. "We're going to take full advantage of the opportunity, if you catch my drift."

"I know how stressful running a business can be," Grace said while they waited for their train to arrive. Extra trains were available after the games to service the departing crowds, but the additional cars hadn't started running yet. "I don't blame you for taking some time for yourselves. I need to start doing more of that."

Despite Grace's assertion that she wanted to spend more time out of the office, Dakota half expected her to change her mind about dinner once Joey and Whitney begged off. When they arrived in Williamsburg, they parted ways with Joey and Whitney with kisses and good-bye hugs outside the subway exit. Joey and Whitney headed for the sex toy shop they planned to visit, and Grace started walking in the opposite direction.

"The restaurant's this way," she said, beckoning for Dakota to follow her. "I hope you're hungry."

"I'm starved."

And the more time she spent with Grace Henderson, the hungrier she became.

❖

By the time Grace and Dakota arrived at La Tigra, the dinner rush was over and the kitchen had run out of half the items on the menu. The restaurant was so small it seated a maximum of thirty people, and the chef, who was also the owner, crafted his meals on two portable burners in a small area behind the checkout counter instead of on a commercial stove in a well-appointed kitchen.

Grace loved the place's quaint, cozy charm. Oversized black-and-white photographs of Honduras hung on the walls, and *punta* music played on a boom box strategically placed on a small wooden shelf above the bathroom door. If the food was as good as the ambience, she would definitely be coming back for more. Since their options were limited, she and Dakota decided to split the *catrachitas.* Paired with a bottle of palm sap wine, she figured the generous appetizer would be enough to tide them over for the rest of the night.

"Have you had *coyol* before?" Dakota asked after the waitress took their order.

"No, but I'm not much of a beer drinker and it was the only thing on the wine list I haven't had before. Why do you ask?"

"It might not be what you're expecting. *Coyol* isn't like traditional wine. It looks like coconut milk, it's not as alcoholic as regular wine, and depending on how long it was allowed to ferment, it can be sweet or sour. There's also an added bonus. When you drink too much of it, it isn't the alcohol that makes you drunk. It's the enzymes. Exposure to the sun exacerbates the process."

"Meaning?"

"Simply put, if we get blasted tonight and sober up by tomorrow morning, we can get wasted all over again just by walking through a sunbeam."

"Nice try, but I call BS on that one."

Dakota held up three fingers. "Scout's honor. If you like, we could put the theory to the test by polishing off a bottle tonight and going for a walk in Central Park tomorrow."

"It's a deal. I'll meet you at Bow Bridge at noon."

"Cool."

Grace realized what had happened a beat too late. As if allowing Dakota to cleverly corral her into accepting a second date wasn't bad enough, suggesting they meet at one of the most romantic places in New York City was even worse. Bow Bridge had been the site of countless proposals over the years. Filmmakers and tourists alike loved focusing their cameras on its graceful lines as it stretched sixty feet over the tranquil waters of Central Park Lake. Using it as a rendezvous point was only asking for trouble. The kind of trouble she couldn't afford but was finding harder and harder to resist.

"When I agreed to go out with you tonight, I knew I'd be signing up for an adventure," she said. "Tonight has proven to be exactly that."

"A good one, I hope."

Grace was hesitant to comment on how incredibly well the evening was going because she didn't want to risk ruining it. Especially when another outing had been added to the schedule. "I'll let you know tomorrow."

"One bottle of *coyol*," the waitress said, placing a chilled carafe filled with a cloudy white liquid on the table. The two small glasses she set next to the carafe looked more like juice glasses than any wine glasses Grace had ever seen. "Enjoy."

Dakota pulled the rubber stopper from the bottle, half-filled both glasses, then raised the one closer to her in a toast. "To continuing adventures."

Grace tapped her glass against Dakota's and took a tentative sip of the wine. Dakota was right. The *coyol*—sweet, yet earthy—wasn't what she was expecting. Neither was Dakota. She was more. Much more. Any woman would be lucky to have her. Any woman, that was, except her.

"Did you always want to be a model when you grew up?" she asked.

"No way. Sometimes I don't want to be a model even now."

"Then why do you do it?"

"Because the money's good and the perks are even better. I get all-expense-paid trips to some of the most beautiful places in the world, and I haven't had to buy my own clothes in years."

"That sounds like a good deal to me. But if you didn't always aspire to be a model, what profession did you want to pursue?"

"When I was younger, I wanted to be Tony Hawk, the best skateboarder in the history of the sport. I used to take my board everywhere I went. At times, I even slept with it. After I won a couple of amateur competitions, I had dreams of turning pro, competing in the X Games, and getting a bunch of sponsorships, but I broke my arm trying out a new trick and decided to try my luck at a career with less risk of injury."

"Like being a bike messenger in New York City? How's that working out for you?"

"Touché." Dakota rubbed her knee, which had been scraped and bleeding the night she and Grace had met. "I was a finance major in college, and I have the bachelor of business administration degree to prove it, but most corporations wouldn't give me the time of day when Rich and I first moved to New York. They were so fixated on my look that my qualifications didn't matter. I became a bike messenger on what I thought would be a temporary basis. I don't have to tell you how that turned out."

"Do you want to take another crack at making a living in the business world one day?"

"I'm doing it now. I dabble in day trading in my spare time. I'm no wolf of Wall Street, but I've done pretty well. I keep telling myself I'm one bad investment away from losing everything. I'm not, but it makes me be careful with the money I have tied up in the stock market. I could probably retire now if I wanted to, but I'd like to build the coffers a little more before I officially pull the pin. For me, money is like coffee and chocolate. I can't have too much of either."

"For me, retirement is more of a suggestion than a tangible goal. I'm trying to save as much money as I can, but it's not enough to retire on. Not yet, anyway. Call me in thirty years or so."

"You're planning to retire early?"

"My goal is to have options. I want to be like Lillie—working because I want to, not because I have to."

"I like her. She's funny, but there's a hint of truth in everything she says. How long does she plan to keep working?"

"She threatens to retire every January, but she always changes her mind by December. I think she likes the routine. I'm glad she does. We'd be lost without her."

Dakota leaned back to allow the waitress to place a platter of *catrachitas* on the table. "I assume you always wanted to be a tailor when you grew up?"

When Grace sampled some of the food, her tongue went numb from the spices in the hot sauce. She waited until she regained sensation before she answered Dakota's question. "Fashion has always been in my blood. I've been sketching designs since I was four years old, and I've been working for my father in one capacity or another for nearly as long. I love what I do. Even though the clients stress me out sometimes, I can't imagine doing anything else. Are you doing something you truly love, or are you doing something that pays the bills?"

Dakota refilled their glasses. "I'll have to get back to you on that one. I have a love-hate relationship with both my jobs. If the weather's nice, I love being a messenger. If the weather's crappy, I hate it. If the shoot's going well, I love being a model. If I'm working with a bunch of self-involved assholes, I hate it. But my situation's hardly unique. Surely you feel the same way about your job from time to time."

"I do, and having family involved makes it worse. I can't take out my frustrations on them because, one, they're my family and, two, I have to live with them. It makes for some tense dinner table conversations from time to time, that's for sure."

"Have you ever thought about going into business for yourself?"

"I couldn't leave my father in the lurch like that, and it wouldn't make good business sense anyway. Right now, I'm in the perfect situation. My father might own the company, but my name's on the shingle, too. I have a growing roster of clients, I have the freedom to create my own designs, I share in the profits, and I'm not personally responsible for any of the expenses. What could be better?"

"No offense to your father, but you're too talented to work for someone else the rest of your life. Don't you want to be your own boss one day?"

"I will be in due time, but I want to learn as much as I possibly can before that day comes. Is that what you want? To be the captain of your own ship instead of a member of the crew?"

Dakota swirled her drink and stared into its cloudy depths. "I like what I do," she said thoughtfully, "but I want something that's mine. Something I built myself. I just don't know how to go about it."

"You'll figure it out."

"How do you know?"

Grace took another sip of the *coyol*. The unusual beverage was starting to grow on her. So was Dakota. "Because I've seen what you're capable of once you set your mind to something."

Dakota looked momentarily embarrassed by the compliment. Then she wiped her hands on her napkin and handed Grace the souvenir baseball from the Mets game. "I want you to have this."

"Why?"

"I couldn't have made that pitch tonight without you. I want you to know how much what you said—what you did—means to me."

Grace ran a finger along the ball's bright red seams. The ball would serve as a tangible reminder, but she had a feeling she would never forget this night—or the woman who had made it possible.

Chapter Twelve

Dakota normally avoided certain parts of Central Park at all costs. Despite its beauty, Bow Bridge was one of those places. The bridge and the surrounding area were gorgeous. There was no denying their obvious appeal. But watching couples mooning over each other as they crossed the bridge or picnicked under a towering tree always made her feel like she was missing out on something.

She had never lacked for female companionship, even when she lived in tiny Richmond Hill instead of sprawling New York City. Each of the women she had slept with had been exciting and unique. Otherwise, she wouldn't have been drawn to them in the first place. Despite their differences, they all had one thing in common: none of them made her want to drop to one knee, pull out a ring, and vow to be faithful to them for the rest of her life.

Then she met Grace Henderson, and everything changed. She wasn't planning on walking down the aisle anytime soon, but she could already tell one night with Grace wouldn't be enough. She hadn't even kissed her yet and she went to sleep with Grace's image in her head, woke up with Grace's name on her lips. She had it bad, and that definitely wasn't good. Grace didn't date clients and she also wasn't attracted to women who played down rather than accentuated their femininity. That meant Dakota was 0-for-2. She had only one strike left, and she needed to make it count.

As she waited for Grace to arrive, she watched a gondolier slowly pilot his boat and two cuddling passengers along the lake.

Her mind soon wandered from the romantic scene playing out before her to the one she had participated in the night before.

Her date with Grace had been perfect from beginning to end. Well, almost. Ideally, the Braves would have won the game instead of getting blown out, but that was a minor detail that could always be omitted from future recountings of one of the best nights she'd ever had.

She had been so nervous when she had walked out to the mound to throw the first pitch. When she'd felt Grace's eyes on her, her nerves had disappeared even faster than they'd arrived. "Go out there and pretend no one's watching," Grace had said in the tunnel as she talked her through a panic attack. "It's just you and the catcher."

When Dakota had turned to face the catcher, she hadn't noticed the tens of thousands of fans in attendance. She had been aware of only one: Grace. When she had wound up to make the pitch, she would have been satisfied if the ball had ended up in the general vicinity of home plate. Watching the ball smack into the catcher's glove in the heart of the strike zone was a feeling she thought couldn't be topped—until she looked into the stands and saw Grace beaming with pride.

"I did that," she had thought as she walked off the mound. "I put that look on her face."

The feat had felt like the greatest thing she had ever accomplished. Bigger than graduating cum laude from the University of Georgia or being awarded the cover for the September issue of *Vogue*. And the night had only gotten better from there.

During dinner, Grace had seemed genuinely interested in wanting to get to know her. Her questions had been probing and incisive, demanding in-depth answers rather than a quick yes or no. Dakota hated when interviewers asked such questions, especially about her personal life, because she had seen too many of them take her words out of context and spin them to match the narrative they were trying to craft instead of sticking with the truth. With Grace, she hadn't felt like she was being interrogated or treated like a mystery to be solved for the entertainment of curious readers. The give-and-take had felt natural instead of forced. As a result, she had opened up to Grace in a way she never had with anyone else.

She and Rich had heart-to-hearts from time to time, but she usually ended up doing more listening than talking. Not last night. With Grace, she had given as much as she had received. She hadn't told all her secrets, but it was probably only a matter of time before Grace tried to draw out anything she might be holding back. Dakota liked the idea of sharing more than just her body with someone, and that was something she thought she'd never say.

She couldn't speak for Grace, but Grace's admissions had felt pretty personal, too. She wondered if Grace had ever shared them with anyone. She hoped not. She liked the idea of being the only person privy to some of Grace's secrets. Knowing something no one else did made her feel closer to Grace. It made her feel like they were part of something bigger than themselves. Like they were building something that could become much deeper than friendship.

After they drank the last of the *coyol* and polished off the plate of *catrachitas*, Dakota had walked Grace home and bade her good night at the door with a kiss on the cheek. She had longed for more—she still did—but she had convinced herself not to try for too much too soon.

Her breath caught when she looked on the other side of the bridge and saw Grace walking toward her. Her body's reaction reaffirmed what her head already knew: Grace Henderson was definitely worth waiting for.

❖

Grace was pretty sure she had made a mistake, but it was too late to back out now. After she made her way from Brooklyn to Central Park, she met Dakota in the middle of Bow Bridge. "I'm sorry I'm late. My appointment ran longer than I thought it would."

Dakota greeted her with a warm hug, then stepped back to take a look at her. Her gaze skimmed over Grace's face and clothes before it settled on her hair. "You look different."

Grace couldn't tell if Dakota meant her comment to be a

compliment or a critique. She had decided to dress down today. She was sporting a T-shirt, tennis shoes, and jeans instead of the professional attire Dakota was used to seeing her wear, but that wasn't the only change she had made. "I've wanted to do something different for years," she said, patting her hair self-consciously, "but I never had the nerve to follow through."

"What finally pushed you over the hump?"

Grace had been pondering the same question all morning. "I have a standing appointment with my hairdresser every other week and I always get the same thing done every time. When I woke up this morning, I was in the mood for a change."

She had spent the last three hours at the hair salon. Her favorite stylist had nearly dropped her comb after Grace sat in the chair and told her she was finally ready to start making the gradual transition from relaxed hair to natural. She could have expedited the process by shaving her head and allowing her hair to grow out unaided by chemical straighteners, but she was afraid such a drastic alteration to her look would be too much of a shock to her system—and her parents' sensibilities.

"I know my sisters will like what I've done," she said, "but my parents are a different story."

"You don't think they'll approve of the new you?"

If she knew her parents as well as she thought she did, Grace suspected they would have issues with much more than her hair.

"My mother loves to say a woman's hair is her glory. When I sat her and my father down and told them I was a lesbian, the first thing she said was she hoped I didn't plan to cut my hair. The second thing she said was she didn't mind if I dated women as long as both of us looked like one. As for my father, he's apt to say my new twist-outs are better suited for a night at the club than a day at the office. I'm not looking forward to fighting either battle when I get home."

"My opinion might not mean much, but I think you look amazing."

Endorphins flooded Grace's body when Dakota tossed a dazzling smile in her direction. She felt like a runner who had just finished a marathon—giddy from a natural high. "You're good for my ego. I need to keep you around."

"Sounds good to me."

Grace felt physically and psychically lighter as she and Dakota began to walk through part of the 843-acre green space that had been carved out of Manhattan's concrete jungle. Once she had made the decision to cut her hair, she had felt as if a burden had been lifted off her shoulders. She hoped the one on her heart would soon follow. She loved her job and her family, but she sometimes felt she was living her life to please other people instead of herself. What would happen, she wondered, if her family's expectations of her ran afoul of the ones she had for herself? Would she bow to her family's wishes or follow her own path? She had a feeling she might soon be forced to come up with the answers to both questions.

"I didn't keep you waiting, did I?" she asked.

"No, I just got here myself."

Grace examined Dakota's handsome face. Dakota's expression was open and honest, lending her an endearing quality Grace found incredibly appealing. "You're not a very good liar, are you?"

"I'm afraid not. When we were kids, my brother used to call me Saran Wrap because everyone could see right through me."

"You say that like it's a bad thing. I hate when people try to hide who they are or how they feel. With you, I always know where I stand. There's something to be said for that."

Dakota rolled her eyes. "You make me sound dependable."

"Don't you want to be someone people can rely on?"

"Of course, but dependable is safe and comfortable. Dependable is boring. It's not sexy."

Grace pointed out some of the women—and men—who had given Dakota admiring looks as they passed by. "I don't think you need to worry about not being considered sexy. Is that why you're still single? Because you're having so much fun playing the field?"

Dakota's smile gave her away.

"Don't you ever want to settle down?"

"One day, maybe."

"And what would a woman have to do to convince you that she's the right one for you?"

"That's just it. She wouldn't have to do anything. I want to be with someone who gets me. Someone who's willing to accept me for who I am and doesn't make it her mission to try to change me into something I'm not. So far, the only women I've come across who meet those prerequisites were on the hunt for something temporary, too."

"I admire people who are able to identify what they want and go after it, but I don't have the temperament for one-night stands. It takes me a while to warm up to someone enough to let her into my heart or my bed. Haven't you ever met a woman who left you wanting more?"

"Yes."

"What did you do?"

Grace expected Dakota to answer the question like she did most serious inquiries—by making a joke at her own expense. Dakota surprised her by speaking from the heart instead of from the lip.

"I took her for a ride on my bike, then I invited her to a baseball game. I haven't decided what to do next, but I'm thinking a gondola ride might be a good place to start."

After the import of Dakota's words sank in, Grace turned to face her. "Dakota—"

"I know what you're going to say: you don't date clients and I'm not your type. I'm not trying to tell you how to run your business or your life, Grace, but I know you're attracted to me. I felt it the day we met, I felt it last night, and I feel it now. Are you going to look me in the eye and tell me I'm wrong?"

Grace couldn't think straight. Her heart was racing and she felt light-headed. For a moment she wondered if the palm wine she had downed the night before was kicking in again just like Dakota had said it would. She quickly realized the intoxication she was feeling had nothing to do with alcohol. She wasn't drunk. Far from it. She was falling in love. She was falling for Dakota Lane.

The sky opened up before Grace could answer Dakota's

question. Dakota took her hand as they ran for shelter under a nearby tree.

"Take this. You're getting drenched."

Dakota pulled off her T-shirt and held it over Grace's head like a makeshift canopy. Grace was grateful for the added protection from the sudden downpour, but Dakota looked like she was freezing as raindrops soaked her gray sports bra and slowly slid down her bare torso. "Do you want your shirt back?"

"No, keep it," Dakota said. "I'm fine."

Dakota talked a good game, but her teeth chattered as she hugged herself for warmth.

Grace turned around and leaned against her, trying to share some of her body heat. "Better?"

"Better." Dakota wrapped her long arms around Grace's waist and pulled her closer. "At least the sun's shining. It could be worse. At home, when it's raining like this, we say the devil's beating his wife."

"We say that here, too." Grace peered at the bright blue sky through the thick branches overhead. "It should be over soon."

"I'm in no hurry. Are you?"

Grace could feel Dakota's hard nipples poking into her back. It was all she could do not to rub herself against them. Dakota's shivering was already providing enough friction. She didn't need more.

She pressed her body closer to Dakota's. Bad idea. The closer proximity only intensified the sensation. She could feel Dakota's crotch pressing against her back. Dakota groaned when Grace ground her hips against her.

"Jesus, Grace," Dakota said with a shudder. "I know I don't look like any of the other women you've been with, but is that reason enough to walk away from something that feels this good?"

Grace turned to face her. Dakota's eyes were wild. When Grace ran a hand over the rippled muscles in Dakota's stomach, her eyes grew wilder still. Grace put her hand on the back of Dakota's neck, snaked her fingers into Dakota's hair, and pulled her head down until their mouths met in a kiss that was tentative at first but quickly grew in urgency until both she and Dakota were left gasping for breath.

Grace ran a finger over Dakota's lips to keep from tasting them again. If she treated herself to another kiss, she might not be able to stop. She and Dakota were already attracting their fair share of attention. Any more might result in a morals charge. Or, even worse, an exposé on a tawdry gossip website. If that happened, her parents would blow a gasket over the negative publicity. Even worse than they had when Hope showed them the infamous picture of Dakota hooking up with a relative stranger in a nightclub. *"I trust you won't find yourself in similar circumstances,"* Hope had said that day. Now Grace was perilously close to doing exactly that. She moved away from Dakota so she could regain some semblance of control. "I thought you said getting caught in the rain was overrated."

Dakota slowly unspooled a lazy smile. "I guess I was wrong."

"I'm beginning to think I was, too."

A glimmer of hope bloomed in Dakota's eyes. "What are you saying?"

Grace returned Dakota's T-shirt as the rain trickled to a stop. "I'm saying you owe me a gondola ride. Are you going to pay up now or later?"

Dakota put her T-shirt back on and fished some money out of her pocket. "There's no time like the present."

Unfortunately, the present always gave way to the future. As they made their way to the boathouse to hire a gondolier, Grace wondered if Dakota would become part of her future or a fond memory soon relegated to the past.

CHAPTER THIRTEEN

Dakota had an underwear shoot scheduled for Wednesday afternoon. She put in a half day at the messenger agency before she stopped by her apartment long enough to shower and change. Then she took the subway to Martin Gaines's studio in Lower Manhattan for the photo session. After she arrived, she greeted everyone in attendance and headed to the dressing room so she could ditch her street clothes in favor of the first in a series of T-shirts, tank tops, and boxer briefs the client had provided.

She was constantly tempted to don her strap-on when she modeled underwear, but she always resisted the urge. The designers who hired her sought her out because they liked her edge, but when she stepped in front of the camera, she had to make sure those edges were blunt enough to appeal to a mainstream audience. The point, after all, was to move product, not prompt upset consumers to spend their hard-earned money on the competition.

Once the shoot began, she didn't have any problems following Martin's command to look sultry because she had been in a constant state of arousal since she and Grace had gotten caught in the rain in Central Park last Saturday. Four days later, she could still feel Grace's soft, curvy body pressed against her as they took shelter under a tree. As they sought comfort in each other. She could still taste Grace's kiss. Grace's lips were sweet like honey. Her tongue hot like fire.

Dakota ran her tongue over her own lips as she savored the

memory. She hadn't been kissed like that since—Well, never. The kiss she and Grace had shared was like something she had read in a romance novel, but it wasn't like anything she had ever experienced in real life.

She lifted the hem of her form-fitting undershirt and flexed her abs. As Martin pressed the shutter release on his camera, she made sure the label on her boxer briefs was visible so the pictures he took wouldn't be wasted. What good was it to shoot a print ad if potential buyers couldn't tell what brand was being advertised?

"What's gotten into you?" Martin asked as he slowly circled her. "You're on fire today."

If only he knew how right he was. *If I were a dude*, she thought, *I'd have the world's biggest boner right now.* The hungry look the wardrobe assistant was giving her wasn't helping matters much. Dakota cupped her hand against her mound, parted her lips, and gave the camera her best come-hither expression. She was grateful the tight cotton-spandex briefs were black because the seat was soaked. The wardrobe assistant looked like she was about to spontaneously combust when Dakota's fingers came away wet. Dakota had been trying to find relief for days, but her self-administered remedies had made her condition worse instead of better. She needed to feel a woman's touch before she lost her mind.

The wardrobe assistant approached her after Martin mercifully ended the shoot. "I'm Ryan." Dakota's clit twitched when Ryan dipped her gaze toward her crotch. "I'll bet you're hard enough to cut glass right now," she said in a seductive whisper. "Do you want to get out of here and grab a drink?"

Dakota slipped on the robe Ryan offered her. A drink sounded wonderful, but it was plain to see a refreshing beverage wasn't the only thing Ryan had in mind.

Ryan was ready, willing, and able. Three of Dakota's favorite words in the English language. Not so long ago, she would have eagerly accepted Ryan's invitation without giving it a second thought. But something made her hesitate. The idea of sleeping with a relative stranger, no matter how hot, didn't hold nearly as much appeal as the thought of holding out for the woman she had spent the past few weeks getting to know.

"I wish I could," she said, "but I'm meeting a friend for an early dinner."

That wasn't an outright lie, but it did stray pretty far from the truth. She was supposed to meet Aaron at Mainline tonight, but she figured he would be too focused on pumping her for information about Rich and his tour to give her time to eat. Rich was just as bad. He called her after every show to let her know how his performance had gone, but he spent more time asking about the people he had left behind than he did discussing the ones who were accompanying him on the road.

She had told herself not to involve herself in other people's relationships since she had no idea how to maintain one of her own, but she was sorely tempted to tell Aaron to pick a city on the list of tour dates, buy a plane ticket, surprise Rich with a bouquet of flowers after a show, and take him to dinner to see if they could get out of their own way long enough to realize they were meant to be together.

"Some other time, then?" Ryan asked.

Dakota's ringing phone saved her from having to come up with another lie. "I'm sorry," she said when she saw Laird's name printed on the screen, "but I have to take this." She headed to the dressing room and closed the door.

"What does your schedule look like next week?" Laird asked without preamble. "If you can take time off work, I need you to go to Tokyo for two days."

She pressed the speaker icon on her cell phone so she could continue the conversation while she got dressed. "What's in Tokyo?" she asked as she dropped her robe and pulled on her jeans.

"One of the leading whiskey manufacturers in Japan wants you to film a commercial."

That got Dakota's attention. Hollywood celebrities were routinely paid exorbitant amounts to shoot commercials and print ads for products they would never shill in the States. If she accepted the job Laird was dangling in front of her, she doubted she would receive the same kind of compensation Brad Pitt or Leonardo DiCaprio might expect, but she knew it would be several times her usual going rate. Not bad for a couple days' work.

"Surely the messenger agency can find someone else to make deliveries in your absence," Laird said. "Unless, of course, you'd prefer to turn down five figures in order to earn minimum wage. When are you going to quit that job, anyway? I know how much money you pull in on an annual basis. Unless you've blown it all without telling me, it's not like you're hurting monetarily."

"Being a messenger helps me stay in shape and it gives me something to do while I'm waiting for you to tell me my next assignment."

"Whatever works for you. So can I pencil you in for Tokyo or not? The client wants an answer by tomorrow, or they're going to reach out to someone else."

Dakota buttoned her shirt and bent to tie her shoes. Tokyo was one of her favorite cities. She loved the sights, sounds, and energy of the place. She didn't get a chance to visit often, and each time she left, she vowed to return as soon as she could. The trip Laird was proposing was right up her alley—a sweet paycheck, all the sushi she could eat, all the sake she could drink, and a no-holds-barred trip to one of the largest red-light districts in the world.

She didn't think her manager at the messenger agency would mind letting her have the week off. In exchange for the free publicity she garnered for the company each time she mentioned its name during an interview, she was practically able to set her own schedule.

"If Sophie's available, see if the client is willing to work with her instead."

"Let me get this straight," Laird said. "A few weeks ago, you practically held a sit-in outside my office because you were worried Sophie was going to unseat you at Whitaker. Now you're passing up a high-profile gig and throwing it her way?"

Turning down a lucrative ad campaign in order to make a play for someone who wasn't completely certain she was into her seemed foolhardy. Dakota didn't know if she was doing the right thing, but one thing was for sure: she would never be able to forgive herself if she didn't take the chance. "I know it sounds crazy, but at the moment, I have much more incentive to stay here than I do to fly halfway around the world."

"I hope you know what you're doing."

"So do I."

❖

Grace didn't often go out during the week because she didn't like staying up late when she had to get up early to go to work the next day. The occasional dinner date was fine as long as it didn't involve more than one bottle of wine, but a full-fledged night on the town? No way. Unless she wanted to spend more time nodding off at her desk than getting any actual work done. So when Lynette called her late Thursday afternoon and begged her to accompany her to an impromptu street party in Harlem because Monica was working the late shift and she didn't want to go alone, her first instinct was to say no. But she had been wired for days and she needed to do something to burn off the extra energy. Spending a few hours doing all the line dances she had memorized the steps to might do the trick since nothing else she had tried seemed to help. Not even extending her work day from eight hours to ten. The additional hours helped her put a dent in the backlog of orders—the stack didn't seem nearly as daunting as it once did—but they didn't do anything to prevent her brain from filling with thoughts of Dakota. And they definitely didn't stop her body from tingling from memories of that kiss.

The kiss—impulsive, daring, and maybe even a little reckless—wasn't like her. In fact, it was the exact opposite of everything she had always aspired to be. She was calm, rational, and she didn't do over-the-top public displays of affection. So what had prompted her to toss reason aside and risk everything—her family's standing, her reputation, even her own sense of self—for one kiss? Simple. Because being in Dakota's arms had felt so good she didn't want to leave. She had spent the last few days yearning for a return visit. For a repeat of the romantic gondola ride they had taken on Central Park Lake. For a continuation of that kiss.

She couldn't decide whether she should run from what she was feeling or embrace it. Despite her reputation as both a playgirl and a party animal, Dakota seemed to have her head on straight. Smart, successful, and surprisingly humble, she was a great catch. If, that was, she had any interest in being caught.

The idea of being with Dakota intrigued Grace, but it scared her too. She wanted to be something more than a notch on someone's bedpost or a box to be checked on a sexual to-do list. Dakota could promise her a good time, but would those promises extend past the hours she and Dakota spent in bed?

Despite her best efforts, Grace's attraction to Dakota continued to grow. But how could she possibly be with her when there were so many obstacles standing in their way? Even if she threw her rule about not dating clients out the window, Dakota didn't want a relationship and Grace didn't want to settle for something temporary. And if they did manage to find common ground on that front, her family would provide another obstacle that would need to be overcome. Neither her parents nor her sisters would approve of them being together. Faith might eventually come around since she was the most open-minded of the bunch, but Hope would be more difficult to convince—as her comments during the walk to church a few weeks ago had made clear.

Hope didn't seem to have it in her to be happy for someone else unless things were going well in her own life. She hadn't had a serious boyfriend in a while, and the comments from the women at church about the lack of a wedding ring on her finger seemed to sting a little more each week. Grace wished Hope could meet someone she could give her heart to, but was she willing to forgo her own shot at happiness while she waited in vain for her sister to find hers?

Lynette's impatient sigh drew Grace back into the conversation and away from her jumbled thoughts. "I didn't ask you to list the first thousand digits of pi. I asked you a simple yes or no question. Do you want to meet up with me tonight or not?"

"Sure."

"You do?"

"If you didn't think I would say yes, why did you call me in the first place?"

"I knew I'd be able to convince you to give in eventually, but I figured I'd have to do a lot more whining first."

Grace laughed as she shut down her computer. "Then it sounds like I gave in just in time. See you in an hour?"

"If you look out the window, you can see me a lot sooner than that."

Grace crossed the room, stuck her head out the window, and peered down at the street. Lynette waved up at her. Grace waved back, turned off the lights, and set the alarm. "You really weren't planning on taking no for an answer, were you?" she asked after she met Lynette downstairs.

"Have I ever? What's up with you?"

"What do you mean?"

Lynette gave her a long look as they walked down the street. "You look different. You look...happy." She gasped, quickened her pace, and blocked Grace's path. "You're seeing someone, aren't you?" She didn't give Grace time to respond before she hit her with a barrage of questions. "Who is she? What's her name? Where did you meet her? Do I know her? How long have you been an item? And why are you keeping her such a secret?"

"Please stop and take a minute to breathe before you pass out."

Lynette took a deep breath, slowly released it, and fired off another round of questions. "Is it serious? It's not Karin, is it? Ooh, maybe it's Renee. Did you take another look at that incredible body of hers and decide to give her a second chance? I certainly would. Have I mentioned her arms?"

"Yes, you have. And no, I'm not seeing Renee. Or Karin. As a matter of fact, I'm not seeing anyone. I'm just..." Grace allowed her voice to trail off as she tried to determine how to finish her sentence.

"Just what?"

*Spending time with someone who makes me question everything
I thought I knew about what I wanted in life and what I was looking
for in a partner.* "Just making a new friend."

"Oh, damn, girl, you already have enough of those. And the
best one of all is standing right in front of you."

Grace didn't want to compare apples to oranges. Lynette was
the best friend she'd ever had, but Dakota was something else
entirely. Until she figured out what that something was, she decided
to keep it—and Dakota—to herself.

Mainline wasn't the same without Rich around to liven things
up. The club itself was the same, but the crowd was thin and the
energy was flat. Even though it was a weeknight and relatively early,
Dakota had expected a better showing. She turned to Aaron after
she finished her club soda. "Roxxy just sent me a text. She's DJing
a nineties throwback street party in Harlem tonight. Do you want to
get out of here and check it out?"

Aaron looked around the sparsely populated room. "Sounds
good to me. Anything is bound to be better than this." He polished
off the rest of his lemon drop martini as she closed out their tab.
"Roxxy had better play 'Vogue,' though, because that's my jam."

Dakota calculated the tip and signed the receipt. "Every song
in Madonna's catalog is your jam, even the ones where she was just
phoning it in."

Aaron inched an eyebrow toward his prematurely graying hair.
Even though he was only a few months past his thirtieth birthday,
he was well on his way to becoming a silver fox. Rich's pet name
for him was Anderson Cooper, though Dakota hoped he managed to
call out the right name when they were in bed. "People who have the
Backstreet Boys' greatest hits on their MP3 player are not allowed
to hate on Her Madgesty."

"Point taken. I'm glad to see you're feeling better," she said
after Aaron tucked a five-dollar bill into a go-go boy's G-string.

"Not that much better." Aaron's smile faded and the twinkle in his eyes dimmed. He was six foot two and solidly built, but the sadness that enveloped him made him look small. "I miss Rich."

"I do, too."

"When was the last time you talked to him?"

Dakota held the door open for him as they walked out of the club. "Last night. He called me after the show in Dallas."

"How did he sound? Excited, I'm sure, but—"

Dakota placed a hand on his arm. "Yes, he misses you, too."

"Did he say so?"

"He didn't have to."

"I knew it. I mean I didn't really, but I hoped I wasn't the only one feeling this miserable."

Dakota stepped to one side to get out of the path of a woman pushing a dachshund in a baby stroller as she jogged down the sidewalk. "I thought love was supposed to make you feel great, not crappy."

"Sometimes, it can make you feel both at the same time. That's when you know it's real."

Dakota had often wondered how it felt to be in love. Aaron's explanation made it sound like something she would rather avoid at all costs than experience for herself.

"Now that's what I'm talking about," Aaron said after they rode the subway to Harlem and joined the large crowd gathered on West 125th Street.

The road was blocked to everything except foot traffic in all directions. The iconic Apollo Theater and the businesses surrounding it were open, but all the real action was taking place outside. Music and laughter filled the air.

"Oh, my God, I love this song," Aaron said as Roxxy blasted Whitney Houston's version of a tune originally made famous by Chaka Khan. "Let's dance."

"Get started without me. I'm going to say hi to Roxxy and let her know we're here."

"Find me when you're done."

"You got it." Dakota squeezed through the crowd until she

reached the platform set up in the center of the street. She gave Roxxy a hug and waited for her to remove her headphones before she said, "Sweet setup. Not bad for a few hours' notice."

"Yeah, well, I do what I can." Roxxy was wearing a black T-shirt, black jeans, and a pair of white shell-toe Adidas tennis shoes. All she needed was a black fedora and a fat gold chain and she could have doubled for a member of the legendary rap group Run-DMC. She fiddled with the controls on her workstation until Whitney Houston segued into the Notorious B.I.G. "Did you come by yourself?"

"No," Dakota said, nodding her head to the beat, "I 'dragged' Aaron along."

"I'm sure that was hard work. Tell him I don't have Madonna on the playlist tonight, but I'll make it up to him next time, okay?"

"Oh, no, I'll let you be the bearer of that bad news."

"Fine," Roxxy said with a laugh. "Now get out of here. I've got work to do."

"Like picking up one or more of the women who are making eyes at you?"

"Exactly. So I can't have any of them thinking you're my girlfriend."

"Excuse me for cramping your style." Dakota gave her a quick peck on the lips. "And good luck tonight."

"You, too."

Roxxy placed her headphones over her ears before Dakota could tell her she wasn't on the prowl. She climbed off the platform and made her way through the crowd, intending to catch up with Aaron. She stopped in her tracks when she spotted someone else she knew. Grace was dancing with a woman who was rapping the song's lyrics word for word. The woman perfectly fit the mold for the kind of woman Grace had said she was drawn to, but Dakota sensed more of a platonic than a romantic vibe between them.

Dakota walked over to them and tapped Grace on the shoulder. "I never imagined I'd see you here."

When Grace turned around, the expression on her face changed from joyous to guarded. Dakota leaned to give her a kiss on the cheek, but Grace backed away. "What are you doing here?" Grace asked.

Dakota jerked her thumb toward Roxxy. "The DJ is a friend of mine."

The woman Grace had been dancing with bumped Grace's shoulder with her own. "Are you going to introduce me or what?"

Grace looked flustered. "Sorry. I'm forgetting my manners. Lynette Walker, Dakota Lane. Dakota, Lynette."

Dakota extended her hand. "You must be the best friend."

"And you must be the new one."

"Meaning?" Dakota asked.

"I'll tell you later," Grace said. She scanned the steadily growing crowd. "Are you here with someone?"

"Yeah, him." Dakota pointed at Aaron, who was dancing his way down a makeshift *Soul Train* line.

"Looks like you have your hands full. Is that Rich?"

"No, that's Rich's boyfriend. Actually, his ex- and possibly future boyfriend." Grace looked confused—and more than a little uncomfortable. "It's a long story." Was the kiss they had shared a few days ago the cause of Grace's discomfort, or was Grace's unease due to her unexpected presence? Either way, Dakota felt like she wasn't wanted. Not here. Not tonight. And, perhaps, not ever. She was tempted to cut her losses and walk away before she embarrassed herself or Grace any more than she already had, but she didn't want the encounter to come to an end before she said what was on her mind. "I didn't mean to interrupt, but there's a thing I have to attend Saturday night and I was wondering if you'd like to go."

"What kind of thing?" Lynette asked eagerly.

"A photography exhibit in SoHo."

"Did you take the pictures or are you in them?"

"I'm in a few photos but not all." After she answered Lynette's question, Dakota turned to Grace. "Joey's in a few shots, too. She and Whitney are going to be there in case you'd like to hang out with them again."

"Again?" Lynette asked.

Grace cleared her throat. "The four of us went to a Mets game last week. No big deal."

That night had been a very big deal for Dakota. Until now, she thought Grace felt the same way. Was Grace downplaying the events of that night for Lynette's sake or her own?

"I see," Lynette said. "What's the theme of the exhibit?"

Dakota had no clue what Lynette did for a living, but if it involved asking questions, she was really good at her job. "The show's called s/he. It's a celebration of the masculine within the feminine."

"Sounds intriguing," Lynette said.

"It is. The photographer's a friend of mine, so she gave me a sneak preview when she was setting things up. The show's at the Stitchfield Gallery Saturday night at eight. Would you like to come?"

Dakota directed her question to Grace, but Lynette provided the answer. "We wouldn't miss it."

"Great," Dakota said when it became apparent Grace didn't have anything to add to the conversation. "I'll add your names to the guest list. See you Saturday night."

As she walked away, Dakota felt like she was the one who was missing out. Why did Grace seem like she couldn't wait to get away from her when, only a few days before, she hadn't been able to get close enough? Lynette had answered most of her questions tonight, but this was one she couldn't field. Only Grace could. But Dakota wasn't sure she wanted to hear the answer.

Grace wanted to call out to Dakota, but she couldn't speak. She wanted to go after her, but her feet were rooted in place. Dakota had barely made it out of earshot before Lynette turned to her and said, "No wonder you look so happy."

"Don't start." Grace watched as Dakota's friend Aaron greeted her effusively, a far cry from the lukewarm reception she had given her.

"So what's the story, morning glory?"

Grace moved a few feet away from the heart of the party so she and Lynette could talk without having to scream at the top of their lungs. "She came into the office a few weeks ago to commission a suit for her sister's wedding. That's all there is to it. She and I are just friends."

Lynette clasped her hands as if she were praying for a miracle. "Please, please, please tell me 'just friends' is a euphemism for you're allowing that gorgeous creature to do you six ways to Sunday. Because if I were single and she looked at me the way she just looked at you, I'd be dusting off my copy of the *Kama Sutra* and signing up for a slew of yoga classes so I can twist myself into all the appropriate positions without dislocating something."

Grace had seen the voracious look in Dakota's eyes when she had turned to see who had tapped her on the shoulder, but what she remembered most was the expression on Dakota's face. The hurt and confusion that had been so plain to see before Dakota had ended the brief conversation and walked away. Grace hadn't meant to cause her pain, but Dakota had taken her by surprise. She hadn't expected to see her tonight. And she hadn't expected to feel so at odds when she did. The afternoon they had spent in Central Park had drawn them closer. Tonight was the first time they had seen each other since that day. Instead of picking up where they left off, why had she insisted on holding Dakota at arm's length? Worse than that. She had practically pushed her away.

Coming face-to-face with Dakota tonight, she had felt trapped between two different worlds—the one she had grown accustomed to long ago and the new one she was just starting to explore. She hadn't expected the realms to collide so soon. Or so publicly. She wished she had handled it better. Instead of taking charge of the situation, she had let Lynette do most of the talking while she stood in the background wishing she could crawl into a hole and disappear. Dakota deserved an explanation. And she'd give it to her. As soon as she came up with one.

"I don't date clients," she said unnecessarily. Lynette already knew her stance, but she didn't know any other way to broach the subject that wouldn't result in a long, drawn-out conversation that should be conducted in quiet tones on a comfy couch, not shouted in the middle of a crowded street.

"I know you don't. It's a sound rule that makes good business sense because it helps you avoid messy complications in your personal life that could affect your professional life as well. To be honest, though, it's also a bit of a copout."

"How so?"

"Think about it. Refusing to date clients is an easy directive to follow when the vast majority of your customers are men because it allows you to turn them down without telling them the real reason why. It's easier to reject the overtures of a jock with a fragile ego by telling him you don't date clients than it is by saying you have zero interest in the piece of meat between his legs that he's so proud of. That isn't the case this time, though, is it?"

"No." Though it didn't resolve her dilemma, Grace felt marginally better for having made the admission. Her life had always been orderly. Uneventful. Strictly regulated by rules both written and understood. Her interest in Dakota, however, was giving her the urge to break every one. Was she ready for the chaos that would be sure to follow?

"She's obviously attracted to you and you just confirmed you're attracted to her. I don't see a problem."

"Don't you?" Grace dragged her gaze away from the sight of Dakota and Aaron grooving to one of Mary J. Blige's early hits. "You know how hung up my parents are on image and respectability. My mother burst into tears because I cut my hair. How do you think my father would react if I brought a gossip-column fixture like Dakota home?"

Lynette waved her hand dismissively. "It isn't her reputation that's got you twisted. It's her look. You've always been drawn to lipstick lesbians, but Dakota's as butch as they come and she's got you so turned out you don't know which way is up. But let's deal with the issue you are willing to address—your desire for your parents' approval—instead of the one you're trying to avoid. You're your father's favorite. I can guarantee he won't like anyone you date, no matter who it is, because he would rather spend the rest of his life taking care of you than handing off the job to someone else."

"Hope once said she could bring Jesus home and Dad would still say He wasn't good enough."

"Probably, but it isn't a matter of being good enough."

"Then what is it?"

"It's like when a couple tells me they're expecting a baby. I'm happy to hear the news, especially if they've been trying for a long time, but my mind inevitably starts wandering to how that baby got made. I don't know about you, but that's an image of my friends I'd rather not have in my head. It's almost as bad as admitting your parents had sex in order to conceive you and you aren't the product of immaculate conception. Your father's the same way. He wants you to be happy, but he doesn't want to have to picture anyone humping you or your sisters. It doesn't matter whether it's a man or a woman or someone somewhere in between. But that's his issue to overcome, not yours. He can't live your life for you. Only you are allowed that privilege."

"So what are you saying?"

"Your father's your boss. You can defer to him all you want when you're in the office. In the real world, that's a different story. At some point, you have to make a stand, especially if the future he sees for you and the one you envision for yourself are at odds. It's like I tell the kids I look after: don't take your cues from everyone else; stand on your own two feet and teach people to follow your lead."

"That's just the thing," Grace said disconsolately. "I don't know how."

"You can start by asking yourself one question." Lynette took Grace by her shoulders and turned her back toward the party. The Mary J. Blige record had ended, a song by Aaliyah was playing, and Aaron was twerking against Dakota like he was Miley Cyrus posting up on Robin Thicke at the MTV Video Music Awards. Despite her assertion that she was a terrible dancer, Dakota was more than holding her own. She exuded confidence and power. Like most things, they looked really good on her.

"Who would you rather be dancing with tonight," Lynette asked, "me or her?"

CHAPTER FOURTEEN

Dakota felt uncharacteristically anxious. She didn't get nervous before photo shoots or runway shows because she didn't have anything at stake. The designers were the ones who had something to lose if the products weren't received well, not her. She showed up, did her job, and called it a day. Tonight was different. Tonight, she was fully invested instead of only marginally involved. Because tonight she wasn't modeling the latest fashions. Tonight, she was baring her soul.

Jennifer hadn't instituted a dress code for the evening, but Dakota decided to dress up for the gallery show instead of down. She ditched her favored uniform of a T-shirt, faded jeans, and canvas tennis shoes in favor of a multicolor checked dress shirt, a dark blue Jil Sander suit, and leather oxfords.

She checked her look in the mirror, then grabbed her keys and headed to SoHo. The event was supposed to start at eight. She arrived twenty minutes past the scheduled start time to give guests time to trickle in. She wasn't trying to be fashionably late in order to make an entrance. She simply didn't want to stand around waiting for people to show up or her nerves would have ratcheted up even more. If she had delayed her arrival much longer, though, she wouldn't have been able to squeeze through the door. The gallery was packed, filled with invited guests and curious passersby who had wandered in off the street to see what the fuss was about.

She spotted Joey and Whitney parked in front of the open bar. If not for the trademark cycling cap covering her short black hair,

Joey wouldn't have been recognizable. She was wearing black dress pants and a tuxedo shirt instead of a ripped T-shirt and voluminous cargo shorts. By her side, Whitney was wearing a gorgeous beaded dress that would have made 1920s icon Isadora Duncan proud.

Dakota kissed Whitney on the cheek and gave Joey a fist bump. "You two look great."

Joey hooked her thumbs in her red suspenders, which were adorned with illustrations of vintage bicycles. "I have to keep pace with you, don't I?"

"You can try."

"Asshole," Joey said with a laugh.

"I knew the show was a big deal," Whitney said, "but I had no idea there would be this much hoopla." She dropped her voice to a conspiratorial whisper as if she didn't want potential eavesdroppers to think she was being a braggart. "We've been interviewed by two of the local network affiliates as well as a cable news channel."

"I feel like an honest-to-God celebrity," Joey said.

"You look like one, too," Dakota said. "You both do. Thanks for agreeing to do this, dude. Jennifer appreciates it and so do I. The shots turned out great, don't you think?"

"She'll never admit it, but she had a lot of fun once she got comfortable in front of the camera." Whitney pinched Joey's cheeks. "I'm just glad we had a chance to share this gorgeous face with the world."

"Now my image is going to be hanging on some stranger's living room wall," Joey said. "Weird."

"You get used to the idea after a while," Dakota said.

"All in all, I'd rather stick to fixing bikes." Joey raised her plastic cup of red wine in a toast. "I'll leave the modeling up to you."

Dakota made small talk with Joey and Whitney for a few more minutes and greeted several other people she knew before she sought out Jennifer to see how the show was going.

Jennifer Stitchfield, the photographer who had taken the pictures on display, also owned the gallery in which the exhibit was being held. Dakota met her years ago at a party in Chelsea. The gathering, a rooftop get-together thrown by a friend of a friend to mark the end of summer, hadn't been very memorable, but Jennifer had proven impossible to forget.

A couple of inches over six feet tall, Jennifer was one of the few women Dakota literally looked up to. She had flowing auburn hair, green eyes, and an intricate tattoo of trailing ivy etched along her left leg. The first time Dakota laid eyes on her, she had wanted to use her tongue to trace that tattoo from its end point on the top of Jennifer's foot to its point of origin slightly north of her upper thigh. A few hours later, she had done just that.

She hadn't been entirely honest with Grace when she said she had never met a woman who made her long for more than a leisurely roll in the hay and a friendly good-bye the next morning. Jennifer had made her dream of sharing her life and building a future with someone, but it hadn't taken her long to realize she wasn't ready to lay a foundation strong enough to sustain a relationship. She had too many places to see, too many things to do. And, most of all, she needed to prove to herself that she had what it took to hold someone's attention for the long term, not simply pique their interest for one night. So far, she was still waiting for confirmation.

Though she and Jennifer hadn't lasted as a couple, their friendship had remained intact. When Jennifer had explained the theme she planned to explore and asked if she would be willing to participate, Dakota had said yes right away because the subject was personal and she trusted Jennifer to do it justice.

When Dakota caught up with her, Jennifer was affixing a circular orange sticker next to an oversized photograph of Joey with a bike draped over her shoulders like a pair of angel's wings. The sticker let potential buyers know that the photo had already been purchased.

"I knew that one would be the first to go," Dakota said.

"I knew it would sell, too," Jennifer said, giving her a hug, "but it's hardly the first. Look around."

When Dakota scanned the room, she spotted orange stickers everywhere. "Seriously?"

"I know, right? I thought we had a chance to do well tonight. Word of mouth has been really good."

"That explains all the drop-ins. I was afraid they'd only shown up for the free booze."

"So was I until the sales started piling up. I could tell people were looking forward to the show, but this has surpassed all my expectations. The doors have been open a few minutes and we're already almost sold out. Thanks for helping me arrange this, by the way. I couldn't have put this show together if you hadn't hooked me up with the models. And I definitely wouldn't be in this setting without your rather substantial investment."

"I had to put my money somewhere, didn't I? And it's not much of a risk when I know it's going to pay off."

Dakota was part owner of the gallery, but she didn't have a hand in its day-to-day operations. She left that part up to Jennifer and her staff. She simply deposited her share of the profits each month and dropped in every once in a while to take a look at the exhibits and make sure everything was running smoothly. The quintessential silent partner. Except, in this case, she was practically mute. The gallery was Jennifer's baby. Dakota was just a sponsor. The next time she had a chance to go into business with someone, she promised herself, she would do so only if the union felt like a genuine partnership rather than a legal transaction.

Jennifer's eyes misted. "You always believed in me, even when I didn't believe in myself."

"What can I say? I recognize talent when I see it." Dakota used her thumb to wipe away Jennifer's tears. "Where's Trish?"

Patricia "Trish" Harlan, Jennifer's partner for the past two years, wasn't often far from her side. Her stolid personality and serious mien provided the perfect counterpart to Jennifer's ethereal nature and frequent creative flights of fancy. They were an ideal match—even if the crown of Trish's head barely reached Jennifer's shoulder.

"She's taking a head count to make sure we don't get in trouble with the fire marshal."

"Smart move." If they weren't over capacity, they had to be pretty darn close. A violation could result in a substantial fine and could also curtail what was turning out to be a wildly successful evening.

"Babe?" Trish's Westchester-accented voice floated above the growing cacophony as she made her way through the crowd. "Oh, hey, Dakota. What's up?"

"Speak of the devil and she appears." Dakota shook Trish's extended hand. Trish's favorite literary character was Sherlock Holmes, and her tweed-centric wardrobe often seemed inspired by the fictional private detective. "I was just asking about you."

"And I've been looking for you. Photographers from the *Times*, the *Daily News*, and the *Post* just arrived. They want to get some shots of you and Jennifer standing next to your display. Do you mind?"

Dakota liked the idea of being part of an ensemble rather than the headliner tonight, but she knew the publicity that resulted from her impromptu photo shoot would be good for both the exhibit and the gallery itself. "Lead the way."

Instinct urged Dakota to reach for the small of Jennifer's back to guide her through the crowd, but she forced herself to defer to Trish. Looking after Jennifer wasn't her job. Because she had turned down the opportunity when she had the chance. What would she do the next time the opportunity presented itself? Turn her back on it as she had with Jennifer, or finally rise to the occasion?

As she followed Jennifer and Trish through the crowd, Dakota told herself she wasn't looking for Grace. Deep down, she knew better. She had been looking for Grace from the moment she had arrived. So far, she hadn't been able to find what she was looking for. No big surprise where Grace was concerned. After Grace had blown her off two nights ago, she had no idea if Grace even planned to show. Grace's friend Lynette had promised they would be here, but Grace hadn't had much to say.

As she smiled for the cameras and tried to provide articulate answers to the reporters' shouted questions, Dakota felt like she was being watched. Not watched. Consumed. Her skin prickled as if it were on fire. While camera flashes popped like strobe lights, she scanned the room to locate the source of the heat. She found it in Grace's eyes, which were trained squarely on her.

Grace looked so sexy Dakota couldn't help but stare. Her black cocktail dress was simple but stunning. The hem fell just above the knee, showing off her gorgeous legs. The sleeves were long but sheer. Dakota longed to feel the contrast between the warmth of Grace's skin and the coolness of the fabric, but her pride still stung from Grace's recent rejection.

She and Aaron had had a blast at the street party Thursday night, but she had left the event feeling like Grace was a lost cause. Grace's presence tonight restored her flickering hopes. She wasn't ready to give up on Grace just yet, but perhaps it was time to implement a new strategy.

She had already presented her case. As far as she was concerned, there was nothing left to say. Instead of chasing after Grace, she decided to let Grace come to her. A gamble, to be sure, but if it paid off, she could end up hitting the proverbial jackpot.

Grace had read about art shows and photography exhibits in local newspapers and national magazines, but she had never attended one in person. When she and Lynette walked through the doors of the Stitchfield Gallery, she expected to see a few groups of people sipping wine, munching fancy hors d'oeuvres, and making pithy comments in posh accents while they stared at overpriced photographs and prints. Instead, the crowd was almost as large as the one that had attended the street party in Harlem Thursday night and its makeup was just as varied.

On one side of the room, wealthy patrons of the arts in vintage Chanel mingled with art school students in paint-splattered jeans. On another, street hustlers made deals with stockbrokers in Brooks Brothers suits. And in the middle, well-heeled society types conversed with women who were packing something other than silver spoons.

A gallery employee wearing black latex hot pants, a red bustier, a military-style crew cut, and an impeccably trimmed goatee stood in the entryway holding a bowl filled with several felt-tip markers and dozens of blank paper tags. Instead of the usual *Hi, My Name Is*, the small purple and white tags were imprinted with *Hello, My Pronouns Are.*

"Hi, my name's Sinclair. Please take a tag and provide your preferred pronouns. That way, you won't be offended if someone makes an inaccurate assumption."

Grace reached into the bowl and grabbed two tags. The tag affixed to Sinclair's hairy chest read "ze/hir." Grace wrote "she/her" on her own tag and handed the pen to Lynette.

"Is this really a thing?" Lynette asked under her breath.

"Just go with the flow, will you?" Grace replied in kind. She dropped the pen in the bowl after Lynette filled in her tag. "Thanks, Sinclair. Love the outfit, by the way. You look fierce."

"Thank you," Sinclair said with a grateful grin. "And thanks for coming. I hope you enjoy the show."

"I'm sure we will." After Sinclair left to greet another guest, Grace noticed the frown on Lynette's face. "What's wrong?"

"The kids I look after are more concerned with where their next meal's coming from, where they're going to lay their heads at night, and how they can keep their parents from using them as punching bags than they are about whether someone calls them by the wrong pronoun," Lynette said after she checked to see if she had stuck her tag on straight. "Kids are embracing their genders and their sexuality at younger and younger ages these days. I think I need to sign up for a training class to make sure I'm properly equipped to help the ones who would rather be called something gender-neutral rather than gender-specific."

"Or," Grace said, remembering the conversation she'd had with Dakota about the very same subject, "you could simply call them by their names."

"When did you get so enlightened?"

Grace grabbed a cup of wine from a passing cater-waiter's tray. "I'm embracing my inner millennial. The next thing you know, I'll become obsessed with having the latest technology and start having random hookups that are solely about physical rather than emotional attachment."

"I seriously doubt that."

"Yeah, me too." She hooked her arm around Lynette's. "Now let's check out some art."

The gallery space was filled with exhibits showcasing nearly a dozen women. The exhibits in the large rectangular room were uniform—each featured the model's name and a quote attributed to them framed by three photographs, two professional ones and an informal one provided by the model—but the subject of each exhibit was anything but.

Grace moved closer to a nearby exhibit featuring a broad-shouldered auto mechanic named Aubrey West. In the first photo, Aubrey's sinewy forearms were covered in what looked like motor oil, and s/he gripped a battered adjustable wrench like a knight wielding a sword. In the second photo, s/he looked like a greaser from the 1950s. A lit cigarette dangled from hir lips and s/he was wearing motorcycle boots, peg-legged jeans, and a tight white T-shirt with one sleeve rolled up to secure a pack of smokes. The third photo was a grainy eight-by-ten that appeared to have been taken when Aubrey was about ten years old. In it, s/he was holding a plastic pumpkin filled with Halloween candy and s/he was dressed like Elvis Presley in *Jailhouse Rock*.

Grace read the quote printed at the top of the exhibit. "'It's not the appendage that matters. It's the person attached to it.'"

The next exhibit was similarly eye-catching.

"I don't care how tired Monica is when she finishes her shift," Lynette said as she stared at a photo of a woman wearing a leather jacket, skintight jeans, and not much more. "She's putting in overtime when she gets home."

Grace winced. "Remember what you said about not wanting to imagine your friends having sex? Ditto."

"Spoilsport."

Grace perused a few other exhibits before she tried to find Dakota's. She didn't have to search too hard or too long. All she had to do was follow the crowd. Each exhibit seemed to have its fair share of admirers, but only Dakota's was ringed by a horde of reporters, photographers, and camerapeople. Grace observed the spectacle from her position on the fringe of the crowd.

Just like in the other exhibits, Dakota's name was printed on the top of the display. The thought-provoking quote attributed to her read, "Gender isn't about genitals."

Grace lowered her gaze from Dakota's self-professed manifesto to the series of photographs arranged beneath it. In the first photograph, Dakota was wearing a gray T-shirt with the words *Male Model* emblazoned on the front in large black letters. Her thumbs were hooked in the belt loops of her low-slung jeans, giving the viewer a peek at the V-shaped muscle that pointed from her rippled abs to her crotch. She stared at the camera with an almost defiant expression on her angular face. "This is me," the look seemed to say. "Do you have a problem with that?"

The second photograph was decidedly less serious but just as challenging. In it, Dakota lay on her stomach on a messy bed wearing nothing but a well-positioned sheet that covered her hips but left the tantalizing arch of her back on full display. Her arms were folded in front of her, hiding her breasts from view. Her hair, normally so perfect, was tousled. Tufts of it stuck out in weird angles all over her head. Her eyes were hooded, her smile sly. Her expression this time seemed to say, "You've taken enough pictures. Now will you please put the camera down and come back to bed?"

Thursday night, Dakota had referred to Jennifer as a friend. Based on the postcoital photograph on display, Jennifer seemed more like a friend with benefits.

Since the third photograph was smaller, Grace couldn't see it clearly from where she was standing. She moved closer to get a better look. The photograph, like the ones in the other models' exhibits, charted an early step in Dakota's evolution from tomboy to androgynous adult. The picture showed Dakota standing in front of a campfire holding a can of beer in one hand and flipping the bird with the other. Even though she couldn't have been much older than fifteen, she looked even more like a rock star than the one printed on her oversized T-shirt.

"Dakota, over here! Dakota, this way!"

The photographers calling Dakota's name drew Grace's attention from the display itself to the scrum taking place in front of it.

Dakota and a gorgeous redhead were standing with their arms around each other's waists and smiles on their faces. The redhead's tag read "she/her"; Dakota's tag read "whatever I feel like on any given day." Grace didn't know if the redhead was Dakota's date or the photographer who had come up with the idea for the exhibit. Based on the interaction between them and the sexually-charged images on display, the answer to both questions was likely one and the same.

Grace had never seen Dakota look more stunning, either in print or in person. Dakota was wearing a fitted dark blue suit and a colorful button-down shirt. The shirt was unbuttoned halfway to her navel. Depending on your point of view, the striations in her bare chest marked either the rise of her breasts or a set of well-developed pecs.

Grace felt a potent mixture of jealousy and desire. She wanted to undress Dakota. Slide her hands inside Dakota's expensive designer clothes and slowly unwrap her like a treasured gift. She wanted to tell the redhead to get away from Dakota and stop touching her in such a familiar way because Dakota was hers. Then she wanted to push her way through the crowd, pull Dakota's mouth down to hers, and stake her claim. But how could she do either when she kept telling everyone who would listen—including herself—that Dakota wasn't her type? When Dakota kept saying she was built for one-night stands, not relationships.

Dakota might not have been what Grace was looking for, but in this setting—in that suit—she was all Grace could see. The realization shook Grace to her core.

That was the moment Dakota turned and looked at her. Grace saw raw hunger etched on Dakota's face. Felt it in her own gaze. As Dakota stared at her as if she were the only woman in the room, Grace no longer doubted her feelings. No matter how often or how adamantly she tried to deny it, she wanted Dakota Lane. Whether for one night or the rest of their lives, the duration no longer mattered. She wanted to be with her. Now. Tonight.

She moved forward, caught up in the combined momentum of the swell of the crowd and the emotions churning inside her. A hand gripped her arm as if offering her a lifeline.

"Grace, hi." She turned to see Joey and Whitney standing in front of her. "Dakota said you might be here tonight," Joey said, releasing her grip on her arm. "I thought we might have missed you."

"No, we just got here a few minutes ago. This is my friend Lynette Walker. Lynette, I'd like you to meet Joey Palallos and Whitney Robbins. They're friends of Dakota's. Joey owns a bicycle shop in Williamsburg and Whitney runs a bar slash restaurant in the same building."

"Joey's also one of the models on display tonight," Whitney said proudly.

"So I heard," Grace said after Lynette, Joey, and Whitney exchanged pleasantries. "I haven't had a chance to view everything yet, but I love what I've seen so far." She craned her neck as she sneaked a peek at the rest of the exhibits. "Where's yours?"

"I'll show you," Whitney said.

Joey begged off. "I've stared at my own image long enough for one night. You guys go ahead. I'm going to find the bathroom, then refill our drinks. Since everyone's staring at Dakota right now, neither line should be too long."

"Do you want me to go with you?" Whitney asked with obvious concern.

"I think I should be okay here, babe."

"Are you sure?"

"When she and Jennifer were remodeling this place, Dakota insisted on unisex bathrooms. Much less room for confusion that way." Whitney still didn't look convinced, so Joey took her hand and gave it a squeeze. "Go ahead. I'll catch up to you in a few."

Whitney watched Joey make her way through the crowd. "Logic says she should be safe in a setting like this, but I can't help but worry. I have to accompany her to the bathroom most of the time to vouch that she hasn't wandered into the wrong one by mistake or on purpose. Most people fixate on her short hair and the way she dresses and assume she's a teenage boy playing a prank."

"You don't have to explain yourself to me," Lynette said. "My partner Monica goes through similar hassles all the time. She's a guard at Rikers, a job that requires her to subvert every ounce of her femininity in order to earn the inmates' respect. Even though she's almost as stacked as Dolly Parton, she still gets sideways glances when she uses a public restroom while she's in uniform."

"You never told me that," Grace said incredulously. Lynette normally talked about every facet of her life, whether the subject was fit for public consumption or something most people considered an issue that should be kept private. Yet she had never mentioned the bombshell she had just casually dropped into the conversation. "Why didn't you say anything? Did you think I wouldn't be able to relate?"

"No, nothing like that. Even though Monica doesn't dress, look, or act masculine of center outside of work, she still gets painted with the same brush from time to time based solely on her profession. It's one of her sore spots. She doesn't like talking about it with me, let alone anyone else. But that's okay. I knew what I was getting into when I agreed to be in a relationship with her." Lynette slowly lifted her shoulders and let them fall. "How could I possibly complain about something I signed up for? I'm not going to stop loving her just because shit gets hard sometimes."

"I hear you," Whitney said. "Sometimes I think how easy life might be if I had fallen for someone else, but I didn't, did I? Now I get the best of both worlds. The hardness of a man and the softness of a woman all in one person."

"Preach, girl." Lynette waved her hand over her head as if she were testifying in church. "You are telling the story of my life."

In order to be with Dakota, Grace knew she would have to be willing to agree to the same emotional contract Lynette and Whitney had entered into with their respective partners. But was she as willing as they were to sign her name on the dotted line? Lynette and Whitney had only put their hearts at risk. She, on the other hand, had much, much more at stake.

"Have we scared you off yet?" Whitney asked as if reading her mind.

"I don't scare easily."

"If you truly mean that," Lynette said, "what are you waiting for? I can find my own way home, you know."

Good, Grace thought. *Because I might not make it to mine before the sun comes up.*

CHAPTER FIFTEEN

After she fulfilled her obligations to the press, Dakota headed to the bar to get some liquid refreshment. "I would offer to buy you a drink," she heard a familiar voice say, "but I hear they're free around here."

Dakota tried and failed to suppress a smile as she turned to face Grace. "I don't have a problem with free. Do you?"

Grace pursed her lips. "That depends on what's being offered."

Dakota accepted her drink from the bartender and placed a couple of bills in the tip jar. "You look beautiful tonight," she said to Grace, "but I don't need to tell you that, do I?"

Thanks to her four-inch heels, Grace was almost Dakota's height. She didn't have to stand on her tiptoes as she pressed her lips close to Dakota's ear. The feel of Grace's breath on her skin sent a shudder down Dakota's spine. Her head swam from the scent of Grace's perfume. From the warmth of Grace's voluptuous body. Close enough to touch, yet still so far away. "The only thing I want you to tell me tonight is how good my dress looks on your bedroom floor. Do you think you can manage that?"

Grace's words made Dakota's knees go weak. "I can manage it, yes, but can you handle it?"

Grace raised her plastic cup of white wine to her full, luscious lips. "Try me and see."

Dakota almost beat a path to the door so she could run out into the street and hail a cab, but she convinced herself to stay put. She had been down this road before, and she didn't want to get her hopes up again only to have them dashed. She didn't want to feel like she had at the street party. Elated to see Grace, then crushed by her rejection. Grace's eyes burned with desire, but she needed to be sure Grace was enthralled by her instead of the exhibit. "I thought you came here with someone."

"I did, but I doubt Lynette would mind if I left with someone else. Can you say the same?"

Dakota followed Grace's line of sight until her gaze landed on Jennifer talking with a cluster of guests standing in front of a display featuring a long-haul truck driver from Jersey City. "If you mean Jennifer, I'm confident her wife will see her home. And as much as I would like to take you to my place right now and show you the lovely view of my bedroom ceiling, we need to talk about Thursday night, don't you think?"

"I have several excuses I could use to explain my behavior, but I don't feel like trotting any of them out so I'll stick with the truth. I didn't expect to see you that night, I panicked, and I didn't know what to do."

"But you do now?"

"No, but I know what I want."

"And that would be?"

Grace looked her squarely in the eye. Dakota admired her directness. Her willingness to face things head-on instead of shrinking from a challenge. "To wake up in your arms."

Dakota swirled the ice in her vodka tonic to disguise the fact that her hands were shaking. Not from fear. From anticipation. She would love to give Grace what she was asking for, but she didn't want either of them to wake up with regrets. "I thought you didn't do one-night stands."

"I don't, but a journey of a thousand miles begins with a single step, doesn't it? I want to take that step with you." Grace trailed a fingertip along the opening of Dakota's shirt. "Why don't we start with tonight and work on tomorrow when it comes?"

Dakota stilled Grace's hand before the tantalizing movements made her come on the spot. "On one condition."

"Name it."

"Do you remember the effect you had on me during our fitting?" Grace's eyes darkened, letting Dakota know she remembered all too well. "I will leave with you right now, no questions asked, if I get to measure you."

Grace drained her drink and set her empty cup on the bar. "What are we waiting for?"

They took a cab to Greenwich Village. After Dakota paid the fare, they slid out of the car and began to climb the three flights of stairs that led to Dakota's apartment. The trip took an unplanned detour at the top of the first landing when Grace pushed Dakota into a corner, grabbed her by her lapels, and said, "I can't take another step until I kiss you."

Grace moved toward her and kept coming until their bodies touched up and down. The contact brought back memories of the moment they had shared in Central Park, but the kiss Grace pressed to her lips made the previous one seem like an innocuous peck on the cheek. When Grace's mouth met hers, Dakota didn't sense hesitation this time. Only desire.

The kiss was sweet at first. Soft and warm like a freshly lit fire just beginning to take hold. Then it took a sexy turn that Dakota wasn't expecting. Not so soon. Grace captured Dakota's lower lip between her teeth and drew it into her mouth. The spike of pain, followed by the gentle, soothing pressure, made Dakota's adrenaline surge. When Grace slid her fingers in gentle circles over the sensitive spot on the nape of Dakota's neck while she stroked Dakota's throbbing lip with the tip of her tongue, Dakota wanted to hike up the hem of Grace's dress and take her right there in the stairwell.

She gently pushed Grace away before she lost all sense of propriety. Then she took Grace by the hand. "Upstairs," she said with a growing sense of urgency. "Now."

The climb was a workout on most days, but Dakota doubted the exertion was the reason she felt breathless as she unlocked her apartment door and ushered Grace inside. The rules of etiquette dictated she should show Grace around the place and offer her a drink before or after the grand tour, but she decided to throw the rules out the window. She and Grace fell on each other the instant she closed the door behind them.

As Dakota explored Grace's mouth with her tongue, Grace slid Dakota's suit jacket off her shoulders and let it fall to the floor. Even though it was no longer fashionable to do so, Dakota always tucked the hem of her dress shirts into her pants because it made her feel more dressed up, not like she woke up, threw something on, and walked out the door without bothering to comb her hair or brush her teeth.

Grace tugged at Dakota's shirt until the hem pulled free. Grace let the shirt fall open, but she didn't remove it. She reached into the opening and slipped her hands inside. Teasing, touching, exploring, but not uncovering. Dakota leaned against the door and closed her eyes as Grace's hands slowly slid across her skin. The first time she'd had sex with a woman, it had been as fast and furious as the movie of the same name. This was different. Slow. Deliberate. Like torture, but in the very best way.

"Whitney was right," Grace whispered as she cupped Dakota's breasts in her hands. "This really is the best of both worlds."

"Fuck." Dakota arched her back when Grace pinched her nipples. The pressure, bordering on the edge of pain, was exquisite.

"Does that feel good?" Grace asked as she nuzzled the side of Dakota's neck.

"What do you think?"

Grace unbuckled Dakota's belt, unbuttoned her pants, and yanked her zipper down. Then she reached inside the fly of Dakota's boxer briefs. Dakota gritted her teeth when Grace slid her fingers through her wetness. And when Grace trapped her swollen clit between two fingers, Dakota nearly came apart. "I think," Grace said, painting a line of kisses along Dakota's collarbone, "you got started without me."

"Let's see what I can do to get you caught up." Grace squealed in surprise when Dakota lifted her off the floor. She kicked off her shoes and wrapped her legs around Dakota's waist as Dakota carried her to the bedroom. Dakota gently placed Grace on the bed and lay on top of her. After Grace hooked her leg around hers to draw her closer, Dakota licked her lips in anticipation of what was about to happen.

"I hate to horn in," Dakota heard someone say, "but I figured I'd better make my presence known before things got too hot and heavy in here."

"Fuck!"

Startled by the intruder, Dakota and Grace leaped off the bed. While Grace held a death grip on her sides, Dakota grabbed the Louisville Slugger leaning in a corner and brandished the bat as a weapon.

"Wait a second, Dakota," her unexpected visitor said. "Calm down. It's me, Brooke."

Dakota thought she was imagining things until she saw that her sister really was standing in her doorway instead of cooling her heels in Richmond Hill while she decided who should sit next to whom at her wedding reception. She lowered the bat, then turned to make sure Grace was okay. Grace nodded to indicate she was fine. She seemed shaken up and more than a little mortified by being seen in such an intimate position by a stranger. Both reasonable reactions.

"I'm sorry," Dakota said in a whisper.

Grace shook her head. "Not your fault."

Dakota turned to face her sister. "What are you doing here, Brooke?" she asked while she buttoned her shirt and fastened her pants. "And how did you get in here in the first place?"

"It's good to see you, too, big sister." Brooke turned her back while Dakota and Grace pulled themselves together. "I told your building superintendent I was planning a surprise party for you and I convinced him to let me in. I've been making myself comfortable in Rich's room while I waited for you to come home, but it looks like the surprise was on me." She peeked over her shoulder to check Dakota and Grace's progress. She turned to face them again when she saw they were done. "Are you going to introduce me, or would you rather I do it myself?"

Dakota wanted to hit rewind rather than provide introductions, but she forced herself to remember her manners. "Brooke, this is my friend Grace. Grace, this is my sister Brooke."

"Congratulations on your upcoming wedding," Grace said.

"Thank you," Brooke said. "I'm sorry we couldn't have met under different circumstances, but I was born two weeks late and my timing's been lousy ever since."

"No need to apologize." Grace smoothed her dress with the heels of her hands. Dakota admired Grace's composure. She didn't know how Grace managed to remain so dignified despite the two of them having been caught in the act like a couple of randy teenagers making out in the backseat of a car on lovers' lane. "How long will you be in town?"

"Actually, I haven't decided yet." Brooke reached into the hall and dragged a large rolling suitcase into the room. "That depends on how long Dakota lets me stay."

Dakota felt the faint stirrings of alarm. She was the impulsive one in the family. Brooke was the one who always planned things out months in advance. For Brooke to make a pilgrimage to New York on the spur of the moment with what looked like several weeks' worth of clothes in tow meant something was wrong. Terribly wrong. "What's going on, B?"

Brooke's blue eyes, normally so bright, lacked their usual luster. "It's...complicated."

Grace gently cleared her throat. "You two obviously have a great deal to talk about, so I'll let you get to it."

"Grace, wait." Dakota trailed her to the living room. "Let me walk you to the subway."

"You don't have to do that." Grace stepped into her shoes, grabbed her purse off the table in the entryway, and touched up her lipstick in the mirror next to the door. "I think I can find the way."

"But—"

"Stop." Grace put a finger on her lips. "All I want to do right now is get out of here, but it has nothing to do with you. This isn't good-bye. It's to be continued. I wanted tonight to happen as much as you did, but your sister obviously needs you more than I do. Go to her. Be there for her. I'll still be here when you're done." She flashed an embarrassed grin. "Next time, let's make sure we check the apartment first to make sure we're alone."

"Good idea." Dakota was relieved to hear that the interruption hadn't managed to change Grace's mind about the reason they had come here tonight.

"You missed a button."

Dakota looked down to see one side of her shirt was significantly higher than the other. She unbuttoned her shirt and started over. "Yeah, well, I never learned to dress myself."

"Apparently not. Come by the office on Monday. You've lost some weight since our initial fitting. I think I need to adjust my numbers before I start making your suit."

"Okay. I'll stop by at lunch." Dakota opened the door and leaned against the jamb. "May I call you tomorrow?"

"You'd better." Grace wiped her lipstick off Dakota's mouth with her thumb. "That Southern tongue of yours is more talented than you let on. I want to see what else it can do."

And Dakota couldn't wait to show her. But first she had to find out why Brooke had decided to hop on a plane and fly several hundred miles without telling her she was coming.

"Okay, little sister," she said once she and Brooke were alone. "What did you do this time?"

❖

Grace's phone rang as soon as she reached the street. Confident it was Dakota on the line, she accepted the incoming call and put her earbuds in without bothering to check the phone's display. "Is it tomorrow already?"

"What in the world are you babbling about?" Faith asked.

Grace fought down a pang of disappointment not quite as acute as the one she had felt when Dakota's sister made her presence known a few minutes ago, but close. She had wanted to crawl into a hole when Brooke had walked in on her and Dakota making out on the bed. She didn't know how she had managed to hold what she hoped passed for a semi-intelligent conversation with Brooke after that. All the comportment lessons her mother had given her and her sisters over the years must have finally taken hold.

Thank God I was paying attention.

Dakota and Brooke sounded a lot alike, but they didn't have much of a family resemblance. Brooke was attractive in a Southern belle kind of way, but she obviously looked like one parent and Dakota another. It was the same way in her family. Hope and Faith both took after their father while she bore the most resemblance to their mother.

"Sorry," she said. "I thought you were someone else."

"No shit, Sherlock. I didn't think you meant to use your sexy voice on me."

"I don't have a sexy voice."

"No, you don't, but that was a nice try."

"Whatever." The word had already spilled out before Grace remembered Dakota had used the same one to describe her preferred pronoun. Dakota's gender might be fluid, but her body had felt oh-so-solid as she writhed under Grace's touch, then settled her weight on her.

"Where are you?"

"Greenwich Village." Grace paused to window shop at a store that sold vintage clothing. The store was closed, but she vowed to make a return trip to buy the colorful Pucci sheath that caught her eye—and to finish what she and Dakota had started tonight.

"But I thought the art exhibit Lynette dragged you to was in SoHo."

"It was."

When Faith had stopped her on her way out of the house to ask why she was wearing one of her best dresses, Grace had said Lynette had wrangled an invitation to a gallery show. Even though Lynette had provided the RSVP, the invitation had been extended to her. Grace wished she had been more forthcoming about her plans for the evening, but she hadn't wanted to deal with any of Faith's inevitable follow-up questions. Would she ever be able to stop treating Dakota like a dirty little secret, or was this the way things would always be? Subterfuge was exciting in the short term, but it often proved tiresome in the end. She wanted Dakota, but she wanted a relationship more, and Dakota had professed to having an aversion to those. Perhaps it was a good thing Brooke had arrived when she did. She might have prevented Grace from making a big mistake. An exciting and incredibly sexy mistake, but a mistake nevertheless.

"So what are you doing in—Ah, I see. Dakota lives in Greenwich Village, doesn't she?"

"How do you know that?"

"I think I read that in *People*. Or was it *Us Weekly*? Anyway, did she show you a good time? And more importantly, is it bigger than a breadstick?"

"None of your business and none of your business." Grace smiled as she remembered holding Dakota in her hands. Shuddered as she remembered the feel of Dakota's hard clit pulsing between her fingers. She brought her hand to her nose. Her fingers still smelled like Dakota. Did they taste like her, too? She resisted the urge to take her fingers into her mouth. She wanted to taste Dakota's essence direct from the source, not secondhand. Would one taste be enough, or, as she suspected, would it prove to be addictive? "Did you call just to harass me, or did you have a real reason for reaching out?"

Faith suddenly turned serious. "Come home as quick as you can. Dad wants to have a family meeting."

"At eleven o'clock on a Saturday night?"

"That's what I'm screaming. He said it's a last-minute thing and he didn't set it for earlier because he wanted to give Hope time to get home from her shift. She's on her way and I didn't have anything planned for tonight except cramming for an exam in one of my summer school classes. That just leaves you. When can you be here?"

"As soon as I catch the next train. What's the meeting about?"

"I was going to ask you the same thing. You're a lot closer to Dad than Hope and I are. I thought maybe he'd told you he had finally decided to retire and was planning to use the meeting to make the official announcement."

Even though she and her father worked side by side, Grace wasn't privy to any of his secrets. That was her mother's role. One she had no desire to take on. Yet she couldn't help feeling as if she had been left out of the loop. If something was going on with the business, shouldn't she already know what it was instead of being forced to hear about it the same time as everyone else? "If he has decided to go that route, he didn't say anything to me. I doubt that's what the meeting's about. If Dad planned to turn the company over to me two years ahead of schedule, I think he would have made sure I had all my ducks in a row, don't you?"

"Yes, but what else would he have to talk about other than work? He and Mom have been together way too long and are still too crazy about each other to even think about getting a divorce. And they're both as healthy as horses, so I don't think he plans to say either of them is dying from some dreaded disease. Be honest. Are you being straight with me right now, or are you blowing smoke up my ass so you can act all surprised when Dad hits us with his big news?"

"Trust me, whatever he has to say will be just as much of a surprise to me as it is to you."

Grace turned toward home, wondering—and dreading—what would be in store for her when she arrived.

CHAPTER SIXTEEN

"What makes you think something's wrong?" Brooke asked. After she followed Brooke to the kitchen, Dakota pointed to the bottle of pale pink liquid sitting on the granite counter. "Because you always break out the Strawberry Hill whenever you've done something you wish you hadn't."

"What can I say? I learned from the best. You used to live on this stuff back in the day." Brooke opened the screw-top bottle and poured a generous amount of the contents into a red plastic cup. "Would you like some?"

Dakota wrinkled her nose. "No, thanks. My tastes have changed since high school."

"I noticed. They've gotten a lot more expensive. And varied." Brooke looked past the high-end kitchen appliances and cut her eyes toward the bedroom. If she hadn't dropped in out of the blue, Dakota would be in there right now acting out a few of her favorite fantasies. "So who's Grace?"

"My tailor. She's making me a suit to wear to your wedding."

Brooke leaned against the counter as she sipped her wine. "Why do you need a new suit when you have a closet full of them? Don't look so surprised. I've been here for almost two hours. I had plenty of time to raid your closet. Unfortunately, I didn't find anything I might want to wear. Kevin, on the other hand, would kill for one of your suits. If he were two inches shorter and about forty pounds lighter, that is. Did you buy all those?"

"No, they're essentially hand-me-downs. Freebies from photo

shoots and runway shows. I didn't want to wear any of them on your big day. I wanted something special. That's where Grace comes in."

"You've been outshining me all my life. You're not planning to do it on my wedding day, too, are you?"

"Of course not."

Brooke looked skeptical. "Is Grace going to be your plus-one? If she is, Mom and Dad will freak."

"Why? Because she's African American?"

"No, because you've never bothered to bring anyone home before."

"I know, and there's a good reason for that."

"Which is?"

"Don't play dumb, Brooke. You know the score. You, Mom, and Dad have made it perfectly clear how you feel about my 'choices.' I'm used to the drama, but I would never subject someone else to it. Especially someone I care about."

"So you're serious about her? I probably should have guessed that from the expression on your face when I walked into your bedroom tonight. If looks could kill, Kevin would be planning my funeral right now instead of our wedding. Not that he's done much help with the wedding planning. The organizer and I have done the bulk of the work. The only things he's done are buy the ring and pop the question."

Dakota sidestepped Brooke's question about the status of her relationship with Grace because she didn't know the answer. She was starting to develop feelings for Grace, but she didn't know where they would lead. Before she and Grace were so rudely interrupted, tonight's encounter was shaping up to be much different from all the others she had experienced in the past. Not a quickly forgotten one-off, but an experience she would remember for the rest of her life. She could still feel Grace's hands on her. See the look in Grace's eyes when she explored her body. Hear the sound of Grace's voice when she paused on the landing and said, "I can't take another step until I kiss you." The kiss that followed had been a revelation. It had made Dakota realize why people wrote sappy love songs or broke into tears when they finally got a chance to say, "I do." Despite Grace's assurances that they would pick up where they left off, Dakota wondered if she would ever get the chance to feel that connected to someone—to *Grace*—again.

"We're supposed to be talking about you, not me," she said. "And I do have actual wine glasses if you'd like to use one. And real wine, too, instead of that antifreeze you're drinking. Would you prefer red or white?"

"You don't have to put on airs for me. I'm good."

"Are you sure?" Dakota arched an eyebrow after Brooke drained her cup and refilled it close to overflowing. "If you think you're going to hurl, make sure you aim for a hard surface, okay? Because that shit is impossible to scrub out of anything porous."

"I'll keep that in mind if I start to feel the urge." Brooke looked her up and down. "God, you look more and more like Dad every time I see you."

"And you look just like Mom." Like Townsend, Dakota had their father's dark hair and lanky body. Brooke had inherited their mother's blond hair, short stature, and soft features. Dakota's and Brooke's personalities were as different as their appearances. Dakota had a tendency to shock while Brooke had always aimed to please. Yet another reason why Brooke's visit was so out of character. "Do Mom and Dad know where you are? Does Kevin?"

"What they don't know won't hurt them."

"What?"

"I'm kidding," Brooke said as she headed to the living room. "I just wanted to see the look on your face when I finally managed to pull the rug out from under you for once. Since you asked, yes, I told everyone where I was going. I just didn't say how long I planned to stay."

"How long do you think you'll be here?" Dakota asked warily. As Benjamin Franklin famously said, fish and houseguests had a tendency to stink after three days. When the guests were family, it usually didn't take that long for the odor to start.

Brooke sat cross-legged on the couch. She had been a cheerleader in high school. Seven years removed from her last split-lift, she still had both the perky attitude and the required flexibility.

"I'm not sure. I always heard that planning a wedding was stressful, but I didn't know it would be this bad. I needed to get away for a while. I needed to take some time for myself that didn't involve cake tasting, dress fittings, menu planning, or seating arrangements. Do they have paintball up here? If they do, maybe we can play a few games tomorrow to blow off some steam."

"If you don't slow down, the only thing you're going to be doing tomorrow is nursing the world's worst hangover." Dakota took Brooke's half-empty cup from her and placed it safely out of reach. "Let's get down to business. Are you here because you came to see me or because you're having second thoughts about getting married?"

Brooke looked at her, mouth agape. "How do you do that?"

"Do what?"

"I haven't seen you face-to-face in almost six months—we've barely spoken during that time—but you're able to talk to me for five minutes and know exactly what's on my mind? I lived in the same house with you for eighteen years and you're still as much of a mystery to me as you ever were." Brooke plunged her hands into her hair. She looked like she wanted to tear her long locks out by the roots. Instead, she pulled them up and away from her face, then slowly let them fall. "Why is it that you know me so much better than I know you?"

"I don't mean to be harsh, but when did you ever try to get to know me? All I ever got from you was judgment and recrimination, not understanding. You never wanted to know what I was feeling. All you wanted to do was tell me how what I was experiencing adversely affected you." Dakota liked being in control. At the moment, she had a decided lack of it. She hugged her knees to her chest while she rode out an overwhelming feeling of hopelessness. "I know you because you're my sister and I love you, Brooke. Can you honestly say the same thing to me?"

"Of course I can. I might not know how to show it, but I love you more than anything in this world, Dakota. Mom and Dad do, too. They're just too set in their ways to accept anything out of the norm. And you are definitely out of the norm."

"I've never aspired to be just like everyone else, Brooke. I just—"

"Wanted to be you. Yes, I know," Brooke said with a melodramatic eye roll. "I've heard that more times than I can count."

"Because it's true."

"I'm not saying it isn't. Stop being so defensive. I'm on your side."

"Are you? Because it doesn't look that way from here."

Brooke sighed and closed her eyes, taking a mental break from a conversation that was growing heavier by the moment. "When I was a little girl," she said when she finally opened her eyes again, "you were my hero. I wanted to be you when I grew up. But when you came out to everyone and I saw how Mom and Dad reacted to the news, I didn't want to be anything like you."

Dakota had never wanted to be anyone's role model, but Brooke's words had unexpected sting. She flinched involuntarily when they hit home. "I can't blame you for trying to protect yourself," she said shakily, "but I wish you'd had my back. No matter what was going on between us, I always had yours."

"I know." Tears welled in Brooke's eyes. "I'm sorry I wasn't stronger. I'm sorry I wasn't a better sister, but I didn't want Mom and Dad to turn their backs on me like they did to you." She picked at the frayed hem of her jeans. "Now I'm wondering if I'm still doing the same thing."

"What do you mean?"

"Am I marrying Kevin because I love him?" Brooke hesitantly met her eye. "Or, even after all these years, am I still trying to prove that I'm not you?"

❖

Grace climbed the steps of her brownstone and opened the front door. Her parents and sisters were waiting in the living room when she walked in. Faith met her in the entryway. "It's about time you showed up." Faith dragged her toward the couch practically before she had time to close the door. "Let's get this party started."

"I'm so glad I have your permission to commence."

Faith sank back onto the couch. "Sorry, Daddy. I didn't mean to steal your thunder."

Grace examined her family members' faces. Despite Faith's attempt to lighten the mood, everyone looked much too serious. She set her purse on the side table and tried to ignore the knot of anxiety taking up residence in her gut. "What's going on, Dad?"

"Well," he said, sounding like a long-winded preacher who was just getting warmed up, "I have some news."

"What kind of news?" Hope asked. "You're not sick, are you?"

Grace's spirits sank. Like Faith, she had discounted that possibility. Even though her parents moved slower than they once did, in her mind, they would always be indestructible. Had a doctor's diagnosis confirmed that they were mere mortals after all?

"Nothing like that," her mother said. "Stop beating around the bush, Clarence, and get to the point."

"I had a visitor today," he said. Grace found it telling he couldn't bring himself to look her in the eye. "A developer came to see me."

"What did he have to say?" Grace asked. She had been dreading an announcement like this, yet it seemed about to come to pass.

"His company wants to buy the building and convert it into luxury condos. He made me a rather substantial offer."

"How much money are we talking about?" Faith asked pragmatically. "Enough for you to buy a nice car and pay off a few bills, or enough for you to retire on?"

"If I accept the offer, I wouldn't have to worry about any of your respective futures because they would be secured. He offered me ten million dollars."

"Split five ways, that's two million apiece," Hope said.

"Ooh," Faith said. "Look who showed up for math class. But why are you assuming an even split? Dad and Grace have put in more work at the company than we have. And you don't want to leave Lillie or any of the other employees out in the cold, do you?"

"Of course not," Hope said rather unconvincingly, "but family comes first." She turned to their father to seek his support for her theory. "Isn't that what you've always said, Daddy?"

"That's why I called this meeting tonight. I didn't say yea or nay today. I just listened. A decision this important shouldn't be made by one person. I wanted to put it to a vote."

"I vote yes," Hope said almost as soon as he got the words out.

"And I second that emotion," Faith said.

"What about you, Grace?" her mother asked.

"Majority rules, remember?" Grace felt the couch—and the world—shift on its axis as Hope turned to look at her. "If you make the right choice, you can cast the deciding vote."

"Don't pressure her. Give her time to think."

Grace's heart raced as she weighed her decision. Even though her sisters were practically bursting at the seams, she didn't share their enthusiasm. She wanted to do right by them, but she had to do what she felt was best. Not just for her. For the whole family. "I vote no."

"Why?" Hope sounded like she was about to cry.

"That building—that company—is our family's legacy. That's something you can't put a price on."

"Shoot," Hope said. "Ten million dollars sounds like a pretty good price to me."

"I agree with Grace." Her mother flashed a wink of solidarity while Hope pouted like a petulant child.

"That means you have the deciding vote, Dad," Grace said. "Which way are you going to go?"

"I'm not sure yet," he said with a weary sigh. "I started my own business for two reasons: to provide for my family and to leave something behind after I'm gone. I have a chance to do both those things, but not at the same time."

"Which of your goals is more important to you?" she asked.

"That's what I have to take time to figure out. I told Mr. Phillips I'd get back to him in a few weeks. This is something I'm going to have to sleep on for a while." He pushed himself to his feet with a grunt of effort. "Pray on it, too."

"While he's on his knees," Hope said after the meeting adjourned, "I hope he reaches out to all the saints and apostles, too. God knows all the things I could do with that check."

"I hear you," Faith said. "Money might be the root of all evil, but I'd love to show the devil how good I could be with two million dollars in the bank."

Grace turned to go upstairs so she could try to absorb all of the night's events in peace, but Hope blocked her path.

"Why didn't you say yes when you had the chance? If you had, the decision would have been made and we wouldn't have to wait two weeks just to hear Dad say he's chosen to side with you as usual. I could have gotten paid instead of having to keep busting my ass for the next thirty years."

"Dad's put his blood, sweat, and tears into the company for forty years. Are you really willing to watch everything he's worked for vanish with the stroke of a pen?" Grace asked.

Hope answered the question with one of her own. "Do you want him to work for the rest of his life? You might think he's Superman, but he's not. He's getting older every day. If he accepts this deal, he and Mom can finally do all the traveling they've always wanted to do but were never able to because he couldn't drag himself away from the shop. Let Dad rest on his laurels, Grace. I know he promised the company would go to you one day, but this decision isn't about you."

"It's not about greed, either."

"I don't have to explain my motivations to you."

"Then why are you asking me to explain mine to you? Even though you're the oldest, that doesn't mean you can bully me into bowing to your will."

"And being Dad's favorite doesn't mean you can sweet-talk him into bowing to yours."

"Is that what you think I'm trying to do?"

"It's what you've always done. Every time you wanted something, all you had to do was ask Dad and say pretty please. But things are different this time. He's got to answer to all of us, not just you. If you want to run a company so badly, start one of your own. As if anyone would buy your stuff except the current collection of misfits you've got lined up outside your office."

"Watch your mouth."

"Or what? You're going to call your girlfriend and tell her to come over here and kick my ass? Or is she your boyfriend? Sometimes, I can't quite tell. As long as you know the difference, I guess it doesn't matter what anyone else thinks, does it? You promised Dad you wouldn't spend time with her outside the office, but Faith had to drag you out of her bed to get you here on time for the meeting."

Grace shot a glance at Faith, who held her hands up to indicate she hadn't betrayed her confidence.

"Faith didn't say anything," Hope said. "She didn't have to. You gave yourself away by coming home reeking of cheap white wine and a redneck who got lucky. Do you plan to tell Dad what you're up to, or do I have to do it for you?" She plucked a dark brown hair from Grace's sleeve and held it up to the light before disdainfully tossing it aside.

"Seriously? You're going to tell Dad on me? Is that really the best you can do? Because you sound like a six-year-old right now."

"Make fun of me all you want, but we both know I'm not known for making idle threats. Do you really want to test my patience when the future of the company—Hell, when all of our futures are at stake?" Hope arched an eyebrow as she waited for a response to her question. "I didn't think so," she said when she saw that none was forthcoming.

Grace wanted to slap the smug expression off Hope's face. She didn't realize she had moved to do exactly that until Faith stepped between them. "Stop arguing before Mommy and Daddy hear you. It would break Daddy's heart to see you fighting like this. And over what? A little bit of money?"

"Whose side are you on," Hope asked, "hers or mine?"

As her eyes darted back and forth between Grace and Hope, Faith looked trapped. "I'm not on anyone's side. I want to get paid as much as you do, Hope, but family is worth a lot more than a few zeroes on a check. And no matter how we feel about each other at the end of the day, we're still family, right?"

"Speak for yourself. Tonight, I've had about as much as I can take of each member of my so-called family." Hope stomped out the door and slammed it behind her.

"Are you okay?" Faith asked.

Grace didn't know how to answer. The argument with Hope had left her shaken. The mean, hurtful things Hope had said to her—and about Dakota—were comments she would have expected to hear from a stranger in the street, not from someone who shared her last name. "Do you think she's right?"

"About what?"

"About any of the things she said."

"Don't mind her. Thanks to Daddy's big announcement, all she can see right now are dollar signs. Everything will work out once he makes his decision."

Grace shook her head. "No, that might actually make things worse. Hope will be fine if Dad decides to sell. If he doesn't, she'll never let me live it down. She'll blame me for every little thing that goes wrong in her life from here on out. For the promotion she thinks she deserves but doesn't get. For all the things she could have but can't afford to buy. And no matter if Dad decides to stay in business or sell out, she'll never be comfortable with the idea of Dakota being in my life in anything other than a professional capacity. Perhaps not even that."

"So what? Hope has always preferred to point fingers at someone else rather than look in the mirror and place the blame where it belongs. Having a few dollars in the bank won't change that. If you want to be with Dakota, don't worry about what anyone else has to say about it. Go for it. I know blood's thicker than water and all that, but blood also stains."

If she wanted to be happy, Grace slowly began to realize, she would have to start by coming clean. With her father, with Dakota, and with herself.

CHAPTER SEVENTEEN

After Brooke spent the night downing three-quarters of a bottle of Boone's Farm Strawberry Hill by herself, Dakota expected her to wake up the next morning with the hangover from hell. Instead, Brooke rolled out of bed at six a.m., showered, dressed, and walked to the coffee shop on the corner to pick up two mocha lattes and a bag of chocolate croissants. Then she started pestering Dakota to find a place for them to play paintball. The last things on Dakota's mind were food, caffeine, or extreme sports. She would rather finish the conversation she and Brooke had left hanging in the balance the night before, but Brooke shoved a cup of coffee in her hand and a croissant in her mouth and said, "Are we going to do this or what?"

Dakota reached for her tablet computer. A brief Internet search led her to Xtreme Sports, a company in Long Island City that afforded customers a chance to participate in a variety of activities without having to deal with the elements. The cavernous building housed venues for laser tag, rock climbing, trampolining, and indoor skydiving. As she took a sip of her rapidly cooling coffee, she was tempted to book sessions for all four disciplines, but she wasn't that foolhardy. If her protective equipment failed while she was playing paintball, the most she could end up with were a few bruises. If something went wrong while she tried her hand at the other sports, she could end up in traction. And find herself out of not one job but two.

"Sounds perfect," Brooke said when Dakota showed her the screen. "Let's go."

"Not so fast. The place isn't even open yet. Give me a chance to take a shower and make a few calls first. We can't play by ourselves, you know."

Xtreme Sports opened at ten on Sundays. Dakota called Joey, Whitney, Aaron, Roxxy, and a few other friends and asked them to meet her and Brooke there at noon, giving the early starters plenty of time to finish their matches before her group arrived.

Paintball was a game in which players eliminated their opponents from play by hitting them with small oil and gelatin pellets filled with dye. Both the technology and the various strategies involved were used by military, law enforcement, and security organizations to supplement their training programs. The various styles of games included elimination, capture the flag, ammunition limits, capturing objects of interest hidden on the playing field, and defending or attacking a particular location. Depending on the type of game chosen, players could compete for as little as a few seconds or up to several days.

Even though she hadn't played in years, Dakota didn't think her strategic skills had deserted her in the meantime. Playing paintball was like riding a bicycle. Once you learned how, the ability didn't leave you. She decided against the longer-lasting scenario play and opted to book a couple of rounds of capture the flag. That would give Brooke plenty to time to get her aggressions out but wouldn't take all day. Dakota had better things to do than trying to avoid getting pelted with dye packs. Like meeting up with Grace so they could pick up where they'd left off last night.

After everyone arrived at the venue, divided into two teams, and appointed captains, Dakota began the game confident she and the members of her squad would do well. The fact that she was the game's first casualty came as a surprise, though not a complete shock. She was too distracted by all the things she and Brooke had left unsaid to concentrate on steering clear of the opposition. After Roxxy tagged her in the shoulder with a pellet filled with yellow dye, she headed to the small area designated for eliminated players.

She removed her helmet and protective goggles, sank to the padded floor, and listened to the outing she had arranged take place without her.

Barked commands were mixed in with peals of laughter, making the game seem serious and frivolous at the same time. Dakota felt much the same way. As she sat with her elbows on her knees and her head in her hands, she didn't know whether to laugh or cry. Everyone else seemed to be having the time of their lives, but she felt miserable. She couldn't stop thinking about what Brooke had said to her the night before. About growing up envying her, then deciding she wanted to be nothing like her. She and Brooke had lived under the same roof and, for a time, had even shared the same room, but the distance that yawned between them now was much more than geographical. She didn't know how to bridge the gap.

Trying to avoid getting lost in her own thoughts, she fished her phone out of her pocket and powered it on. She pulled up the list of recent calls and scrolled down to Grace's number. She was dying to hear Grace's voice, but the timing was off. Given the hour, Grace was most likely at church or having lunch with her family. Dakota didn't want to take a chance on interrupting either venture. She pulled up her boss's number instead. Depending on how long Brooke decided to stay, she might need to take a few days off from her day job in order to play tour guide. Her phone rang before she could place the outgoing call. When she checked the display, she saw Laird's number printed on the screen.

"When you gave Sophie the gig in Japan, did you know she'd decide to stay?" he asked without preamble.

That got Dakota's attention. "She's not coming back to New York?" she asked, sitting up straight. "She just got here."

"Apparently, her stay is meant to be short-lived. As in it's already over."

"You're losing me."

"I just got a text from Ruben," Laird said patiently. "Sophie finished shooting the commercial this morning."

"And?"

"Not only did the client flip for her, the director did, too. So much so that he offered her the lead role in his next movie. Some straight-to-DVD action film with cheaper production values than a high school play, most likely. Please tell me you aren't harboring similar ambitions."

"I'm not planning to become a distaff Steven Seagal or a twenty-first century Cynthia Rothrock, if that's what you're asking."

"Wonderful. Can I have that in writing?"

Though she was happy to hear she could stop looking over her shoulder to see if Sophie was gaining on her, Dakota decided to play it coy. "That depends. Are you offering to renegotiate my contract?"

"I wasn't planning on it, but since Sophie opted out of hers, we have some wiggle room. I should have known there was a reason Ruben insisted on having a ninety-day right of rescission written into Sophie's deal. The two of them were playing me the whole time. She never intended to become part of the team. She just wanted to use the company's status to raise her profile. Now she's dumping us to move on to something bigger and better. Allegedly. The last swimmer who made a splash as an actor was Johnny Weissmuller, and he didn't have to say much more than 'Me Tarzan, you Jane.'"

Dakota didn't point out that action films were known more for spectacular stunts than witty dialogue. As long as Sophie—or her stunt double—could look good pretending to fight off a horde of bad guys, she wouldn't have to do much in order to carry a film. Even a straight-to-DVD one with cheaper production values than a high school play. "Before he became a celluloid badass, Jason Statham was a competitive diver. Does that count?"

"You couldn't resist twisting the knife, could you?" Laird asked with a hint of mirth in his voice.

"If you toss me a fat pitch, what do you expect me to do except hit it?"

"Save the sports analogies for a direr situation. I think it's safe to say we've got this one under control. So when can you come in and sign the new agreement?"

Dakota stopped trying to temper her excitement. She had never been any good at playing mind games. Why should she start now? "Is tomorrow too soon?"

"After the day I've had, tomorrow can't come soon enough. I'll have our legal team get to work on the new contract. Lucky for you, I'm in the mood to reward loyalty. Congratulations. You're about to break the bank."

"I like the sound of that." Dakota ended the call and slipped her phone into her pocket.

"What was that about?" Brooke asked as she took a seat next to her.

"I just got a rather substantial raise."

"Is it large enough for you to buy one of those fancy penthouse apartments in Manhattan?"

"Do you have any idea how much those places cost?"

"Of course I do. I know it's been a while since you were home, but there's a newfangled invention called cable TV that allows country bumpkins like me to see what goes on in big places like New York City."

Dakota rolled her eyes as Brooke exaggerated her natural Southern accent to comical proportions. "Just because I can afford something doesn't mean I have to run out and buy it. Except for bottle service, of course. A party isn't a party without that."

"Aside from overpriced booze, are you saving your money for a rainy day, or are you sitting on it like Ebenezer Scrooge? You don't have to blow it all at once, but you can't take it with you either."

"All I know is I'm not looking to upgrade. I like where I'm living just fine."

"I love your neighborhood, and your apartment's cute, but what will you and Rich do if one of you meets someone? Your place is barely big enough for two people, let alone three or more."

"Then I guess it's a good thing neither of us is looking to bring anyone else into the fold."

"Have you told Grace that?"

Dakota didn't want to discuss her and Grace's burgeoning relationship with Brooke or anyone else. Not until she'd had a chance to experience it for herself first. "She knows I'm not the marrying kind," she said, hoping to put the subject to rest.

"And she's okay with it?"

"I wouldn't say that."

Brooke frowned. "Then why are you chasing after her if you can't give her what she wants?"

"Because I want her. Isn't that reason enough?"

"If you're looking for a random hookup, yes." Brooke carefully examined Dakota's face. "But I can see you're already well past that."

"If you say so."

"I know so. And for what it's worth, I think you do, too."

Dakota wasn't used to dissecting her relationships. Hell, she wasn't used to having relationships that lasted long enough to dissect. Her typical entanglements had the life span of a fruit fly. This was different. It was exciting. And a little bit scary, too. Like riding the world's tallest roller coaster without being securely strapped into her seat. She didn't want to jinx what was happening, so she changed the subject rather than talk about it. "Who tagged you?" she asked, eyeing the telltale blue stain on Brooke's leg.

"Aaron. I was starting to like him. Now I'm not so sure." Brooke laughed. "Aren't we a pair? I came up with the idea to play paintball. You planned the excursion. Now everyone is enjoying the benefits of our labor without us."

"Look at the bright side. This gives us an opportunity to spend more time together. That's one of the reasons you came to New York in the first place, isn't it?"

"I guess." Brooke's smile slowly faded until it was nothing more than a distant memory.

"Are we going to talk about what you said last night, or are we going to keep pretending last night never happened?"

"I know which of those options I'd choose," Brooke said with a sigh, "but I'm sure you'd select the opposite just to be contrary."

"Me? Surely you have me mistaken for someone else."

"I know exactly who I'm talking to, Dakota Louise Lane, so don't try to sneak anything past me."

"I'm not the one who's keeping secrets. You are. Do you plan to share some of them with me, or do you want to keep wasting time?"

"Is that what I am to you? A waste of time?"

"That's not what I meant and you know it. Goddammit, Brooke, just talk to me. Tell me what's on your mind. Tell me the real reason you're here."

"I already told you why I'm here. I needed to escape the wedding preparations for a few days, and I wanted to spend some time with you."

"Me? The person you have no desire to emulate?"

Brooke closed her eyes as if she couldn't stand seeing the truth. "That didn't come out right."

"So here's your chance to fix it. Go ahead. I'm all ears."

"You're not making this easy for me, are you?"

"You've always had it easy. Maybe you'd be better off if I'd been tougher on you."

"How could you have been? You left, remember? You sat us down, told us how things were, and took off to chase after some girl you were hot for instead of sticking around to help us deal with it. Now you're up here doing whatever the hell you want without stopping to think how it might affect us or how we might feel about it."

"It's my life, Brooke. It doesn't have anything to do with you. That was the case then and it's still the case now."

"Is it? Do you have any idea how many times I've been asked inappropriate questions by people who think anything you do or say is fair game for analysis? Do you have any idea how many people assume I'm a lesbian because you are? Do you have any idea how many times I've asked myself the same question?"

Instead of giving an immediate response, Dakota gave herself time for the import of Brooke's words to sink in. "You've been boy crazy since you learned to talk. When did you ever question your sexuality?"

"Do you remember Lauren Chapman?"

Dakota nodded. "She was your best friend when you were in elementary school."

"I met her when I was in kindergarten," Brooke said wistfully.

"After Mom dropped me off on my first day of school, I cried because I wanted to go home instead of spending my day surrounded by a bunch of strangers. Lauren gave me a hug in the hall outside our classroom and told me everything would be okay. She and I were constant companions for the next seven years."

"When you were twelve, her father got a job with a tech company and moved the family to Seattle. I remember how devastated you were when she broke the news to you."

"At the time, I thought I was so upset because I was losing my best friend. When you came out the next year, I realized she meant much more to me than that. She wasn't just a friend. She was the first person I ever truly loved."

"Did you ever tell her so?"

"No."

"Why not?"

"Because it wouldn't have made any difference. If she didn't feel the same way about me as I did about her, I didn't want to know. And if she returned my feelings, there was no way her father would have turned down a six-figure salary just so Lauren and I could be together."

"Were you still dealing with those feelings when I came out the following year?"

Brooke nodded. "That's one of the reasons I was so affected by the things you said. In a way, it felt like you had stolen my thunder. You felt comfortable enough to define yourself as something I couldn't bring myself to. And when Mom and Dad turned on you, I was glad I had opted to keep my feelings to myself. Having you around made it easier for me to deal with everything. Even if it may have seemed like I couldn't stand you at times."

"Do you care to rephrase that?"

"Okay, all the time."

"Are you still attracted to women?" Dakota asked after she and Brooke shared an uneasy laugh.

"No, Lauren is the only one I've ever thought of in that way. I got in touch with her on social media a few years ago. Partly out of curiosity. I started thinking about her after I received a friend request from a former classmate. I wanted to know if she looked the same as I remembered."

"Does she?" Dakota had barely been able to recognize some of the former classmates that had sent her friend requests over the years. Time was a cruel mistress, and she had apparently been a complete bitch to more than a few people.

"She has the same smile, but everything else has changed. I'm sure she can say the same about me. I follow her posts, but there's a disconnect. It's like when someone you have only a passing acquaintance with sends you a Christmas card with a family newsletter stuffed inside. You read the newsletter because it's right there in front of you, but you don't know anyone mentioned in it enough to care about the milestones they achieved during the year. When I see the pictures of Lauren, her husband, and their kids pop up on my feed, I don't feel the spark I did when we were younger. Maybe it was just a phase. Maybe it was just a crush. Maybe it was more. I don't know. I was tempted to send her a wedding invitation, but I thought it would have been weird since we haven't seen each other in so long."

"Have you told Kevin?"

"That we won't be getting an extra toaster oven?"

"No, that you used to have feelings for Lauren."

"He and I told each other about our respective sexual histories when we started becoming serious because it's the responsible thing to do in this day and age, but I didn't say anything about my attraction to her because my bond with her was emotional rather than physical. I don't want him to ever feel like I'm keeping secrets from him or hiding part of myself, but I honestly don't know how he would react if I told him. I don't want to risk what we have if I don't have to."

"Don't worry about how he might react to hearing about something that happened more than a decade ago. Just ask yourself one question. Do you love him? Because it doesn't matter who meant what to you in your past as long as he's the one you want in your future."

Brooke rested her head on Dakota's shoulder. "I knew there was a reason I came to see you." Dakota leaned the side of her head against the top of Brooke's, enjoying the kind of closeness she and her sister hadn't experienced since they were kids. "I missed this," Brooke whispered. "I miss you."

Dakota swallowed around the lump in her throat. "We shouldn't wait so long to get together next time. You're not getting any younger, you know."

"That goes double for you, party animal."

"I'm not partying nearly as hard as I used to."

"Because of Grace?"

"No, because of me. The last few times I've gone out have been kind of disappointing. It felt like I'd already been there and done that, so why should I do it again?" In fact, she'd had much more fun sitting at a baseball game with Grace or conversing with her over a platter of appetizers than she had popping bottles in the latest hot new club. One felt like a performance; the other felt real. But how long would the feeling last?

"Mom and Dad's fortieth anniversary is in September," Brooke said. "Townsend and I are throwing a party for them. Nothing fancy. Just a sit-down dinner with family and a few of their closest friends. I made reservations at their favorite restaurant, the seafood place on Lazzaretto Creek they used to take us to on our birthdays."

Dakota smiled at the memory of past family outings to the dockside restaurant that served some of the best and freshest seafood in the country. Every time they walked in, she, Brooke, and Townsend would press their faces against the oversized aquarium in the lobby. The one teeming with all sorts of colorful tropical fish. And no matter what the weather was like, they would always insist on getting a table outside so they could watch shrimpers cast their nets from the dock or fishing boats return to shore carrying their latest hauls. Dakota had dined in several five-star restaurants since then, but despite the ritzy establishments' elaborate settings and exorbitant prices, none of them compared to the humble family-owned restaurant on Tybee Island where she sat at butcher paper–covered tables, servers dumped buckets of piping-hot steamed shrimp in front of her, and she discarded the shells by tossing them in the round hole cut in the center of the table.

"Can I add you to the guest list?" Brooke asked. "Even if they haven't said it, I'm sure Mom and Dad would love it if you came."

Dakota hoped Brooke was being honest instead of projecting her newfound fuzzy feelings on someone else, but there was no way she could know for sure unless she was willing to make the effort. Unless she was willing to risk getting hurt in order to heal.

"Sure," she said. "Pencil me in." Players began to drift off the course after the first paintball game came to an end. Brooke's team had been victorious, but Dakota felt like the real winner. After all these years of forced separation, she finally had her sister back. Perhaps the rest of her family would soon follow. "Are you ready for the next round?"

Brooke shook her head and pushed herself to her feet. "I've got to book a flight. My wedding won't plan itself, you know," she added with a wink. She wrapped her arms around Dakota and squeezed her tight. "I love you, big sister."

Dakota was taken aback by the unexpected display of affection. She hesitated before she returned the pressure—and the sentiment. "I love you, too, little sis."

"Thanks for listening."

"Thanks for letting me in."

"Give me a call when you'd like to return the favor."

Dakota could tell Brooke was being sincere instead of paying lip service. "I'll do that."

She eagerly awaited their next heart-to-heart talk, but there was one conversation she was looking forward to even more: the one she would soon be having with Grace. She had never been willing to bet her heart on anyone. Until now. With Grace, she felt like going all in. Now that she had admitted it to herself, it was time to share the news with Grace. And as far as she was concerned, that time couldn't come soon enough.

❖

The service was running long and Grace's stomach was growling. She glanced at her watch, more focused on the chicken and waffles she planned to have for brunch than she was on the topic of today's sermon—a long-winded rumination on the difference between faith and belief. After more than ninety minutes, she still wasn't sure which was which. Or why one was more important than the other. When her phone buzzed, she reached for it like a drowning woman being thrown a lifeline.

"Unless that's Jesus himself," her mother said under her breath, "I suggest you let that call go to voice mail."

"It might be important," Grace said as her phone continued to vibrate. She pulled out her trump card. "It could be work."

Her mother covered her hand with her own. "In case you've forgotten," she said, drawing Grace's hand out of her purse, "let me remind you that Sunday is supposed to be a day of rest. Work can wait until tomorrow."

"At this rate, we'll still be sitting here listening to Reverend Davis speak when tomorrow comes."

Her mother covered her mouth with her program to hide her smile.

"For a while there, I thought I was going to have to separate you two," Grace's father said when the service finally ended. Her mother and sisters were already making their way to the restaurant, but her father had asked her to stay behind while he greeted Reverend Davis and his wife and congratulated Reverend Davis on "yet another fine sermon." Grace had come close to rolling her eyes on that one, but she had somehow managed to hold herself in check. As she suspected, her father had an ulterior motive for asking her to perform a chore normally allotted to her mother. "Last night's announcement probably took you by surprise."

"To say the least."

"And I'm sure you're waiting for an explanation for why I didn't tell you first."

"An explanation would be nice, but it isn't required."

Her father smiled as he chucked her under her chin. "You and Faith have always been the peacemakers in the family. That's what makes this so hard. I want to do right by everyone, but no matter what I decide to do, at least two of the women I love more than anyone in this world will be mad at me."

"You've fielded offers before—none as lucrative as this one, of course—but you turned all of them down without giving them a second thought. Why are you losing sleep over this one? Is it the amount of money involved?"

"Yes and no. The money's eye-opening, but it's more a matter of timing. I want your mother and me to be able to enjoy my retirement, which we can't do if I keep putting it off. And I want you and your sisters to be able to enjoy yourselves without breaking your backs to make a living, which the money would allow you to do. Are Faith and Hope responsible enough to handle having access to that much disposable income at once? I have my doubts about that, but one of the hardest parts of being a parent is allowing your children to learn from their mistakes."

"This could be a rather expensive learning opportunity, don't you think?"

"That it could. On the other hand, it could also give you the push you need to do what you really want to do."

"I already am, Dad."

"Yes, but you could do more."

"I don't understand."

Her father stopped walking and turned to face her. "When you took on your new roster of clients, I had my doubts about where you—and the company—were headed, but I can see how happy servicing them makes you. And how happy meeting with you makes them. Instead of continuing my legacy, why don't you establish your own?"

"That's what Hope said."

"Though not in the same terms, I'm sure," he said with a knowing smile.

"No, not even close."

"The two of you have always been like oil and water. I keep hoping in vain you'll find a way to mix."

"Keep hoping. It'll probably happen the same day the lions finally lie down with the lambs."

"And what a glorious day that will be for all concerned," her father said, sounding remarkably like Reverend Davis. "In all seriousness, you're about to establish your own company. Be the face of your own brand. You can't afford to have any slipups, either personally or professionally. Are you ready to be your own boss? I've got to warn you it feels different when everything falls on your shoulders instead of someone else's."

"That's what I'm afraid of. What if I'm not cut out to be the person in charge? What if I'm meant to be the second-in-command?"

"Just keep doing what you've been doing. Play by the rules you've set for yourself, conduct yourself professionally, treat your clients with respect, and be careful who you associate with. Take care of those things and you'll be fine. Better than fine. You'll be great. Better than I ever dreamed I could be. I can't ask for any more than that." He placed his hands on her shoulders and gave them a squeeze. "Spread your wings, baby girl. It's time for you to fly."

Grace's father had given her many things over the years, but she felt like she had finally received the one thing he had never granted. The one thing she had always wanted most: permission. But permission for her to run her business the way she wanted didn't seem to extend to her personal life as well. He had told her to be careful who she associated with, but all she had heard was *Stay away from Dakota Lane.*

"I have an announcement to make," her father said after they joined her mother and sisters at the restaurant.

"Another one?" Hope set her tea down with such force some of the contents sloshed out of the glass onto her hand.

"Yes. Another one."

"What is it this time?" Faith asked.

"Your sister has decided to go into business for herself."

Grace felt like the center of attention after her mother and sisters turned to stare at her. Each had questions, but Hope's rose above the din. "Where did she get the money to do that?"

"I've decided to accept Mr. Phillips's offer," her father said.

"You did what?" her mother asked, her protests nearly drowned out by Hope and Faith's squeals of delight. "Is that what you two were conspiring about while we were sitting here waiting for you to show up?"

"Grace didn't try to sway me one way or the other," her father said. "In the end, I decided to do what was best for the family. The *entire* family."

Hope raised her hands heavenward. "Thank you, Jesus, Mary, *and* Joseph."

"Does that mean we have to start paying rent?" Faith asked.

Her father spread his napkin in his lap as he prepared to tuck into his meal. "If you want to continue living under my roof, it does. Consider it a reverse allowance."

"I'm down," Faith said with a shrug. "It's cheaper than moving out. What about you, Grace? Are you planning to stick around or find a place of your own?"

"I'm not sure yet." The answer depended on how much money she'd have left after she found a retail space to rent and got her business up and running. Even though it would be cheaper to stay put, she was looking forward to being on her own in more ways than one.

"If you leave," Faith said, "I'm calling dibs on your room. I've been waiting *years* to say that."

"I thought the third floor was too hot for you."

"It is, but I'll be able to afford the air-conditioning."

Grace was sad to realize Henderson Custom Suits was coming to an end, but she was glad to see everyone in her family laughing, joking, and having a good time without the usual undercurrent of tension. "When one door closes," she said to herself, "another one opens."

It was time to put the past behind her and start planning for the future. But the questions she had yet to address were the ones she needed to answer most. She was about to become busier than she had ever been as she helped shutter one business and embarked on another. For the next few months, if not years, her life wouldn't be her own. Would she have time to find a place in it for love? And if she did, would there be a place in it for Dakota?

With her life in flux, she would need someone steady at her side. Someone who was in it for the long haul. Dakota didn't appear to possess either of those qualities. Grace might be able to look past that deficiency in the short term, but would she be able to do so for years to come? Before her father decided to sell the company, she might have been willing to take that risk. Now she couldn't afford to. Emotionally or financially. When she committed herself to someone, she needed to be sure the sentiment was returned. If not, everything she was trying to build could come crashing down around her.

Play by the rules you've set for yourself, her father had advised her.

Stringent though they might be, the principles she lived by had gotten her to this point. On the verge of a potentially lucrative career she could direct herself without having to answer to anyone else. She was so close to being able to live out her dreams. She couldn't abandon her principles now. Not when she needed them most. All she needed to do was ignore the fact that her heart kept trying to tell her she needed Dakota more.

CHAPTER EIGHTEEN

The revised version of the contract Whitaker Models offered Dakota seemed relatively straightforward, but she read the entire document three times before she initialed the bottom of each page and signed and dated the last one. When she was done, Laird handed the executed contract to his assistant so she could make a copy for Dakota to keep for her records. Then he extended his hand across his desk. "It's a pleasure doing business with you."

"Believe me, the pleasure's mine." Under the new terms of her contract, both her appearance and hourly fees had almost doubled. "Sorry, I can't," she said after Laird's assistant Marilyn offered her a celebratory glass of champagne. "Even though I'm clocked out, I'm technically still on the job. I can't drink until after five."

"More for me." Laird raised both glasses in a toast, downed the contents of one, and leaned back in his chair. "It's five o'clock somewhere," he said, propping his loafer-clad feet on a corner of his desk. "I would offer to take you to lunch, but thanks to the contract you just signed, you can afford to treat me in the manner in which I'm accustomed. Where would you like to go? I might have to pull some strings, but I should be able to get us a table at Griffin Sutton's new place."

"I'd love to give it a try, but I have another appointment I need to get to and I can't afford to be late."

"What kind of appointment?"

"Relax," she said after Laird nearly choked on his second glass of champagne. "My meeting's not with a rival agency. My sister's getting married in a few weeks and my tailor needs to take a new set of measurements before she starts working in earnest on the suit she's making for me to wear to the ceremony. I've got to take the train to Brooklyn so she can do what she needs to do before I head back to work."

Laird arched his manicured eyebrows. "You have your own personal tailor? Even I don't have one of those. Color me impressed. Is yours any good?"

"She's the best I've come across."

"That probably means you're sleeping with her, but leave me her name and number anyway. She might be able to help me spruce up my wardrobe. I want to add some unique pieces to help me stand out from the crowd. I can't walk around looking like everyone else, can I?"

With his vast collection of garish ties and gaudy dress socks, Laird didn't have much to worry about in that regard. Thanks to his expensive tastes, he was guaranteed to be responsible for several lucrative sales, which would mean more money and more exposure for Grace and her father.

"Happy to oblige." Dakota jotted Grace's contact information on a notepad and slung her messenger bag over her shoulder. "Considering all the referrals I keep sending her way, she should put me on the payroll."

"I know you're being only half-serious, but that's actually not a bad idea. With her design skills and your contacts in the fashion industry, a business partnership could be a win-win for both of you."

Dakota liked the idea of working side by side with Grace, but the scenario seemed unlikely to take place as long as Grace's father was standing in the way. He had been working for himself for so long, Dakota doubted he would be willing to take on a partner, silent or otherwise. "Thanks for believing in me, Laird. And for respecting my judgment enough not to put restrictions on me."

When he offered to revise her contract, she had expected him to ask the legal department to throw in a codicil or three requiring her to quit her day job and/or limit her extracurricular activities. Much to her surprise, the contract he had presented to her hadn't included any such language.

"Though it might not look like it from a distance, you've got a good head on your shoulders, Dakota. Savvy business sense, too. Thanks for choosing to stick by us even when you thought we weren't sticking by you."

"Like you said, we're family, right?"

"That we are. Before you go," he said, rising from his seat, "promise me one thing."

"What?"

"If you wake up one morning and decide you want to do something other than this for a living, please give me more than twelve hours' notice."

"You've got a deal."

When Dakota reached Grace's office, she felt like she had left one party for another. The mood was so festive she was surprised there weren't streamers dangling from the ceiling.

Grace was with a customer, so Dakota approached the de facto reception desk. Lillie was supposed to be manning the phones, but her headset was draped across her shoulders and she was dancing in her seat to the Stevie Wonder song playing on the radio at her feet.

"What's going on?" Dakota asked.

"Haven't you heard?" Lillie asked, snapping her fingers to the beat. "We're going out of business."

Dakota's heart lurched. She had just found this place and it was already going under? "The company's closing its doors? Since when?"

"Since yesterday. We haven't set the official date yet, but we're not taking any new orders either. Grace's father sold the building to some rich developer who's buying up the block so he can build condos or some such. Mr. Henderson signed the papers this morning. In a month or two—three at the latest—everyone in here is going to be out of work."

Dakota looked around the room. No one seemed adversely affected by the turn of events. The dire news Lillie had just delivered didn't match the festive vibe. "And you're okay with that?"

"You bet I am. I've been working here for more than half my life. I'm sure I'll shed a tear or two when we complete the last order, but I don't expect to be crying long. With the severance package I've been promised, I won't have time for tears. I'm going to be set for life. It's not Kardashian money, but it's way more than I need to get by."

"What are you going to do with all your riches now that you don't have to worry about making ends meet?"

"Whatever I want to, child. Whatever I want to. I won't stray too far, though. I'll still be around if Grace needs my help. If she can find a space to rent that doesn't cost an arm and a leg, she's planning to open her own shop."

"Really?" When Dakota had asked Grace if she planned to start her own company one day, Grace had seemed content to sit back and wait for her father to hand her the reins to his. Had Grace changed her mind, or had her father's decision to sell prompted her to be more proactive? "That's awesome."

"Yes, it is. And long overdue, if you ask me," Lillie said in a conspiratorial whisper. "News like that calls for a celebration, don't you think?"

"You read my mind."

"You'd better be glad I can't. If I could, I might have to bend you over my knee and spank you. On second thought, I'd better not. You might like it too much. We wouldn't want to make Grace jealous, would we?"

Dakota gave Lillie a kiss on the cheek. "You know you'll always be the only woman for me."

"You're a mess, you know that?" Lillie said with a girlish giggle that belied her advanced years. "An absolute rascal. I might have to follow Grace to her new shop just so I can see you from time to time. You're not planning to take your business elsewhere, are you?"

"I wouldn't dream of it."

Even though she had been a customer for only a short time, Dakota felt invested in the company's success—and especially in Grace's. She cared about Grace and wanted to see her do well.

Striking out on her own wouldn't be easy for Grace. Operating a business that catered to a niche market never was. Dakota wanted to support her in any way she could. Perhaps she should make her investment financial as well as emotional. The venture was risky, but the upside was enormous.

Laird was right. With her contacts and Grace's design skills, they could make an unbeatable team. In more ways than one. She smiled to herself as an idea began to take root.

When she and Grace had dined at La Tigra a few weeks ago, Grace had asked her if she wanted to be the captain of her own ship one day instead of a member of the crew. *I want something that's mine*, she had said in response. *Something I built myself.*

If she played her cards right, perhaps she and Grace could build something together. Not just a business, but a life as well.

The sound of Lillie's raucous laughter drew Grace's attention away from her consult with her customer, a seven-year-old whose father had brought him in for the final fitting for the suit he planned to wear during his upcoming piano recital. Grace's heart skittered in her chest when she spotted Dakota standing in the reception area. She had been simultaneously anticipating and dreading Dakota's visit all day. The moment had finally arrived, and she didn't know how to react.

She was glad to see Dakota—especially in the form-fitting cycling gear she was sporting as she chatted with Lillie—but she wished she could put off the conversation they needed to have. Not the one about Dakota's order. Grace was on solid ground as long as the subject was work. It was when she allowed her focus to shift to more personal matters that she started to feel like she didn't have a leg to stand on.

She had heard the classic "it's not you, it's me" speech more times than she could count, but she was used to being on the receiving end instead of the one delivering the address. She didn't know if she would be able to get her point across without making a royal mess of things. She valued Dakota's friendship. Would they be able to hold on to it after Grace told her that a platonic relationship was the only kind they could ever have? Would Dakota still want to be her friend knowing she could never be her lover?

Intellectually, Grace knew she was doing the right thing by ending things before they went too far. She didn't have time for a relationship, and Dakota wasn't interested in one to begin with. Once she became the face of her own company, she would have too much at stake to risk attaching her livelihood to someone with a tarnished reputation. All she needed to do was figure out a way to express that sentiment without driving a wedge between her and Dakota that couldn't be removed. They could still have a relationship. Just not the kind either of them was looking for.

Grace ran her hands over her customer's narrow shoulders, checking for imperfections in the seams. Finding none, she turned him to face the floor-length mirror bolted to the wall. "How does it feel?"

Zaire turned this way and that to check his reflection. "Good," he said with a snaggletoothed grin. "How do I look, Dad?"

Ahmad Hawkins, a single father who had been working a series of back-breaking jobs to support himself and his son since his ex decided she would rather be single and free than a wife and mother, beamed with pride. "You look like a million bucks, little man." Tossing Grace a wink, he added, "I'm just glad you didn't charge me that much."

"I wouldn't dare treat one of my best customers that way."

"I appreciate it." Ahmad had been coming to the shop practically since the day Zaire was born. Willing to make the ultimate sacrifice, he often went without so he could provide his son with whatever he needed. He didn't spoil Zaire by any means, but he definitely made sure Zaire never wanted for anything. He wiped his hands on his dirty work pants, reached into his back pocket, and pulled out a wrinkled envelope. "The recital's Friday night. I picked up two extra tickets in case you and your sister would like to come. I know Z would love to see you two there."

"Oh, he would, would he?"

"Okay, maybe I would, too."

Ahmad had had a crush on Hope since the first time he set foot in the shop. Grace had long thought his gentle nature could provide the perfect remedy to soothe Hope's sharp edges, but Hope refused to give him the time of day. Her official excuse was she didn't want anyone else's sloppy seconds, though Grace suspected Hope might choose to sing a different tune if Ahmad did something more lucrative than ride on the back of a trash truck for a living.

"I'm not sure about Hope's work schedule. She might not be able to make it that night." In truth, Hope had called in sick that morning and probably intended to do so until the funds from the real estate closing were disbursed. If her employer lost patience, she could be out of a job on Friday. If not sooner. "Even if she can't attend, I'll definitely be in the crowd. I wouldn't miss a chance to see the next Thelonious Monk do his thing."

"To hear Z tell it, he's not the next anyone. He's the first Zaire Hawkins." Ahmad ran a hand over Zaire's close-cropped hair, then gave Zaire a nudge toward the door. "Go get changed, little man. Make it quick. I've got to drop you off at daycare before I head back to work." After Zaire scampered to the bathroom to change back into his play clothes, Ahmad held out a work-roughened hand. "Thanks for everything you and your father have done for me and Zaire over the years," he said, swallowing Grace's hand in his firm grip. "I'm going to hate seeing this place close. It's been part of the neighborhood for so long the block won't be the same without it. Once you get your new shop up and running, be sure to let me know where it is so I can keep Z looking fly."

"I'll be contacting everyone on the client list to let them know where they can find me if they choose to follow me to the new location."

"Hit me up and I'll be sure to come through." Ahmad tucked his hard hat under one arm and grabbed his work gloves off the cutting table. "See you at the recital Friday night?"

Grace held up the envelope containing the tickets. "I wouldn't miss it."

"Cool. And be sure to tell your sister I said hello."

"I'll do that." Though she doubted it would do any good, she would still make the effort. Relations between her and Hope had shown a slight improvement since her father announced he planned to sell the business. She and Hope weren't besties by any means, but they hadn't exchanged cross words in days. That was a new record for them. Perhaps the phrase *father knows best* applied in real life, too, not just on classic TV shows.

"Is it my turn now?" Dakota asked after Ahmad left.

"Thanks for being so patient. I didn't keep you waiting long, did I?"

"Lillie kept me entertained. I hardly noticed the delay. I'm just glad you were the one running late this time instead of me."

Grace knew Dakota's comment was a humorous reference to their first meeting, but she didn't feel like laughing. She should have followed her instincts that day. If she had, this situation would be a hell of a lot easier to deal with. Dakota would have remained nothing more than a customer, not whatever it was she had started to become.

Grace wrapped her measuring tape about Dakota's waist. She nodded when her assumption proved correct. Dakota's waist size had changed by three-quarters of an inch. Not a huge number, but enough to make a difference in the way the pants would fit. "I'll take these new numbers into account, and I should be able to have your suit ready by the end of next week. I'll text you or send you an email to schedule your final fitting. If adjustments need to be made, I should be able to get them done in a day or two. If not, you'll be all set for the wedding."

"Perfect."

"Pardon me, young man, but I don't think we've met." Grace started when her father tapped Dakota on the shoulder. She hadn't heard—or seen him approach. "I'm Clarence Henderson," he said, sticking out his hand. "Who might you be?"

"Dakota Lane."

"The person responsible for all those referrals?"

"That would be me."

Grace's father pumped Dakota's hand enthusiastically. "My

mistake. I'm pleased to meet you, young *lady*. Living with four women, you'd think I would be able to recognize one when I see her. I guess my eyes aren't as good as they used to be."

Grace was mortified by her father's mistake. And the more he talked, the more he kept compounding the gaffe. "Dad!"

"I seem to be digging myself into an even deeper hole, don't I?" he asked with a chuckle. "I just wanted to introduce myself and thank you for your business."

"You're welcome, sir. I hear congratulations are in order."

"Grace told you the news?"

"She didn't get a chance. Lillie spilled the beans before she could. Lillie also suggested I should take Grace to dinner to celebrate, and I wholeheartedly agree." Dakota turned to Grace. "Would you like to go back to La Tigra so we can try some of the dishes Whitney recommended? If we go early enough, they might actually be available this time."

"This time?" Grace's father asked.

"Dakota and I went there a few weeks ago. I've always wanted to try it out, and Dakota graciously offered to accompany me so I wouldn't have to dine alone," Grace said, trying to cover for Dakota's unintended faux pas. She remembered that night fondly. She and Dakota had spent several hours opening up to each other. Sharing their hopes and dreams. How ironic that the place where they had essentially introduced themselves might also be where they said farewell. "Will your sister be joining us?"

"No," Dakota said, "she caught a flight home this morning."

"That was a quick trip. Were you able to help her solve whatever crisis drove her to come here?"

"We had a good talk. Several, in fact. I'm sorry she interrupted us Saturday night, but I'm glad she came. Her visit gave us a chance to clear the air."

Grace could tell how much Brooke's visit meant to Dakota. Her eyes were just a little bit brighter, her smile just a little bit wider today. "I'm happy for you."

"I could say the same thing to you."

Grace's father cleared his throat. "I'll let you two talk," he said, extricating himself from the conversation. "It was nice meeting you, Dakota. Grace, we'll speak later, yes?"

"Of course," Grace said, though she had a feeling she might not want to hear what he had to say. She had promised him she wouldn't see Dakota in anything other than a professional capacity, and Dakota's comments had made it clear she had been doing exactly that. Few things got under her father's skin like dishonesty, and she had just been exposed as a liar. A bad one, at that.

"Have you thought of a name for your company yet?" Dakota asked.

"I've barely had time to catch my breath, let alone think about branding or trademarks."

"I can imagine. Instead of going out to dinner, why don't we get together someplace more private? Meet me at my place tonight after work. We can order takeout and split a bottle of wine while we wait for the food to be delivered."

"That sounds like the perfect way to end what's bound to be a long day."

As long as the topic of conversation didn't leave them with a bitter taste in their mouths.

CHAPTER NINETEEN

Dakota headed home as soon as her shift was over. She had asked Grace to meet her at her apartment at eight. That left her a little less than two and a half hours to straighten the place up before Grace arrived. Brooke's unannounced arrival and abrupt departure had left her apartment looking like a hurricane had hit it. Not a wimpy Category One or Two. More like a Four or Five. She tidied up as best she could, hit the common areas with a few liberal shots of air freshener, and peeled off her sweaty work clothes so she could take a shower.

"Oof," she said when she caught a whiff of her ripe jersey. "Too bad today isn't laundry day."

She gave her dirty clothes a few spritzes with the deodorizer and closed the hamper lid tight so the competing odors of fresh sweat and artificial lavender wouldn't escape. After she scrubbed herself clean, she patted herself dry, wrapped a towel around her waist, and headed to the kitchen to open a bottle of red wine so it would have time to breathe before Grace arrived.

When she was satisfied with both the amount and quality of her prep work, she placed her collection of takeout menus on the coffee table and returned to her bedroom so she could find something to wear. Opting for comfort rather than style, she slipped on a pair of board shorts and a T-shirt featuring the cartoon image of the Lady Chablis, the late drag performer whose antics in a best-selling true-crime novel and the Clint Eastwood–directed movie based on it had helped make Savannah a tourist mecca.

Grace rang the buzzer a few minutes before eight. "I'm sorry about this afternoon," she said after Dakota ushered her inside.

"That thing with your father? Don't be. It happens all the time." Dakota closed the door and twisted the locks into place. In Richmond Hill, few people panicked if they forgot to secure the doors before they left the house. Here, things were different. In her old neighborhood, everyone looked out for each other. In New York City, it was every man for himself. An unlocked door was an open invitation for someone to rob you blind, not pay you a friendly visit.

"You weren't offended?"

Dakota strode to the kitchen and poured two glasses of wine. "Your father made an honest mistake. No harm, no foul."

Grace looked at her hard. "Do you really feel that way, or are you just trying to make me feel better?"

"I've heard worse, believe me." Dakota handed Grace a glass of wine and settled on the couch. Grace sat next to her. Despite their relatively close proximity, Grace felt distant. Like she was a million miles away instead of only a few feet. Dakota chalked it up to the awkward encounter they'd had with Grace's father that afternoon. No matter how young or old you were, your parents always found a way to embarrass you from time to time. Clarence Henderson was no different in that respect. Even though she had tried to assure Grace she didn't have any hard feelings over the incident, Grace didn't seem to be buying what she was selling. "I can usually tell when people are genuinely confused or if they're simply trying to be confrontational. Some people get off on being assholes. Your father was trying to be a gentleman. I could probably learn a lesson or two from him."

"I think you're doing just fine on your own."

"Thanks for the compliment, but I'm still mad at you."

"What did I do?"

"It's more like what you didn't do. Why didn't you warn me you hadn't told your father about us? If you had given me a heads-up, I wouldn't have asked you out in front of him."

Grace grimaced. "Sorry about that."

"Were you intentionally keeping him in the dark, or did you simply forget to clue him in?"

Grace swirled her wine glass and stared into its depths like a fortune-teller studying a set of tea leaves. "I promised him I wouldn't see you."

"I suspected as much." Dakota took a sip of her wine and let the rich, oaky liquid rest on her tongue for a few seconds before she allowed it to slide down her throat. "I'm not the kind of person most women choose to take home to meet their parents. What convinced you to make me your dirty little secret?"

Grace set her glass on the coffee table. "Shortly after you and I met, one of my sisters showed my parents pictures of you and some woman in a rather compromising position."

Dakota felt like kicking herself. No matter how hard she tried, she couldn't escape her past. Though she wasn't ashamed of the things she had done, she wasn't necessarily proud of them either. Now her past was coming back to haunt her when all she wanted to do was give it a decent burial. "That one mistake is going to keep biting me in the ass for the rest of my life. I would say I was young and dumb, but I can't because the incident you're referring to wasn't that long ago." She carefully set her glass next to Grace's and leaned forward as she took Grace's hands in hers. "What I will say is the person in those pictures isn't who I am anymore. It's taken me a while to get to this point, but I have my priorities in order. And tonight, my only priority is pleasing you."

"I appreciate the sentiment, but that's not the reason I came here tonight. We need to talk."

"I know. And we will. Later. I promise."

Grace stared at her, her expression almost plaintive. "Dakota—"

Dakota placed a finger against Grace's lips to still them. "At the moment, all I want to do is show you how much I care about you. How much I want you. Will you let me do that?"

"Dakota." Grace brushed Dakota's hand aside.

"What?"

"Shut up and kiss me."

Dakota was more than happy to oblige. Sliding across the

couch, she closed the distance between them. Then she cradled Grace's face in her hands and gently pressed their lips together. Unlike the rigid posture she had borne when she arrived, Grace's mouth was soft and yielding. With a soft moan of acquiescence, she parted her lips and allowed Dakota entry.

Dakota slowly slid her tongue across Grace's, tasting the sharp tannins of the wine they had shared, along with something sweeter. Something indefinable but intoxicating. Dakota deepened the kiss. She wanted more. She wanted Grace. Just Grace and no one else. She had never been able to say that before. And now that she was able, she couldn't say it often enough. Words didn't matter at this point, however. It would do no good for her to tell Grace she could trust her not to walk away once the night was over. She needed to show Grace how much she wanted to stay. In her arms. In her life. In her heart. Not just tonight. For all the days to come.

"I thought there was supposed to be measuring tape involved," Grace said after Dakota led her to the bedroom, reached into a drawer in her nightstand, and pulled out a bottle of almond-flavored massage oil.

"Not tonight. Tonight, I don't want to measure that beautiful body of yours. I want to worship it."

Dakota turned Grace toward the wall. Then she languidly lowered the zipper on Grace's dress, pushed the soft material off Grace's even softer shoulders, and allowed the dress to pool at Grace's feet.

"These need to go, too."

Dakota hooked her thumbs in the waistband of Grace's black lace underwear and pulled them off. When Grace kicked off her shoes and turned to face her, Dakota's mouth went dry. Other parts of her, however, grew very, very wet.

"You look so good I don't know where to begin."

"I'm sure you'll think of something." Grace stepped toward Dakota and pressed her body against hers. She slid her hand over the spot at the nape of Dakota's neck that always drove Dakota wild before she threaded her fingers in Dakota's hair. Her nails scraped lightly against Dakota's scalp. The sensation made Dakota's nerve endings go haywire. And that was before Grace kissed her with a passion bordering on ferocity, then lay facedown on the bed with her round hips in the air. "Does this give you any ideas?"

Dakota swallowed hard. "Several, but I think I'll start with the first thing that comes to mind."

She stripped off her T-shirt and shorts and straddled Grace on the bed. She reached behind her, grabbed the bottle of massage oil, and squeezed a line of it down the center of Grace's back. The oil warmed as the user worked it into someone's skin, but it was initially cold to the touch. Grace hissed and arched her back as the frigid liquid trickled down her spine.

Dakota set the bottle down and used the sides of her hands to spread the oil over Grace's neck, shoulders, sides, and lower back. Then she began to knead Grace's tense muscles. Gently at first, then with steadily increasing pressure. Grace closed her eyes and sighed as her body began to respond to Dakota's touch. Dakota heard Grace's breathing slow. Felt her tight muscles start to loosen.

"Does that feel good?"

Grace didn't open her eyes. "Mmm," she said lazily. "That feels amazing."

Dakota grabbed the bottle of massage oil and squeezed some into her palm. After she rubbed her hands together, she placed them on Grace's hips. She kneaded the tender flesh, entranced by the smoothness of Grace's skin. Grace's breath hitched when Dakota slipped an oil-slicked finger between her ass cheeks and teased the sensitive folds. Grace groaned deep in her throat and pushed against Dakota's hand.

"Relax," Dakota said, turning her attention to Grace's legs. "I'm just getting started."

She massaged the back of Grace's thighs before she slid down to her calves and then to the soles of her feet.

"You are so good at this," Grace said with a sigh of contentment. "I think you missed your calling."

"I'm glad you think so."

Dakota rolled Grace onto her back and slowly worked her way up from Grace's feet to her knees. By the time she reached the gentle curve of Grace's thighs, she could tell how close Grace was to losing control. She was right there with her, but she was determined to make the moment last. It had taken them far too long to reach this point to get into a rush now.

Dakota slid her hands along Grace's inner thighs and parted her legs. Grace gasped and lifted her hips off the bed. Dakota clenched her tongue between her teeth to keep from flicking it against Grace's engorged clitoris.

"Dakota," Grace said, her voice aching with desire, "I need you."

"Soon," Dakota promised.

Her hands felt molten as she placed them on Grace's full breasts. Grace's pebbled nipples were the color of dark chocolate, but they tasted much, much sweeter. Dakota worshiped them with her mouth, teased them with her tongue, then rolled them between her forefingers and thumbs, eliciting a sound halfway between a groan and a whimper.

"Dakota, please."

Hearing the urgency in Grace's voice, Dakota covered Grace's body with her own. Feeling Grace's skin against hers nearly sent her over the edge, but she was determined to allow Grace's needs to come first. She explored Grace's mouth with her tongue in the same fashion she had explored Grace's body with her hands. Slowly. Reverently. Thoroughly.

Grace grabbed Dakota's hips and pulled her closer. "I need you inside me. Now."

Unwilling to take the time to grab her strap-on and buckle herself into the intricate harness it fit into, Dakota slid her hand through Grace's wetness and slipped first one finger, then two inside her.

"Yes," Grace hissed, grinding against her. She wrapped her legs around Dakota's, drawing Dakota in even deeper.

Dakota could feel Grace's smooth walls flexing against her fingers. Her hand was trapped between their bodies, giving her distended clit some much-needed friction.

"Don't come yet," Grace said. "I want to take you with my mouth."

Dakota rubbed her thumb against Grace's clit as she continued to thrust her fingers inside her. "Word of warning: you can't say things like that if you expect me to hold out."

"I'll keep that in—Oh, God."

As a keening cry escaped her lips, Grace arched her back so far Dakota thought it might break. Warmth flooded Dakota's hand, mirroring the glow she felt surrounding her heart. Though she hadn't realized it at the time, this night, this moment, and this woman were everything she had been waiting for. And they were just getting started.

❖

Grace had expected Dakota to be a skilled and attentive lover. Practice made perfect, as the old saying went, and Dakota had had more than her fair share of opportunities to hone her technique. Even with that in mind, reality had greatly exceeded all of Grace's lofty expectations. She felt the pressure to equal if not surpass Dakota's performance.

She flipped Dakota onto her back and devoured her with her eyes. Dakota's body looked as it had been carved from polished marble, but she appeared all too human as she submitted to Grace's visual inspection. Grace trailed a finger across Dakota's narrow hips. "What's wrong?"

Dakota propped herself on one elbow and ran her free hand through her hair, which was still damp from the shower she had taken before Grace arrived. "I'm not used to feeling this exposed."

"You expose your body all the time." In some of the print ads Grace had seen, Dakota had often had more skin than clothes on display. And in the oversized photo hanging in her ex-lover's gallery, Dakota had been wearing nothing at all. In that picture, Dakota had seemed more than happy to put herself on display. "What makes tonight different?"

"Because I'm spending it with you."

Grace paused as she traced the lines and ridges in Dakota's rippled stomach. "Tonight means that much to you?"

"You mean that much to me." Dakota's arresting eyes glowed so brightly they seemed to be lit from within. "Tonight means everything. *You* mean everything."

Oh, how Grace wished she could believe her. She wished tonight could mark the beginning instead of the end, but Dakota had made it clear on more than one occasion that she wasn't interested in anything remotely serious and definitely nothing long-term. Tonight would be the only night Grace could allow them to be together in this way. As much as Grace wanted Dakota, she couldn't keep coming back for more knowing they could never be more.

Grace splayed her fingers and placed her hand in the center of Dakota's chest. Dakota's heart was beating with the desperation of a caged bird trying to break free. "Tell me how to please you. Tell me what you want."

Dakota bit her lip as she pondered the question with the dedication of a little boy who had been asked what he wanted for Christmas and was determined not to say the wrong thing. "I want to watch you go down on me."

Grace cupped her hand against Dakota's cheek and gave her a reassuring smile. "It sounds like we want the same thing."

Grace kissed her. Dakota's lips tasted like almonds, a residual effect of the sensuous massage she had treated Grace to a few moments before. Grace still felt the effects of Dakota's tender ministrations. Both the ones that had been applied during the massage and after. Though her skin wasn't bruised, her soul bore the marks.

She kissed her way down Dakota's body, taking several pit stops along the way. In the hollow of Dakota's throat, the slight indentation above her collarbone, the undulating plain of her stomach, and the shallow well of her navel.

As Grace moved lower, Dakota's legs fell open as if on their own accord. Grace settled between them. She took a deep breath, inhaling the musky scent of Dakota's arousal. The act she was about to perform was as familiar to her as breathing, but she felt like she was about to do it for the first time. Because she had never done it with someone like Dakota.

Dakota stared intently at her as Grace grazed her teeth against the close-cropped hair at the apex of Dakota's thighs. Dakota's eyes widened the closer Grace came to her ultimate destination. Grace parted Dakota's labia with her fingers and touched the tip of her tongue to the head of Dakota's clit. Dakota groaned deep in her throat as Grace slid her tongue along the length of her shaft. When she took Dakota into her mouth, Dakota threw her head back and howled her approval.

As Grace continued to stroke her, Dakota grew harder and longer, filling her mouth.

"Yes," Dakota said breathlessly. "Just like that."

Grace dragged her tongue through Dakota's juices, savoring the earthy taste before she turned her attention back to Dakota's clit. Dakota growled when Grace flicked her tongue against the tip. Her cries grew even more guttural as Grace increased her pace. Dakota thrust her hips against Grace's mouth, matching her rhythm.

As the end neared, Grace looked up. She wanted to see the effect she was having on Dakota, not just hear it. She wanted to watch her come. The sight was glorious.

Dakota's handsome face twisted into a rictus of pleasure as her clit throbbed and pulsed against Grace's lips. Grace thrust her tongue inside her, feeling Dakota's smooth muscles spasm around it.

Her ears rang from the sweetest serenade she had ever heard. To her heart, the sound was more like a dirge. A memorial to the most memorable—and the most painful—night of her life.

❖

Dakota kissed Grace long and hard, then drew her into her arms and held her close. "I need to go to the living room and grab the menus so we can order dinner, but I don't want to move. Even if I did, I doubt my legs would support me. What are you in the mood for? Thai? Mexican? Chinese? Italian? Greek? Whatever you want, I think it's safe to say I've got you covered. Rich and I aren't what anyone would consider the world's best cooks, so we're on a first-name basis with most of the food delivery guys in the neighborhood. Which one would you like me to call?"

"Dakota, slow down." Grace lifted her head, her expressive face a mask of almost unbearable sadness.

"Aren't you hungry?"

"Yes, I am, but forget about dinner. We need to talk."

Dakota felt an unwanted sense of dread. "That sounds ominous."

Grace covered herself with the sheet as she rested her back against the headboard. "I've loved spending time with you the past few weeks, and tonight was amazing—"

Dakota's heart sank even lower. "But?" she prompted her, uncertain if she really wanted to hear Grace's answer to her question.

"But I'm about to close one business and start a brand-new one, which means I'm about to take on a slew of new responsibilities. I won't have time to—"

Dakota drew her knees to her chest to protect herself from the verbal slings and arrows Grace was lobbing at her. "Are you dumping me?"

"I wouldn't put it that way."

"Then how would you put it?"

Grace sighed as if her heart was breaking. Dakota didn't know if that was truly the case in Grace's situation, but it definitely was in hers. "It would be pointless for us to continue whatever it is we're doing. I'm not going to have the time to devote to a relationship, and you're not interested in one."

"I'm interested in you."

"That's not enough for me, and you know that. That's what I came over here tonight to tell you. I never meant for any of...this to happen."

"I didn't have to twist your arm to convince you to go to bed with me, Grace. You came of your own free will. And quite loudly, I might add."

"I know I did. And I will treasure this night for the rest of my life, but—"

Dakota finished the sentence for her. "You don't want me *in* your life. If that's how you feel, I'm not going to try to change your mind. Just do me one favor before you go."

"What?"

"Be honest with me. It's not your increased workload that's driving you away. It's something more fundamental, isn't it? Something I can't change and you can't bring yourself to accept." Grace lowered her eyes, confirming Dakota's theory. Giving life to her fears. "I'm sorry I'm not woman enough for you."

Grace opened her mouth to respond, but her rebuttal seemed to die on her lips. Without a word, she gathered her discarded clothes and sought refuge in the bathroom. Dakota heard the faucet running as Grace gathered water in the sink. When she heard the bathroom door open a few minutes later, she turned and faced the wall so she wouldn't have to watch Grace leave.

"I'll text you when your suit's done," Grace said softly. "I'll understand if you decide you'd rather not meet with me for your final fitting. When the time comes, let me know what you'd prefer and I'll ask my father to be on standby in case you'd rather deal with him instead of me." She paused as if she were waiting for Dakota to respond. Dakota couldn't bring herself to look at her, let alone speak. The pain was too great. "I'm sorry it had to end this way. Good-bye, Dakota."

Dakota waited until she heard the front door close before she allowed her tears to fall. This was why she had never been willing to embark on a relationship. This was why she had never truly shared herself with anyone. Because she was afraid that the women who went to bed with the illusion wouldn't want to wake up to the reality.

She had thought Grace was different. She had thought Grace cared for her. All of her. When they had made love tonight, Grace had known exactly what to do and say to make her feel comfortable, desired and loved. In all her forms. But none of it was real. Grace liked the surprise inside the box, but she couldn't get past the packaging.

While she had listened to Grace say the words that had broken her heart in two, Dakota had been tempted to beg for a chance to prove her wrong—to prove they belonged together—but she had forced herself to hold her tongue. Hadn't she already done enough to prove herself? Didn't Grace already know what she was about?

"Why should I fight for someone who isn't willing to fight for me?"

She picked up her phone and scrolled through her list of contacts. If she wanted, she could have someone else here in a matter of minutes. But what was the point in that? Though another woman could replace Grace in her bed, she wouldn't be able to evict her from her heart.

She found the number she was looking for and held the phone to her ear.

"Hey, sis," she said when Brooke picked up. "I'm sorry to call you so late, but do you have time to talk?"

❖

Grace hadn't meant to sleep with Dakota tonight. She had gone to Dakota's place hoping to end things before either of them got hurt. Instead, she had accomplished exactly the opposite. Now both of them were suffering. And it was all her fault.

She could still see the look on Dakota's face when she had told her it was over. She could still hear the pain in Dakota's voice when Dakota had asked her to explain the reason why.

She had wanted to refute Dakota's arguments, but she hadn't been able to because, deep down, she had known what Dakota said was true. As much as she wanted to get past her issues over the way Dakota lived her life—the way Dakota lived her truth—she couldn't stop tripping over the hurdle.

She knew her father would be waiting up for her when she got home, but she didn't feel up to facing him. She'd already had one emotional conversation tonight, and she didn't think she could handle another one. All she wanted to do was crawl into bed and begin to put this night behind her. Or try to.

Her father was sitting on the couch when she unlocked the door. The TV was on, but it was watching him instead of the other way around. "I was just resting my eyes," he said after he jerked awake.

"Of course you were."

He looked at her and frowned. "Are you okay?"

"I ended it. It's over."

She didn't bother explaining what she meant. She didn't have to. She could tell he already knew. To his credit, he didn't ask her to provide details. He simply walked over to her, wrapped his arms around her, and gave her a kiss on her forehead. "Don't worry, baby girl. One day, you'll meet a woman who's right for you."

Grace rested her head against his chest, hoping he was right. Hoping she hadn't already met—and lost—the love of her life because she hadn't been brave enough to accept her for who she was.

CHAPTER TWENTY

A little over a week after Grace slept with her and kicked her to the curb, Dakota received a text from her. Even though she knew the message was most likely business-related and not personal, she couldn't stop her heart from racing when she saw Grace's name printed on her phone's cracked screen. She couldn't stop hoping the message was an invitation to make things right, not set up an appointment to check the fit of the suit she had ordered nearly six weeks before.

Your suit's ready, the message said. *The fitting should take about fifteen minutes. When would you like to come by?*

Dakota wanted to get the ordeal over with as soon as possible, but she had two more deliveries to make before she would be able to take a break. Even though she longed to see Grace, being in close proximity with her would be tantamount to torture. Feeling Grace's hands on her would bring back memories best left forgotten.

Tell your father I'll be there in an hour, she texted back.

Will do.

Dakota stashed her phone in the pouch on the back of her jersey, locked her bike outside a skyscraper on Wall Street, and headed inside. Riley Nichols, one of the uniformed security guards patrolling the lobby, smiled when she saw her approach. Riley was usually good for a few insider tips and a quick round of athletic sex in the supply closet, but Dakota wasn't interested in either for a change. She had more than enough money to get by, and after Grace, the next woman she slept with would only pale in comparison.

"See you later, Riles," she said after she made her delivery.

She headed to her next stop a few streets away, then caught the train to Brooklyn. After Lillie buzzed her into the building, she stepped into the elevator with mounting trepidation. How would Grace react when she walked into the office? More importantly, how would she? Her mutilated heart had barely begun to heal. Now she might be about to rip open the wound again.

She needn't have worried. When she walked into the workroom, Grace's father rose to meet her, but Grace was nowhere in sight. Dakota could smell the faint aroma of Grace's perfume in the air, but Grace's desk and work area were empty.

Dakota couldn't hide her disappointment. Seeing Grace would have hurt, but not seeing her—knowing Grace was purposefully avoiding her—hurt even more.

Seeming to recognize Dakota needed support, Lillie gave her a hug. "It's good to see you, baby."

"It's good to see you, too."

"Miss Lane? I've got your order right here." Clarence Henderson held up a crisp white dress shirt and an impeccably tailored robin's-egg blue suit. "Once you get changed, we can get started."

In the bathroom, Dakota took off her cycling gear and began to put on the clothes Grace had made for her. The shirt fit perfectly. Roomy through the shoulders but fitted at the waist. The sleeves ended right at her wrists instead of a few inches above or below them.

She tried on the pants next. Like the shirt sleeves, the hems were the perfect length. The waist wasn't too loose or too snug, meaning she wouldn't have to cinch her belt extra tight to keep her pants from falling off or lower her zipper a few inches after she pigged out on a big plate of chicken wings.

When she slipped on the jacket, she discovered the forgiving material afforded her plenty of freedom of movement. She didn't feel like she was wearing a suit. She felt like she was wearing a second skin.

The small mirror over the sink only allowed her to see herself from the chest up. She returned to the office and stood in front of the full-length mirror attached to the wall so she could see the whole picture. What she saw took her breath away. The questions that had seemed so invasive during her first meeting with Grace had served their purpose well. Grace had used her answers to get to know her. To find out what made her tick. Then she had created a suit to match. Dakota had never looked or felt more like herself. And it was all thanks to Grace.

She could feel the care and love that had gone into crafting the suit. She could see it, too. In the unique touches here and there as well as the attention to detail throughout. And especially in the pride exhibited on Clarence Henderson's face.

"This is, without a doubt, the best work she's ever done," he said, slowly looking her over. "I don't see any adjustments that need to be made. Do you?"

"No, sir. I wouldn't change a thing."

"Neither would I." He held the jacket's lapel between his fingers, smiling at either the feel of the material or, more likely, the understated elegance of his daughter's design. "When is the wedding supposed to take place?"

"Next weekend. I'm flying home tomorrow so I can help my sister with some of the last-minute preparations. Her wedding planner's supposed to be taking care of everything, but I'm sure there'll be something that falls through the cracks. My main tasks will be drafting a speech to deliver at the reception and making sure the bride gets to the venue on time."

"Two worthwhile endeavors, to be sure, though one is much more important than the other."

"Yeah, my speech is going to be the highlight of the week. Once I write it, that is."

Mr. Henderson laughed from his gut instead of his chest. The latter would have meant he was only being polite. The former meant he was genuinely enjoying their conversation. He seemed like a cool dude. Dakota wished she'd had an opportunity to get to know him better. For him to get to know her. The real her, not the distorted version Grace's sister had presented. Now it was too late.

He held out his hand. "Tell your sister I said good luck."

"I will."

She turned to leave, but he didn't let go.

"I don't know the full story of what happened with you and Grace. Though my daughters might say otherwise, I make it a rule not to get involved in their romantic entanglements. I've been around long enough to know that if two people are meant to be together, they will eventually find their way back to each other."

"I don't know if that's true in Grace's and my situation, but at the very least, you've given me a great idea for a speech."

He gave her hand a final squeeze. "We've all got to start somewhere."

And Dakota knew exactly where to begin.

❖

Grace lingered in the fabric room until her father poked his head in the door to let her know the coast was clear.

"It's safe," he said. "You can come out of hiding now."

"I wouldn't call it hiding."

"No? Then what would you call it?"

"Choosing not to cause a scene." She hopped down off the bolster of merino wool she had been sitting on. "How did the fitting go? Did Dakota like the suit? Do I need to make any changes to it?"

"The fitting went well, she loved the suit, and it's perfect as is. Does that answer all of your questions?"

"Not even close." Because she was the only person who could provide the answers to the rest of her long list of queries, and she had chosen to ignore rather than address most of them.

"She seems much different in person than she did on Hope's phone," Grace's father said with a bemused chuckle. "It just goes to show you can't judge a book by its cover."

The comment struck a chord in Grace because it made her realize she had been doing exactly that. She had judged Dakota based on the way she presented herself and the questionable behavior attributed to her rather than by the things she had personally seen and heard her do. She should have chosen to base her opinion of

Dakota on the way she conducted herself with those she cared about or the honorable way she treated everyone she came across, whether they were a friend or a stranger.

The Dakota she had gotten to know didn't mesh with the images of the drunk wild child cameras had caught puking in alleyways or hooking up with random women in public restrooms.

She had used her concerns about Dakota's reputation to mask her fear. She had been afraid of what others might say if she began a relationship with Dakota, but she had been even more afraid of the way Dakota made her feel. Dakota brought chaos to her orderly life. She never knew what to expect from her. Much to her surprise, she liked it. No, she loved it. She loved the uncertainty. The mystery. And more than anything else, she loved the woman—the *person*—behind both.

When a wedding invitation came across her desk a few days later, she knew the perfect way to tell her so.

CHAPTER TWENTY-ONE

Dakota stared at the empty seat next to hers. When she had arrived in Richmond Hill and sent Grace an invitation to Brooke's wedding, she hadn't really expected her to show. Storybook endings like that one were reserved for fairy tales and romance novels. Her life didn't resemble either of those things. It never had and probably never would.

Brooke's wedding and reception hadn't been held in a church but at a popular outdoor venue only five minutes from downtown Savannah. Brooke and Kevin had exchanged their vows in a flower-covered gazebo while their one hundred fifty guests looked on and the limbs of two hundred-year-old oaks swayed in the breeze. The stately three-story mansion that housed the reception was almost as old as the majestic trees shading it. Sophisticated but not too over-the-top, the venue served as the perfect locale for Brooke and Kevin to start their new life. A little bit country. A little bit city. Just like the two of them.

Despite Brooke's last-minute freak-out, she and Kevin were perfect for each other. Dakota could tell from the way they looked into each other's eyes when they said "I do" and how they couldn't stop giggling each time guests clinked their silverware against their water glasses, signaling for them to kiss. Dakota had never wanted a love like that. Now she didn't know if she could live without it.

"May I have this dance?"

Dakota looked up from her half-eaten plate of rubbery chicken and soggy vegetables when her sister tapped her on the shoulder.

Brooke looked stunning in her beaded off-the-shoulder wedding dress. She had ditched the veil she had worn down the aisle earlier that afternoon, but she was still clutching her bouquet. The traditional first couple's dance and the bride's dance with her father were out of the way. The garter and bouquet tosses were yet to come. Dakota planned to be a safe distance away when flowers and undergarments started flying through the air, but she and her sister had never been closer.

"I'd be honored."

Dakota pushed her chair back from the table and followed Brooke to the dance floor, where several couples were cutting a rug to the strains of the Bruno Mars/Mark Ronson song the five-piece cover band was playing.

"Thanks for that great speech you gave," Brooke said as she held her bouquet in one hand and the hem of her wedding dress in the other. "I didn't know whether to laugh or cry."

Dakota raised her voice so Brooke would be able to hear her over the music. "Neither did I."

"You look amazing in that suit. I told Dad you look just like him."

"What did he say?"

"He said, 'Thanks, but even in my prime, I never looked that good.'"

"Yeah," Dakota said with a laugh. "That's what he told me, too. He changed his tune after Mom pulled out a picture from when they first started dating. He and I could have passed for twins."

"Told you."

Instead of greeting her with his usual handshake or fly-by hug when he had picked her up from the airport a few days ago, her father had wrapped her in a bear hug and held on so long she had started to wonder if he planned to let go.

Her mother had been almost as bad. "I don't know what you did," she had said, "but thank you for bringing Brooke back to us."

"That's what families are for, right?"

Dakota had been so happy she had burst into tears right there in the airport. Her father had thrown his arm around her shoulder and offered an unusual brand of comfort. "I know the Braves stink this year, but they're not that bad, are they?"

Dakota had laughed through her tears. "Can't hit. Can't pitch. I don't think they can get much worse."

Her father had given her shoulder a squeeze. "Don't worry. There's always next season."

In just a few minutes, all the animosity that had built up over the years had vanished. Her homecoming hadn't been what she expected, but it had been everything she needed. Well, almost.

"I'm sorry Grace didn't show," Brooke said as the band switched from an up-tempo song to a ballad, "but are you having a good time?"

Dakota tried not to sneeze when Brooke placed the hand holding the bouquet on her shoulder and nearly shoved the roses halfway up her nose. "This is the best wedding you've ever thrown."

"Silly." Brooke smacked her with the collection of peach, pink, and ivory roses. "This is the *only* wedding I've ever thrown. And hopefully, the last. I take that back. There might be a wedding ceremony in your future one day. I'd be more than happy to help with that."

"I'll keep you in mind, but I highly doubt your skills will be needed."

"Don't be so sure." Brooke glanced over Dakota's shoulder and jerked her chin in that direction, indicating Dakota should follow her line of sight.

When Dakota turned around, she saw Grace standing at the edge of the dance floor. Grace was wearing a colorful sheath dress that looked remarkably like the one Dakota had seen on display in the vintage clothing store near her apartment. The dress was molded to Grace's curves. She looked beyond gorgeous, but her presence was so ephemeral Dakota thought she must be a mirage. She had to be real, though, because the crowd parted like the Red Sea as she slowly walked past them.

"Don't just stand there," Brooke said, giving Dakota a push in the right direction. "Meet her halfway."

Dakota tried to think of something witty to say, but she must have used all her best lines in her speech because all she could come up with was "You came."

"I'm sorry I missed the wedding," Grace said. "My flight was delayed by a thunderstorm. We had to circle the airport for over an hour before we were allowed to land."

"That's par for the course during summer in the South. We get pop-up storms every afternoon. They're loud and obnoxious, but they don't usually last long. Would you like to dance?"

"I thought you'd never ask."

Brooke, who had found a willing partner to take Dakota's place, gave her a high five as they passed each other on the dance floor. Townsend's thumbs-up from his perch in front of the open bar was a bit more understated but equally appreciated.

Dakota gripped Grace's right hand with her left and placed her right hand in the small of Grace's back. Grace placed her free hand on Dakota's chest and slid it up to her shoulder. Dakota never thought she would feel Grace in her arms again. She shuddered at the rightness of it.

"You look handsome," Grace said with a smile. "New suit?"

"Yes, as a matter of fact. A very beautiful woman made it for me."

Amazing might be the more appropriate adjective. Because every word in the country song the band was playing seemed to apply to Grace. She was amazing, and Dakota was completely amazed by her.

"I hear you're starting your own business," she said as they moved to the music. "Are you looking for a partner, by any chance?"

"No, because I've already found her."

Dakota's heart soared, but she didn't allow it to completely take flight. She couldn't. Not yet. She needed to be sure. "Why did you come? The wedding favors are cool, but I doubt they're worthy of a three-hour flight."

"Perhaps not, but you are. I came because I wanted to clarify something. The night we parted ways, you said you were sorry you weren't woman enough for me."

Dakota remembered that night. And Grace's silent confirmation that what she had said was true. Tonight, almost as if it had been scripted, the band chose precisely that moment to take a dramatic pause, adding emphasis to Grace's words as Grace looked deep into her eyes.

"Dakota, you're all the woman I need."

Tears welled in Dakota's eyes as she heard the validation she'd thought she would never receive. Experienced the love she'd thought she would never feel. Her brother's piercing whistle kicked off a round of cheers. Families were like that. They could be embarrassing, even maddening at times, but one thing was certain: they never stopped surprising you.

"I love you, Grace."

"I love you, too. Now shut up and kiss me."

Dakota smiled at the woman who had so thoroughly captured her heart. "Your wish is my command."

EPILOGUE

One Year Later

While Dakota made sure the models knew who would be following whom on the runway and ran them through their paces to see if they finally had their timing down, Grace peeked into the audience.

Her parents and Dakota's mother and father sat side by side in the front row. Dakota's sister and brother, her sisters, and their siblings' respective partners sat next to their parents. Brooke and Kevin. Townsend and Haley. Faith and her boyfriend Reed. Hope, her new husband Ahmad, and her stepson Zaire.

Hope had put up a fuss when Grace had dragged her to Zaire's piano recital the previous June. She had spent the first few minutes after they had arrived saying how much she couldn't wait to leave. But that was before Ahmad had walked over to where they were sitting and asked if he could join them.

"Trash Man cleans up *good*," Hope had said under her breath. She and Ahmad had hit it off right away. They had been inseparable ever since and had been married for a little over three months. Just long enough for Grace's mother to start asking when they planned to make her a grandmother. Since they couldn't seem to keep their hands off each other, a new addition to the family would probably be coming sooner rather than later.

Faith didn't seem to be in a rush to follow Hope down the aisle. She and Reed, her study partner from one of her college courses, were growing more serious by the day and he kept pressuring her to move in with him, but Faith was content to continue living at home. As she so colorfully put it, she wanted to finish school and earn her degree before she worried about "all that real-world stuff." Funny how having money set aside for the future always made planning for it easier to deal with.

Lynette and Whitney were on the other side of the room, talking animatedly with each other behind press row as they waited to give moral support to Monica and Joey, who would be participating in the show.

Grace was overjoyed she and Dakota had been able to blend their families and friends so well. She had expected to encounter a few rough patches as everyone got to know each other, but it had been smooth sailing all the way.

She waved at Rich and Aaron after they stepped out of Roxxy's DJ booth and took their seats. After Rich had returned from his lengthy tour, he had moved out of the apartment he and Dakota had shared for almost seven years and moved in with Aaron. Dakota hadn't lived alone long, however. Less than a month later, Grace had taken Rich's place. She and Dakota had talked about finding more space one day, but, like Faith, Grace was in no hurry. She didn't care how much square footage she and Dakota had as long as they were together.

Letting the curtain fall, she turned back to the chaos taking place behind the scenes. The small dressing room in the back of Mainline, the venue she had rented for the night, was a whirlwind of activity. A dozen models milled about, anxious for the show to begin, while Lillie, Tracy, and the other members of the support staff made sure the suits the models were wearing were free of wrinkles and loose threads.

"Okay," Dakota said, clapping her hands to get everyone's attention. "We've almost got it. Let's run through this one more time. Just because this is our first runway show doesn't mean we have to look like we've never done it before."

"Speak for yourself," Austin said, sparking a round of nervous laughter.

"I'll deal with you later, counselor." Continuing her pep talk, Dakota said, "Relax, have fun, and don't be afraid to be handsome."

Aside from Dakota, there were no professional models in the show. The lineup was composed of willing amateurs like Austin—legacy customers from Henderson Custom Suits, along with new ones from Henderson+Lane Designs, the company Grace and Dakota had started after Grace's father shuttered his.

The business, headquartered in a small shop near Grace and Dakota's Greenwich Village apartment, had been in operation for almost six months. Initial sales had been steady and were growing stronger all the time, spurred by good word of mouth and a strong social media presence. It didn't hurt, of course, that one of the company's cofounders was part of the fashion industry. Dakota's contacts had offered invaluable advice when the company was in its infancy. Now that it was up and running, Grace and Dakota could count most of them as customers rather than consultants.

Though she still modeled, Dakota had finally given up her day job as a bicycle messenger so she could concentrate on their joint business venture and, like Grace had many years before, work as an apprentice tailor. Grace loved watching Dakota grow into her new role. Dakota was bright, creative, and eager to learn every possible thing she could about being a tailor. She was the perfect partner. Both in business and in life.

"What are you thinking?" Dakota asked as they prepared to start the show.

Grace looked around the room. "I'm wondering how I got so lucky. To be able to do what I love with the person I love? It doesn't get any better than this."

"Luck has nothing to do with it. Some things are meant to be." Dakota kissed her and squeezed her tight. "You and I, we're tailor-made."

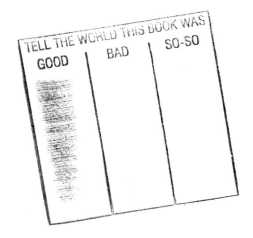

TELL THE WORLD THIS BOOK WAS

GOOD	BAD	SO-SO

About the Author

Yolanda Wallace is not a professional writer, but she plays one in her spare time. Her love of travel and adventure has helped her pen fifteen globe-spanning novels, including the Lambda Literary Award–winning *Month of Sundays* and the Lambda Literary Award finalist *Date with Destiny*, written as Mason Dixon. Her short stories have appeared in multiple anthologies including *Romantic Interludes 2: Secrets* and *Women of the Dark Streets*. She and her wife live in beautiful coastal Georgia, where they are parents to two children of the four-legged variety.

Books Available From Bold Strokes Books

A More Perfect Union by Carsen Taite. Major Zoey Granger and DC fixer Rook Daniels risk their reputations for a chance at true love while dealing with a scandal that threatens to rock the military. (978-1-62639-754-5)

Arrival by Gun Brooke. The spaceship *Pathfinder* reaches its passengers' new homeworld where danger lurks in the shadows while Pamas Seclan disembarks and finds unexpected love in young science genius Darmiya Do Voy. (978-1-62639-859-7)

Captain's Choice by VK Powell. Architect Kerstin Anthony's life is going to plan until Bennett Carlyle, the first girl she ever kissed, is assigned to her latest and most important project, a police district substation. (978-1-62639-997-6)

Falling Into Her by Erin Zak. Pam Phillips, widow at the age of forty, meets Kathryn Hawthorne, local Chicago celebrity, and it changes her life forever—in ways she hadn't even considered possible. (978-1-63555-092-4)

Hookin' Up by MJ Williamz. Will Leah get what she needs from casual hookups or will she see the love she desires right in front of her? (978-1-63555-051-1)

King of Thieves by Shea Godfrey. When art thief Casey Marinos meets bounty hunter Finnegan Starkweather, the crimes of the past just might set the stage for a payoff worth more than she ever dreamed possible. (978-1-63555-007-8)

Lucy's Chance by Jackie D. As a serial killer haunts the streets, Lucy tries to stitch up old wounds with her first love in the wake of a small town's rapid descent into chaos. (978-1-63555-027-6)

Right Here, Right Now by Georgia Beers. When Alicia Wright moves into the office next door to Lacey Chamberlain's accounting firm, Lacey is about to find out that sometimes the last person you want is exactly the person you need. (978-1-63555-154-9)

Strictly Need to Know by MB Austin. Covert operator Maji Rios will do whatever she must to complete her mission, but saving a gorgeous stranger from Russian mobsters was not in her plans. (978-1-63555-114-3)

Tailor-Made by Yolanda Wallace. Tailor Grace Henderson doesn't date clients, but when she meets gender-bending model Dakota Lane, she's tempted to throw all the rules out the window. (978-1-63555-081-8)

Time Will Tell by M. Ullrich. With the ability to time travel, Eva Caldwell will have to decide between having it all and erasing it all. (978-1-63555-088-7)

Change in Time by Robyn Nyx. Working in the past is hell on your future. The Extractor series: Book Two. (978-1-62639-880-1)

Love After Hours by Radclyffe. When Gina Antonelli agrees to renovate Carrie Longmire's new house, she doesn't welcome Carrie's overtures at friendship or her own unexpected attraction. A Rivers Community Novel. (978-1-63555-090-0)

Nantucket Rose by CF Frizzell. Maggie Jordan can't wait to convert a historic Nantucket home into a B&B, but doesn't expect to fall for mariner Ellis Chilton, who has more claim to the house than Maggie realizes. (978-1-63555-056-6)

Picture Perfect by Lisa Moreau. Falling in love wasn't supposed to be part of the stakes for Olive and Gabby, rival photographers in the competition of a lifetime. (978-1-62639-975-4)

Set the Stage by Karis Walsh. Actress Emilie Danvers takes the stage again in Ashland, Oregon, little realizing that landscaper Arden Philips is about to offer her a very personal romantic lead role. (978-1-63555-087-0)

Strike a Match by Fiona Riley. When their attempts at matchmaking fizzle out, firefighter Sasha and reluctant millionairess Abby find themselves turning to each other to strike a perfect match. (978-1-62639-999-0)